U0080535

開企，

是一個開頭，它可以是一句美好的引言、
未完待續的逗點、享受美好後滿足的句點，
新鮮的體驗、大膽的冒險、嶄新的方向，
是一趟有你共同參與的奇妙旅程。

Pocket English

老外都醬說

職場英語

Instructions

全書使用說明

01 隨身應急情境句

73 個職場熱門話題，1500 個常用的道地職場常用句，盡可能地涵蓋了職場人士會遇到的各種情境，融合了表達每個話題必備的關鍵句，讓你在每個場合都能夠遊刃有餘地運用英語。

SECTION 01

自我介紹，展示才華
Self-Introduction, Showing Your Skills

隨身應急情境句　Track 001

1 It is a great honor to have this opportunity to introduce myself here.
我很榮幸有這個機會在這裡作自我介紹。

2 I am of great honor to stand here and introduce myself to you.
我很榮幸在這裡向您介紹我自己。

3 I would like to answer whatever you may raise, and I hope I can make a good performance.
我樂意回答你們所提出的任何問題，希望我能表現出色。

02 萬能好用句型

針對經常用到的職場短句進行整理，歸納出最常用、最經典的必備句型，讓你可以自由套用，在職場上運用英文能夠更有效率。

萬能好用句型

- It is a great honor to have this opportunity to introduce myself here. 我很榮幸有這個機會在這裡進行自我介紹。
- I hope I can make a good performance. 希望我能表現得十分出色。
- I am a graduate of .... 我是……的畢業生。
- My major is .... 我的主修是……。
- I majored in .... 我主修……。
- My speciality is .... 我的專長是……。
- I like ..., and it is one of my specialities. 我喜歡……，這是我的專長之一。

03 職場應答對話

73 個職場常見情境對話，預先做好萬全準備，讓你在各種職場情境中不再感覺沒話說或者不敢開口，徹底擺脫語言貧乏的困況！

職場應答對話

✦ 我的專業背景 My Major Backgr

Annie So, Jeff, why do you think you would be an a pany?
安妮 那麼，傑夫，為什麼你認為自己能夠成為對 人呢？

Jeff Well, I have an MBA from one of the top univ UK, and I also think that my background in psyc ally be utilized when assessing potential mark the best way to promote our clients' products.
傑夫 我在英國的一所頂尖大學拿到了 MBA 學 己的心理學專業背景在評估潛在市場和 的產品的最佳方案時，能發揮作用。

Annie How is psychology useful?
心理學要怎麼發揮作用？

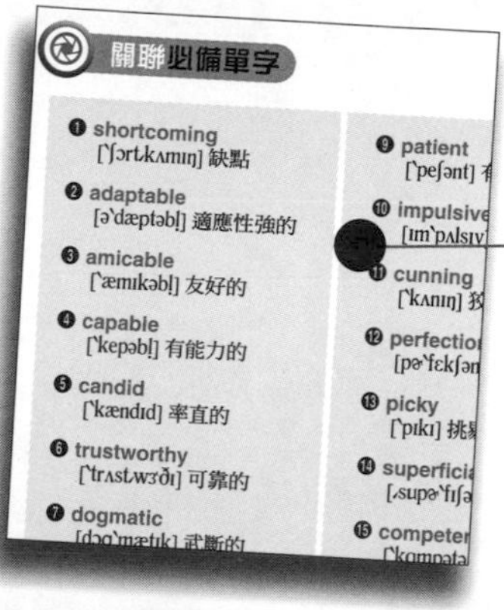

04 關聯必備語彙

每個話題都列出了使用頻率較高的語彙，並同時列出語彙的音標和常見釋義，力求減輕學習者的記憶負擔，提高吸收效率。

05 專業貼心便條

解讀各種職場話題所涉及的職場文化，在了解文化及背景差異的同時，幫助學習者克服在職場中可能會體驗到的各種疑惑和不安。

面試結束
After the Interview
Track 007
隨身應急情境句
I am wondering whether I am qualified for the job.
我想知道我是否能夠勝任這份工作。
Do you think I am the person for the job?
您覺得我是這份工作的合適人選嗎？
Do you think I am competent for the position?
您覺得我可以勝任這個職位嗎？

06 最純正美語發音

隨書附贈學習 MP3，純正美語錄音，建議學習者邊聽邊模仿，不但能加深對英語的記憶和理解，同時可以培養語感，進而做到英語脫口而出！

前 言 PREFACE

征戰職場必備英語！

本書針對職場英語所需取材十分廣泛，內容絕對實用，全書總共 11 個章節，依序為：「Ch1 求職面試、Ch2 職場新人、Ch3 日常事務、Ch4 工作進行時、Ch5 跟同事相處、Ch6 辦公電話、Ch7 舉行會議、Ch8 談判高手、Ch9 業務精英、Ch10 遇到特殊情況、Ch11 休閒時光」。這 11 個章節共收錄 73 個職場熱門話題，盡可能地涵蓋了職場人士會遇到的各種場景，讓讀者朋友在每個場合下都能夠遊刃有餘地運用英語。同時，本書編排小巧，便於隨身攜帶和查閱學習，是每位渴望成為職場英語達人的讀者朋友必不可缺的會話書。

本書的內容

✦ 隨身應急情境句

本部分主要包含一些與職場話題相關的常用應急口語句，讓讀者朋友更切實地融入話題語境。

✦ 萬能好用句型

本部分摘錄了職場中最常用的句型，幫助讀者朋友脫口說出最道地的英語口語。

✦ 職場應答對話

本部分的對話場景都是職場中極可能會遇到的，這樣可以幫助讀者朋友在各種場景中不再感覺沒話説或者不敢開口，徹底擺脱語言貧乏的囧況！

✦ 關聯必備語彙

每一話題都列出了使用頻率較高的詞彙，幫助讀者朋友記住常用詞彙，同時也兼顧減輕記憶負擔，只列出詞彙的音標和常見釋義，提高學習效率。

✦ 專業貼心便條

本部分解讀了該話題所涉及的職場文化，在了解文化及背景差異的同時，也希望能幫助學習者克服在職場中可能會體驗到的各種疑惑和不安。

本書特色

✦ 英文母語使用者編寫，道地實用

本書全部英文內容都由外師編寫，語言純正道地，風格時尚流行，可以讓讀者朋友盡情感受英語語言文字的魅力，體驗英語學習的樂趣。

PREFACE

✦ 課程規劃完整，學習循序漸進

本書按照句子 → 句型 → 對話 → 語彙 → 專業貼心便條的順序進行編排，讓讀者朋友可以採用階梯形方式進行學習，循序漸進，增強學習效果。

✦ 純正美語錄音，衝擊完美聽覺

本書都是純正美語錄音，讓大家全方位感受原味英文的氛圍，加深對英語的記憶和理解，培養語感，從而做到脫口而出！

最後，衷心希望廣大讀者朋友能從本書中學到自己需要的語言和知識，成為一名職場英語達人。持之以恆，多加練習，相信你一定能夠掌握一口標準流利的英語口語，擁有一個絢爛的職場生涯。

振宇英語中心

目 錄 CONTENTS

CHAPTER 01 求職面試・The Job Interview

CHAPTER 02 職場新人・The Office Newcomer

CONTENTS

CHAPTER 03 日常事務・Daily Affairs

CHAPTER 04 工作進行時・Working Time

CHAPTER 05 跟同事相處・Getting Along with Your Co-Workers

CHAPTER 06 辦公電話・Telephone Communications

CONTENTS

CHAPTER 07

舉行會議．Holding a Meeting

CHAPTER 08

談判高手．Becoming a Good Negotiator

CHAPTER 09

業務精英・Being the Best Salesman

CHAPTER 10

遇到特殊情況・Special Circumstances

CONTENTS

CHAPTER 11

休閒時光 · Leisure Time

CHAPTER 01

求職面試 The Job Interview

❶ 自我介紹，展示才華 Self-Introduction, Showing Your Skills
❷ 明確自己的優勢和劣勢 Advantages and Disadvantages
❸ 應聘這份工作的原因 Reasons for Applying for the Job
❹ 簡述自我職業規劃 Career Planning
❺ 對公司的瞭解 About the Company
❻ 期望的薪資待遇 Expected Salary and Benefits
❼ 面試結束 After the Interview

SECTION 01

自我介紹，展示才華
Self-Introduction, Showing Your Skills

隨身應急情境句

Track 001

1. It is a great honor to have this opportunity to introduce myself here.
我很榮幸有這個機會在這裡作自我介紹。

2. I am of great honor to stand here and introduce myself to you.
我很榮幸在這裡向您介紹我自己。

3. I would like to answer whatever you may raise, and I hope I can make a good performance.
我樂意回答你們所提出的任何問題，希望我能表現得十分出色。

4. I am a graduate of Yale University.
我是耶魯大學的畢業生。

5. I graduated from University of California.
我畢業於加州大學。

6. I'd got a master's degree in Harvard University.
我畢業於哈佛大學，獲得碩士學位。

7. My major is economics.
我主修經濟學。

8	I majored in international trade. 我主修國際貿易。
9	My speciality is painting. 我的專長是繪畫。
10	I like taking pictures and it is one of my specialities. 我喜歡攝影，這是我的專長之一。
11	My main interests are reading financial magazines and skiing. 我的主要愛好是閱讀財經雜誌和滑雪。
12	I have kinds of hobbies, such as writing poems, singing French songs, and so on. 我有一些業餘嗜好，比如寫詩、唱法語歌等。
13	I am an optimistic person and have a positive attitude toward life. 我是一個樂觀且生活態度積極的人。
14	I'm quite active and energetic. 我相當積極且充滿活力。
15	I'm always enthusiastic and full of energy, and that's my strongest personality. 我為人非常熱情並且精力充沛，這是我最大的特質。
16	My friends think I am a really easy-going person. 我的朋友們認為我是一個十分容易相處的人。
17	I have the ability to deal with people at all levels. 我能夠跟各種類型的人打交道。

18 I have the ability to operate independently and I also respect teamwork.

我具有獨立工作的能力，也重視團隊合作。

萬能好用句型

- It is a great honor to have this opportunity to introduce myself here. 我很榮幸有這個機會在這裡進行自我介紹。
- I hope I can make a good performance.
  希望我能表現得十分出色。
- I am a graduate of .... 我是……的畢業生。
- My major is .... 我的主修是……。
- I majored in .... 我主修……。
- My speciality is .... 我的專長是……。
- I like ..., and it is one of my specialities.
  我喜歡……，這是我的專長之一。

職場應答對話

✦ 一些特殊的語言能力 Some Unique Language Skills ✦

Mary I see on your resume that you have some unique language skills. Can you please explain them in detail?

瑪麗 我看到你的履歷裡寫著你具備一些特殊的語言技能。可以具體說明一下嗎？

Roger Sure. In college I studied both French and Korean, and after I graduated I continued to study both languages. I am now fluent, so I can do multiple translations.

羅傑 當然。在大學，我學了法語和韓語，畢業後我仍然繼續學習這兩種語言。現在我可以說得很流利，所以我能進行多語言翻譯。

Mary Really? That is very impressive.

瑪麗 真的嗎？那很好。

Roger Thank you. I studied abroad in Seoul one year and did a lot of translation work at the time, so I have a bit of experience.

羅傑 謝謝。我在首爾留學了一年，留學期間從事了很多翻譯工作，所以我有一點經驗。

Mary Seeing as we conduct a lot of business in both Korea and France, I think your language abilities will suit our company well.

瑪麗 有鑒於我們在韓國和法國都有很多業務，我認為你的語言能力非常適合我們公司。

Roger Great!

羅傑 太好了！

- Korean [kəˋrɪən] n 韓語
- multiple [ˋmʌltɪḷ] adj 多重的，多樣的
- translation [trænsˋleʃən] n 翻譯，譯文
- impressive [ɪmˋprɛsɪv] adj 令人印象深刻的
- Seoul [sol] n 首爾（韓國首都）

關聯必備單字

❶ **resume**
[ˋrezjume] 履歷

❷ **interview**
[ˋɪntɚvju] 面試

❸ **candidate**
[ˋkændədet] 求職者

❹ **interviewee**
[ˏɪntɚvjuˋi] 被面試者

❺ **interviewer**
[ˋɪntɚvjuɚ] 面試官

❻ **introduction**
[ˏɪntrəˋdʌkʃən] 介紹

❼ **recommend**
[ˏrɛkəˋmɛnd] 推薦

❽ **opportunity**
[ˏɑpɚˋtjunətɪ] 機會

❾ **graduate**
[ˋgrædʒuˏet] 畢業生

❿ **major**
[ˋmedʒɚ] 專業

⓫ **speciality**
[ˏspɛʃɪˋelətɪ] 特長

⓬ **interest**
[ˋɪntrəst] 興趣

⓭ **personality**
[ˏpɝsəˋnælətɪ] 個性

⓮ **attitude**
[ˋætətjud] 態度

⓯ **background**
[ˋbækˏgraʊnd] 背景

⓰ **hobby**
[ˋhɑbɪ] 業餘愛好，嗜好

⓱ **hire**
[ˋhaɪr] 聘用

⓲ **progress**
[ˋprɑgrɛs] 進步

專業貼心便條

求職者留給面試官的印象是從一份履歷開始的，那如何讓自己的履歷趨於完美，從眾多履歷中脫穎而出呢？

那麼，撰寫履歷的兩點「切忌」，是你務必要知道的：

1. 切忌重點不突出。

雖然列舉了諸多曾經做過的事情，但卻無法讓面試官看出你的專長，倘若如此，則對你非常不利。

2. 切忌千篇一律。

履歷寫得太過平淡無奇，沒有突出你的任何個人特點，這樣的履歷不會給面試官留下較深的印象。

SECTION 02

明確自己的優勢和劣勢
Advantages and Disadvantages

隨身應急情境句

Track 002

1 As for my qualities, I believe I am a highly-motivated and reliable person.
說到我的特質，我認為自己是一個上進心強且值得信賴的人。

2 I'm a person with strong determination.
我是一個有堅定決心的人。

3 My great strength is my confidence.
我最大的優勢是我很有信心。

4 A positive attitude toward learning is acknowledged to be my greatest strength.
積極的學習態度是我最大的優勢。

5 My main advantage is that I can thrive under pressure.
我的主要優勢是能承受壓力。

6 I am always ready to meet challenges. I never give up easily.
我隨時準備好迎接挑戰，從不輕易放棄。

7 I have a strong sense of responsibility and dedication.
我有很強的責任心和事業心。

8	I have a strong sense of my direction towards the goals, and a clear vision of the short-term tasks that need to be achieved along the way. 我清楚地知道自己需要努力的方向，也對在實現目標的過程中需要完成的短期任務具有清楚的認知。
9	I have a strong ability to study things independently. 我的自學能力非常強。
10	I believe my great strength is my willingness to learn and progress. 我認為願意學習進取是我最大的優勢。
11	I am good at English and I enjoy working with people. 我的英文很好，我還很喜歡和別人一起工作。
12	I'd like to share with others as I respect communication. 我願意和他人分享，因為我重視彼此間的交流。
13	To be frank, I think I'm a very creative person. 坦白說，我認為我是一個十分具有創造力的人。
14	As a recent graduate, I lack work experience, but I will use my diligence to make up for it. 作為應屆畢業生，我缺乏工作經驗，但我會用自己的勤奮來彌補這點。
15	I don't have any real experience in marketing, but I am willing and eager to learn. 我沒有市場行銷方面的實際經驗，但我願意並渴望學習。

16	I am not good at math, but I believe I can handle the problem after a period of study. 我的數學不太好，但是我相信經過一段時間的學習，我可以解決這個問題。
17	I believe everyone has his strength and weakness. 我相信每個人都有自己的優勢和劣勢。

萬能好用句型

- As for my qualities, I believe I am ….
  說到特質，我認為自己……。
- My great strength is …. 我最大的優勢在於……。
- … is acknowledged to be my greatest strength….
  ……是我最大的優勢。
- My main advantage is …. 我的主要優勢是……。
- I don't have any real experience in …, but I am willing and eager to learn.
  我沒有……方面的實際經驗，但我願意並渴望學習。
- I am not good at …, but I believe I can handle the problem after a period of study.
  我的……不太好，但是我相信經過一段時間的學習，我可以解決這個問題。
- I believe everyone has his strength and weakness.
  我相信每個人都有自己的優勢和劣勢。

職場應答對話

✦ 我的專業背景 My Major Background ✦

Annie So, Jeff, why do you think you would be an asset to this company?

安妮 那麼，傑夫，為什麼你認為自己能夠成為對公司有價值的人呢？

Jeff Well, I have an MBA from one of the top universities in the UK, and I also think that my background in psychology can really be utilized when assessing potential markets and finding the best way to promote our clients' products.

傑夫 我在英國的一所頂尖大學拿到了 MBA 學位。我也認為自己的心理學專業背景在評估潛在市場和尋找推廣我們客戶的產品的最佳方案時，能發揮作用。

Annie How is psychology useful?

安妮 心理學要怎麼發揮作用？

Jeff Because I can analyze consumers from another perspective than simply their status as consumers.

傑夫 因為我可以從其他角度來分析客戶，而不只是簡單地從他們作為客戶的這個角度來分析。

Annie That does sound like an interesting approach.

安妮 這聽起來似乎是個有趣的方法。

Jeff I believe it is. Being able to have an alternative view of things helps me to think outside of the box and come up with new ideas.

傑夫 我相信是這樣的。從另一個角度思考事情能夠幫助我跳出思維的框架，提出新點子。

- asset [ˋæsɛt] n 有價值的人
- psychology [saɪˋkɑlədʒɪ] n 心理學
- utilize [ˋjutḷaɪz] v 利用
- potential [pəˋtɛnʃəl] adj 潛在的
- analyze [ˋænḷ͵aɪz] v 分析
- perspective [pɚˋspɛktɪv] n 觀點，遠景
- status [ˋstetəs] n 狀況，情形；地位
- alternative [ɔlˋtɝnətɪv] adj 另外的，其他的

關聯必備單字

1. **shortcoming** [ˋʃɔrt͵kʌmɪŋ] 缺點
2. **adaptable** [əˋdæptəbḷ] 適應性強的
3. **amicable** [ˋæmɪkəbḷ] 友好的
4. **capable** [ˋkepəbḷ] 有能力的
5. **candid** [ˋkændɪd] 率直的
6. **trustworthy** [ˋtrʌst͵wɝðɪ] 可靠的
7. **dogmatic** [dɔgˋmætɪk] 武斷的
8. **dedicate** [ˋdɛdə͵ket] 奉獻
9. **patient** [ˋpeʃənt] 有耐心的
10. **impulsive** [ɪmˋpʌlsɪv] 衝動的
11. **cunning** [ˋkʌnɪŋ] 狡猾的
12. **perfectionist** [pɚˋfɛkʃənɪst] 完美主義者
13. **picky** [ˋpɪkɪ] 挑剔的
14. **superficial** [͵supɚˋfɪʃəl] 膚淺的
15. **competent** [ˋkɑmpətənt] 能勝任的
16. **weakness** [ˋwiknəs] 劣勢，缺點

SECTION

03

應聘這份工作的原因

Reasons for Applying for the Job

隨身應急情境句

Track 003

1. What interests you about this job?
   這份工作吸引你的是什麼？
2. Why do you apply for this position?
   你為什麼要申請這個職位？
3. Please tell me the reason for picking this position.
   請告訴我申請這個職位的原因。
4. What made you decide to change job?
   是什麼讓你決定換工作？
5. Can you tell me the reason for leaving?
   你能告訴我離職的原因嗎？
6. Why should I hire you?
   我為何要聘請你？
7. I believe I'm really qualified for the job.
   我認為自己可以勝任這個工作。
8. I think my abilities fit me well for the position.
   我認為自己有能力勝任該職位。
9. I majored in business English, and I'd like to get into foreign trade business.
   我主修商務英語，而且我想從事外貿行業。

10 My previous job is out of my field.
我先前的工作超出我所學的領域。

11 Becoming an engineer was my childhood dream.
當工程師是我兒時的夢想。

12 I would like to work in a foreign-invested company so as to make full use of my English.
我想在外商公司工作，這樣可以充分發揮我的英語優勢。

13 It would be a good place for me to make use of what I learned in the university.
這裡會是我運用大學所學知識的好地方。

14 I think working in your company would provide me with more opportunities for career growth.
我認為在貴公司工作可以得到更多的職業晉升機會。

15 I would like to get a job that is really challenging.
我希望從事一份非常具有挑戰性的工作。

16 I want to be challenged and taking on the responsibilities of this position will help me succeed.
我想要迎接挑戰，而承擔這個職位所賦予的責任將幫助我取得成功。

17 I have three-year experience in this field, and I'm confident that I can do a good job.
我從事這個行業已經三年了，而且我有信心能夠做好這份工作。

18 My major and working experience make me qualified for this particular job.
我的專業和工作經驗使我能夠勝任這份特別的工作。

萬能好用句型

- Why do you apply for this position?　你為什麼要申請這個職位？
- Please tell me the reason for picking this position.
  請告訴我申請這個職位的原因。
- I believe I'm really qualified for the job.
  我認為自己可以勝任這個工作。
- I think my abilities fit me well for the position.
  我認為自己有能力勝任這個職位。
- I majored in … and I'd like to get into ….
  我主修……，而且我想從事……。
- My previous job is out of my field.
  我先前的工作跟我所學的領域不相符。
- … was my childhood dream.　……是我兒時的夢想。
- I would like to work in a foreign-invested company so as to make full use of …
  我想在外商公司工作，這樣可以充分發揮我的……優勢。

職場應答對話

✦ 為什麼是心理學 Why Psychology ✦

Kate　According to your resume, you are qualified for two of our open positions. Why are you applying for this one and not the other?

凱特　根據你的履歷，我們空缺的職位中有兩個你可以勝任。為什麼你選擇這個職位而不是另一個呢？

Barney In my last year of college, I really became interested in the psychological aspects of public policy making, so I decided to focus on that area.

伯尼 在我大學的最後一年，我對從心理學角度分析公共政策的決定特別有興趣，所以我決定要關注這個領域。

Kate Why psychology?

凱特 為什麼是心理學呢？

Barney I took a few psychology courses and found them extremely interesting.

伯尼 我學了一些心理學課程，發現它們特別有趣。

Kate We certainly have need for an employee with that specialized knowledge. Why did you apply with our organization?

凱特 我們的確需要一位具備這種專業知識的員工。你為什麼來應徵我們公司呢？

Barney My advising professor spoke highly of the organization, and so on his recommendation I applied here.

伯尼 我的教授對貴公司評價很高，在他的推薦之下，我到這裡來應聘了。

- psychological [ˌsaɪkəˋlɑdʒɪkḷ] adj 心理學的
- aspect [ˋæspɛkt] n 方面
- specialized [ˋspɛʃəlaɪzd] adj 專業的
- recommendation [ˌrɛkəmɛnˋdeʃən] n 推薦

關聯必備單字

❶ field
[fild] 領域

❷ career
[kə`rɪr] 職業

❸ position
[pə`zɪʃən] 職位

❹ application
[ˌæplə`keʃən] 申請

❺ employment
[ɪm`plɔɪmənt] 雇用

❻ qualification
[ˌkwɑləfə`keʃən] 資格

❼ post
[post] 職位

❽ development
[dɪ`vɛləpmənt] 發展

❾ adept
[ə`dɛpt] 熟練的

❿ vacancy
[`vekənsɪ] 空缺

⓫ requirement
[rɪ`kwaɪrmənt] 要求

⓬ challenging
[`tʃælɪndʒɪŋ] 挑戰的

⓭ engineer
[ˌɛndʒə`nɪr] 工程師

⓮ childhood
[`tʃaɪldˌhʊd] 童年時期

專業貼心便條

禮儀，是影響面試成績的一個十分重要的因素，也是面試致勝的關鍵之一。其實，在面談中，面試官對求職者的總體印象，語言交流只占了其中的 30%，而眼神交流和求職者的形象氣質及身體語言卻占了絕大部分。因此，在面試時，不僅要注意自己的外表和談吐，也要避免一些下意識的小動作和姿態。在與面試官交談時，要表現得誠懇熱情；回答面試官的提問時，應當從容淡定，對自己要講的話應多加思索，切勿信口開河、誇誇其談。

SECTION

04

簡述自我職業規劃

Career Planning

隨身應急情境句 Track 004

1 Where do you see yourself in five years?
你認為你五年之後會在哪裡？

2 What are your career plans for the next five years?
你未來五年的職業規劃是什麼？

3 What are your professional goals for the next five or ten years?
在接下來的五年或十年裡，你的職業目標是什麼？

4 What are your long-term career goals?
你的長期職業目標是什麼？

5 How does this job fit into your long-term career goals?
這份工作怎麼符合你的長期職業目標呢？

6 I have some short-term and long-term career goals.
我的職業目標有短期的，也有長期的。

7 My short-term goal is to work in a reputed company like yours.
我的短期目標是進入一家像貴公司這樣知名的公司。

8	My long-term goal is to become the art director of a magazine. 我的長期目標是成為一本雜誌的藝術總監。
9	My long-term goal is to grow with a company where I can continue to learn, and contribute my efforts and more value. 我的長期目標是繼續學習與公司共同成長，貢獻自己的力量和更多的價值。
10	My ultimate goal is to do risk management for global corporations seeking to invest in foreign nations. 我的最終目標是為在國外尋找投資機會的跨國公司做風險管理。
11	I want to become a client manager in three years. 我想在三年後成為客戶經理。
12	I hope I would take a managerial position in the company. 我希望自己能進入公司的管理層。
13	I wish that I could become an expert in this field. 我希望成為這個領域的專家。
14	I desire to gain more opportunities for my career development. 我渴望得到更多有助於我事業發展的機會。
15	I will work with full dedication and hopefully I could become a senior producer in the future. 我會全心全意地工作，希望日後能成為一名資深製作人。

16 Becoming an executive producer was my dream. And I am dedicated to achieving that goal.
當監製是我的夢想。我會竭盡全力來實現它。

萬能好用句型

- Where do you see yourself in five years?
  你認為你五年之後會在哪裡？
- What are your professional goals for the next five or ten years?
  在接下來的五年或十年裡，你的職業目標是什麼？
- I have some short-term and long-term career goals.
  我的職業目標有短期的，也有長期的。
- My short-term goal is to .... 我的短期目標是……。
- My long-term goal is to .... 我的長期目標是……。
- I want to become … in three years. 我想在三年後成為……。
- I wish that I could become an expert in this field.
  我希望成為這個領域的專家。
- I will work with full dedication and hopefully I could become ....
  我會全心全意地工作，希望能成為……。

職場應答對話

✦ 未來的目標 Future Goals ✦

Ella Tell me more about your future goals, please.
艾拉 請多談一下你未來的目標。

Kevin It has always been my dream to work for an NGO, such as the Brookings Institution or RAND Corporation. I think this research job will give me invaluable experience.

凱文 為像布魯金斯學會和蘭德公司這樣的非政府組織工作，一直都是我的夢想。我認為這份研究工作會帶給我十分寶貴的經驗。

Ella This particular position covers several areas of research in the field of economics. In which area do you have expertise?

艾拉 這個職位涵蓋了經濟學領域裡的多個研究方向。你具備哪一方向的專業知識呢？

Kevin Well, I focused on political economy in college, in particular south-south economic cooperation. I would like to continue research in this area.

凱文 好的，我在大學主要研究的是政治經濟學，具體地說是南部對南部的區域經濟合作。我想要繼續這個方面的研究。

Ella So where do you see yourself in five years?

艾拉 那你認為你五年之後會在哪裡？

Kevin I hope to still be working with your company. I like stability and I think it's important to learn as much as you can from one job.

凱文 我希望還會在貴公司工作。我喜歡穩定，而且我認為從一份工作中學到盡可能多的東西是十分重要的。

- NGO 非政府組織（= Non-Governmental Organization）
- Brookings Institution 布魯金斯學會（美國綜合性政策研究機構，是華盛頓學術界的主流思想庫之一）
- RAND Corporation 蘭德公司（美國非盈利性的研究和諮詢服務機構）
- expertise [ˌɛkspɚˋtiz] n 專業知識
- stability [stəˋbɪlətɪ] n 穩定（性）

關聯必備單字

❶ **managerial**
[ˏmænəˋdʒɪərɪəl] 管理的

❷ **professional**
[prəˋfɛʃənl̩] 職業的

❸ **reputed**
[rɪˋpjutɪd] 知名的

❹ **expert**
[ˋɛkspɝt] 專家

❺ **manager**
[ˋmænɪdʒɚ] 經理

❻ **potential**
[pəˋtɛnʃəl] 有潛力的

❼ **become**
[bɪˋkʌm] 成為

❽ **objective**
[əbˋdʒɛktɪv] 目標

❾ **effort**
[ˋɛfɚt] 努力

❿ **improve**
[ɪmˋpruv] 改善

⓫ **enhance**
[ɪnˋhæns] 加強

⓬ **dedication**
[ˏdɛdəˋkeʃən] 奉獻

⓭ **accomplish**
[əˋkʌmplɪʃ] 完成

⓮ **senior**
[ˋsinjɚ] 高級的

⓯ **plan**
[plæn] 計劃

⓰ **ultimate**
[ˋʌltɪmət] 最終的

專業貼心便條

走好職場的第一步是十分關鍵的，這也是職業規劃的重要內容，每一位職場新人都應非常瞭解自己的 SWOT（strengths 優勢、weaknesses 劣勢、opportunities 機遇、threats 威脅），不要盲從，要做出準確的判斷，清楚自己的目標，並堅定不移地走下去。職業目標應當是切合實際的，同時不要僅局限於個人前途和個人利益方面，要帶有社會責任感，這樣才能獲得真正的認同與尊重。在不同的階段，職業規劃必須根據自身狀況的變化做出相應的調整。

SECTION 05

對公司的瞭解
About the Company

隨身應急情境句

Track 005

1	Why did you choose our company? 你為何選擇我們公司？
2	Why did you select our company as the priority? 為什麼我們公司是你的首選？
3	What do you know about our company? 你對我們公司有多少瞭解？
4	I choose your company because it offers its employees with overseas training opportunities. 我選擇貴公司是因為貴公司為員工提供海外培訓機會。
5	I want to work here because it is one of the leading international trading corporations with a good reputation. 我想在這裡工作，是因為貴公司是國際貿易公司中的領導者，擁有良好的聲譽。
6	Your company is one of the Fortune 500 companies. 貴公司是世界 500 大公司之一。

7	As far as I know, your company has an impressive reputation in the industry. 據我所知，貴公司在業內享有良好的聲譽。
8	Your company is one of the long-established corporate champions in the field. 貴公司是這個領域久負盛名的龍頭企業之一。
9	Your company is well-known internationally for its technical strength. 貴公司因技術實力雄厚而揚名國際。
10	As a multinational corporation, I think your company can offer me more opportunities to work abroad. 作為跨國公司，我認為貴公司會給我提供更多出國工作的機會。
11	The company culture here is a match with my values and personality. 貴公司的文化與我的價值觀和個性很一致的。
12	"Happy work, happy life" is one of our core company cultures. 「快樂工作，快樂生活」是我們公司的核心文化之一。
13	The company will help its employees with long-term career plans. 公司將幫助員工制定長期職業規劃。
14	Do you have any questions you'd like to ask? 你有什麼問題要問嗎？

15	You may ask any questions about the job. 你可以提出任何與工作相關的問題。
16	I'd like to know some details of this position. 我想瞭解這個職位的一些細節。
17	I have questions about the job profile. 我對職位說明有點疑問。
18	I have some questions about performance review. 我有一些關於業績評估的問題。

萬能好用句型

- I choose your company because .... 我選擇貴公司是因為……。
- Your company is one of the Fortune 500companies.
  貴公司是世界 500 強之一。
- As far as I know, your company .... 據我所知，貴公司……。
- Your company is well-known internationally for ....
  貴公司因……而揚名國際。
- The company culture here is a match with my values and personality. 貴公司的文化與我的價值觀和個性是很一致的。

職場應答對話

✦ 公司的全球中心 Global Centers of the Company ✦

Kim Can you tell me more about your foreign centers?
金 能多談一點你們在國外的中心嗎？

Peter Of course. We have seven centers worldwide, this one in D.C., and one each in Beijing, London, Brussels, Moscow, Cairo, and Rome. Each center focuses on a different area of research.

彼得 當然。我們在全球共有七個中心，這個是在華盛頓，其他中心分別位於北京、倫敦、布魯塞爾、莫斯科、開羅和羅馬。每一中心針對的是不同的研究領域。

Kim So if I get the job, would I be travelling to any of the centers?

金 那如果我得到了這份工作，我會到這些中心出差嗎？

Peter Yes, for this position you would travel to Cairo fairly often.

彼得 會的，擔任這個職位的話，妳會常常去開羅出差。

Kim And what other benefits does the organization have for employees?

金 貴機構還為員工提供哪些其他的福利待遇？

Peter You will get to attend numerous conferences, both domestic and worldwide.

彼得 妳會參加很多會議，包括國內的及世界性的。

Kim That is very nice.

金 這很不錯。

關聯必備單字

❶ **impressive**
[ɪm`prɛsɪv] 令人難忘的

❷ **reputation**
[͵rɛpju`teʃən] 名聲

❸ **industry**
[`ɪndəstrɪ] 行業

❹ **corporate**
[`kɔrpərət] 公司的

❺ **priority**
[praɪ`ɑrətɪ] 優先

❻ **organization**
[͵ɔrgənaɪ`zeʃən] 組織

❼ **headquarters**
[ˌhɛdˋkwɔrtɚz] 總部

❽ **international**
[ˌɪntɚˋnæʃənəl] 國際的

❾ **global**
[ˋglobḷ] 全球的

❿ **foreign**
[ˋforən] 外國的

⓫ **corporation**
[ˌkɔrpəˋreʃən] 公司

⓬ **trade**
[tred] 貿易

⓭ **enterprise**
[ˋentɚpraɪz] 企業

⓮ **culture**
[ˋkʌltʃɚ] 文化

⓯ **exceptional**
[ɪkˋsɛpʃənḷ] 卓越的

⓰ **overseas**
[ˌovɚˋsiz] 海外的

專業貼心便條

美國《財富》雜誌每年發佈一次世界 500 強排行榜。一直以來，這個排行榜都是衡量全球大型公司的最著名、最權威的榜單。1930 年，美國人亨利•魯斯創辦了《財富》雜誌，他曾在 1929 年的一次公開演講中說道：「基本上，商業就是我們的文化，因為它就是我們時代的特徵。它控制我們的生活，而同時許可我們去加以控制的就是科學、技術以及環球信用和環境的發展——簡而言之就是現代企業。企業就是我們的生命，它是藝術家、牧師、哲學家、醫生的生活必要條件，因為企業對藝術家或哲學家的生活狀況，具有一種決定性的影響，普通人更是隨時都必須與企業有關係。」

《財富》雜誌還舉辦了一系列的財經論壇，並於 1995 年開始舉辦世界 500 強年會，即《財富》全球論壇，它被視為世界經濟界巨頭「腦力激蕩」、「激發新思維」的良機。

SECTION 06

期望的薪資待遇
Expected Salary and Benefits

隨身應急情境句

Track 006

1 May I ask about your present pay?
我可以問一下你目前的薪資狀況嗎？

2 Can you tell me your monthly salary now?
可以告訴我你目前的月薪是多少嗎？

3 What's your expected salary?
你期望的薪水是多少？

4 What salary range are you expecting?
你期望的工資範圍是多少？

5 My present pay is 200,000 RMB annually plus some allowance and bonus.
我現在的年薪是 20 萬元，還有津貼和獎金。

6 I'm paid 150,000 RMB annually in all.
我的年薪總計 15 萬元。（RMB＝人民幣）

7 I hope my starting salary can reach 5,500 RMB.
我希望起薪能達到 5500 元。

8 I hope my starting salary would be at least 4,000 RMB a month.
我希望起薪不低於每月 4000 元。

9	I require a monthly salary of 5,000 RMB. 我希望月薪能有 5000 元。
10	I'm hoping for appropriate pay according to my ability. 我希望能夠根據我的個人能力給我一份合適的薪水。
11	I expect a salary closely related to the importance of the job. 我希望薪水和工作的重要性密切相關。
12	I accept 3,500 RMB per month during the probation period. 我可以接受試用期月薪 3500 元。
13	I'm quite willing to follow the rules you have here. 我非常樂意遵從這裡的規定。
14	To be frank, it is a little bit less than I expected. 老實說，這比我預期的還要少一點。
15	That's not what I was hoping for. 這和我預期的有些出入。
16	4,000 RMB has reached my bottom line. 4000 元已經是我的底線了。
17	We have all the benefits, such as health care insurance, housing allowance, paid vacation and so on. 我們有很多福利，比如醫療保險、房屋津貼、帶薪假期等等。

18	Is there still room for negotiation? 還有商量的餘地嗎？
19	Is there any chance you would change your mind? 你有沒有可能改變主意呢？
20	There's nothing that can't be negotiated. 沒有什麼是不能協商的。

萬能好用句型

- What are your pay expectations? 你期望的工資是多少？
- I'm paid … annually in all. 我的年薪總計……。
- I hope my starting salary can reach …. 我希望起薪能達到……。
- I require a monthly salary of …. 我希望月薪能有……。
- I accept … per month during the probation period.
  我可以接受試用期月薪……。
- I'm willing to follow the rules you have here.
  我樂意遵從這裡的規定。
- Is there any room for negotiation? 還有商量的餘地嗎？

職場應答對話

✦ 公司的福利待遇 The Benefits of the Company ✦

Paul Tell me more about the benefits of working with the company.
保羅 請再多說一點貴公司的福利待遇。

Ellen As an employee, you'll be receiving excellent health care coverage for you and your family, paid federal holidays, and also five weeks of vacation time per year.

艾倫 作為員工，你和你的家人都會享受完備的醫療保險，有帶薪國家假期，每年也會有五個禮拜的休假。

Paul What about corporate training?

保羅 公司的培訓呢？

Ellen Yes, we offer seminars and special training courses throughout the year for employees to enhance existing skills, or acquire a new one.

艾倫 有的，我們全年都會有討論會和專業的培訓課程來讓員工提升技能，或者掌握一門新技能。

Paul Is there sick leave?

保羅 會有病假嗎？

Ellen Yes, you will have two weeks of sick leave each year.

艾倫 有，每年你能請兩個禮拜的病假。

Paul That all sounds good, but I would really prefer $7,000 per month and four weeks of sick leave.

保羅 這聽起來不錯。但我很希望每個月能有 7000 美元，以及四個禮拜的病假時間。

Ellen I can give you $6,500 per month and three weeks of sick leave. How's that?

艾倫 我可以提供你每個月 6500 美元，以及三個禮拜的病假時間。這怎麼樣？

- seminar [ˋsɛməˏnɑr] n 研討班，討論會
- enhance [ɪnˋhæns] v 提高，增強

關聯必備單字

❶ **allowance**
[ə`laʊəns] 津貼

❷ **pay**
[pe] 薪金

❸ **bonus**
[`bonəs] 獎金

❹ **salary**
[`sælərɪ] 薪水

❺ **annually**
[`ænjʊəlɪ] 每年地

❻ **probation**
[prə`beʃən] 試用期

❼ **insurance**
[ɪn`ʃʊərəns] 保險

❽ **payroll**
[`pe͵rol] 工資單

❾ **raise**
[rez] 增加

❿ **income**
[`ɪnkʌm] 收入

⓫ **wage**
[wedʒ] 工資

⓬ **evaluate**
[ɪ`væljʊ͵et] 評估

⓭ **negotiation**
[nɪ͵goʃɪ`eʃən] 協商

⓮ **workday**
[`wɜk͵de] 工作日

⓯ **premium**
[`primɪəm] 津貼，獎金

⓰ **monthly**
[`mʌnθlɪ] 每月的

⓱ **commission**
[kə`mɪʃən] 傭金

專業貼心便條

一家企業會根據自身的發展決定其薪酬制度，而薪酬制度一般分為崗位、技能、市場和績效導向四種。以崗位為導向的薪酬制度是根據崗位的難度、重要性和對企業的貢獻等來確定薪酬；以技能為導向的薪酬制度主要是根據員工自身能力來定薪酬；以市場為導向的薪酬制度，其薪酬則依據市場來進行確定和調整；以績效為導向的薪酬制度，則是根據員工的工作業績來定酬勞，比如進行績效考核等。

SECTION 07

面試結束
After the Interview

隨身應急情境句

Track 007

1. I am wondering whether I am qualified for the job.
我想知道我是否能夠勝任這份工作。

2. Do you think I am the person for the job?
您覺得我是這份工作的合適人選嗎？

3. Do you think I am competent for the position?
您覺得我可以勝任這個職位嗎？

4. What do you think of me as a purchasing assistant?
您認為我適合做採購助理嗎？

5. Could you give me some suggestions on my performance today?
您能就我今天的表現，給我一些建議嗎？

6. What's your general impression of me?
您對我的整體印象如何？

7. How did my performance impress you?
您覺得我的表現如何？

8. I would be honored if I could work in your company.
如果能在貴公司工作將會是我的榮幸。

9	I am eager to become a member of you. 我渴望成為你們中的一員。
10	Is there any room for my development? 我還有什麼發展的空間嗎？
11	You have limitless potential in the area. 你在這個領域裡擁有無限的潛力。
12	We can see your potential. 我們能看到你的潛力。
13	I believe there will be much more to come from you. 我認為你有很大的潛力。
14	When will the interview results be available? 什麼時候可以知道面試結果呢？
15	When may I expect to hear the results of this interview? 我什麼時候可以得知面試的結果呢？
16	We'll let you know the result sometime next week. 我們會在下個禮拜通知你面試結果。
17	You will be informed of the interview results within one week. 一個禮拜之內會通知你面試結果。
18	Thank you for giving me the opportunity. 感謝您給我這個機會。

19 Thank you for the interview. I hope to hear back from you soon.

感謝您給我面試。希望能很快得到您的回復。

萬能好用句型

- Do you think I am competent for the position?
  您覺得我可以勝任這個職位嗎？
- What do you think of me as ...？ 您認為我適合做……嗎？
- How did my performance impress you? 您覺得我的表現如何？
- I am eager to become a member of you.
  我渴望能夠成為你們中的一員。
- When will the interview results be available?
  什麼時候可以知道面試結果呢？
- Thank you for giving me the opportunity. 感謝您給我這個機會。

職場應答對話

✦ 錄用 A Job Offer ✦

Kevin Hi, may I speak to Tara?
凱文 嗨，我能找一下塔拉嗎？

Tara This is Tara. Who is calling?
塔拉 我就是塔拉。您是哪位？

Kevin This is Mr. Bond's secretary. I'm calling because he would like to extend you a job offer.

凱文 我是邦德先生的秘書。我打電話來是因為他錄用妳了。

Tara Really? That's wonderful.

塔拉 真的嗎？太好了。

Kevin There are some new hire forms that we need you to fill out, as well as a new hire seminar session to attend. It's mandatory for all new employees.

凱文 妳需要填一些新員工入職表格，還要參加新員工培訓。這些是每位新員工都要遵守的。

Tara Sure, you can fax the forms to me at your convenience. When is the new hire seminar?

塔拉 當然， 您方便的時候，可以把那些表格傳真給我。新員工培訓是什麼時候呢？

Kevin We have two options, the first Saturday or third Saturday of each month. You won't be able to begin work until you have completed the training session.

凱文 我們提供兩個選擇，每月的第一個週六或每月的第三個週六。只有完成了培訓，妳才能開始工作。

Tara Okay. Next Saturday will work for me.

塔拉 好的。下週六我可以參加。

- session [ˋsɛʃən] n 會議，講習會
- seminar session 培訓，座談會
- mandatory [ˋmændəˏtorɪ] adj 強制性的，必須遵守的
- option [ˋɑpʃən] n 選擇，選項

關聯必備單字

❶ **performance**
[pɚˋfɔrməns] 表現

❷ **impression**
[ɪmˋprɛʃən] 印象

❸ **gratitude**
[ˋgrætə͵tjud] 感激

❹ **sincere**
[sɪnˋsɪr] 真誠的

❺ **comment**
[ˋkɑmɛnt] 評論

❻ **potential**
[pəˋtɛnʃəl] 潛力

❼ **appreciate**
[əˋpriʃɪ͵et] 感激

❽ **result**
[rɪˋzʌlt] 結果

❾ **beginner**
[bɪˋgɪnɚ] 新人

❿ **eager**
[ˋigɚ] 渴望

⓫ **member**
[ˋmɛmbɚ] 成員

⓬ **contact**
[ˋkɑntækt] 聯繫

⓭ **practice**
[ˋpræktɪs] 練習

⓮ **suggestion**
[səˋdʒɛstʃən] 建議

⓯ **tip**
[tɪp] 建議

⓰ **cautiously**
[ˋkɔʃəslɪ] 慎重地

專業貼心便條

面試的目的其實是讓雇主看到履歷上沒有表現出來的東西，你需要用心體會下面這三個法則，它們可以幫助你博得雇主或公司 HR 的青睞，讓你成功入職。

1. 對自己要有清晰的定位，在面試時要充分展示出自己就是該職位的最佳人選。
2. 對自己將要從事的職業及擔任的職位要充滿興趣和熱情。
3. 對應聘公司及其所提供的職位要做一定的分析，要讓自己的理想跟目標職位一致，讓面試官知道自己十分看重該公司所提供的這個平臺。

CHAPTER

02

職場新人 The Office Newcomer

❶ 主動認識同事 Introducing Yourself to Co-Workers

❷ 領取辦公用品 Getting Office Supplies

❸ 熟悉工作環境 Getting Familiar with the Work Environment

❹ 學習公司規章制度 Learning the Company Rules and Regulations

❺ 參加培訓 Attending Training Courses

SECTION 01

主動認識同事
Introducing Yourself to Co-Workers

隨身應急情境句

Track 008

1	Hello. I'm Andy. I'm here to report. 你好，我是安迪。我是來報到的。
2	Good morning, I am Andy. It is my first day at work. 早上好，我是安迪。今天是我第一天上班。
3	Can I meet my colleagues? 我能見一下同事們嗎？
4	Glad to meet you. I am new around here. 很高興見到你們。我是新來的。
5	Hello, everyone, nice to meet you. 大家好，很高興見到你們。
6	May I introduce myself? 我可以自我介紹一下嗎？
7	Please let me introduce myself. My name's Andy. 請允許我自我介紹一下，我叫安迪。
8	It's my honor to introduce myself to you here. 我很榮幸能在這裡向你們介紹我自己。

9 I am a newcomer here. I just joined the marketing department.
我是新來的。我剛加入行銷部。

10 I'm working in the marketing department.
我在行銷部工作。

11 Hi, I'm Andy, the new guy in the business department.
嗨，我是安迪，業務部的新員工。

12 I've just started working for the company. I'm in the finance department.
我剛來公司工作，就職於財務部。

13 I really appreciate the opportunity of working here. And I'm looking forward to working well with all of you.
我很感謝有機會在這裡工作。希望能夠和大家共事愉快。

14 I'm looking forward to starting working here.
我很期待在這裡工作。

15 I'm very glad that you can join our section.
我很高興你加入我們部門。

16 I'm new here and would honestly appreciate your guidance.
我是新人，真誠地希望你們能夠多多指教。

17 I'm hoping to receive your guidance.
我希望得到你們的指導。

萬能好用句型

- Hello. I'm …, I'm here to report.
  你好，我是……，我是來報到的。
- It is my first day at work.　今天是我第一天上班。
- Glad to meet you. I am new around here.
  很高興見到你。我是新來的。
- May I introduce myself?　我可以自我介紹一下嗎？
- It's my honor to introduce myself to you here.
  我很榮幸能在這裡向大家介紹我自己。
- I am a newcomer here. I just joined ….
  我是新來的。我剛加入……。
- I'm looking forward to working well with all of you.
  我希望能夠和大家共事愉快。

職場應答對話

✦ 我是您的助理 I'm Your Assistant ✦

Celine Hi, I'm Celine. I'll be your assistant. Let me know if there is anything I can do for you.

席琳 嗨，我是席琳。我是您的助理。您有什麼需要的話，請叫我。

Jim Thanks, I'm Jim. I guess this is my office?

吉姆 謝謝，我是吉姆。我猜這就是我的辦公室吧？

Celine Yes, you are on extension 205.

席琳 是的，您的分機是 205。

Jim Can you tell me who else works in the department?

吉姆 妳可以告訴我這個部門裡還有誰嗎？

Celine Sure. Two doors down is Bob Campell's office, and next door is Karen Simpson. Across the hall you have Martin Stephens and Joe Smith. They are all very nice.

席琳 當然。您隔壁的隔壁是鮑勃·坎佩爾的辦公室，隔壁是卡倫·辛普森。走廊對面的是馬丁·斯蒂芬斯和喬·史密斯。他們都很友善。

Jim Where do you guys normally have lunch?

吉姆 你們通常會在哪裡吃午餐？

Celine Sometimes we order in and eat together in the lounge, but we also go out to a sandwich shop nearby sometimes.

席琳 有時我們會訂餐，大家會在休息室一起吃。但我們有時也會去附近的一家三明治店。

Jim Okay, I got it.

吉姆 好的，我知道了。

➲ lounge [laʊndʒ] n 休息室

關聯必備單字

❶ **report** [rɪ`pɔrt] 報到

❷ **introduce** [ˌɪntrə`djus] 介紹

❸ **newcomer** [`njuˌkʌmɚ] 新人

❹ **office** [`ɔfɪs] 辦公室

❺ **department** [dɪ`pɑrtmənt] 部門

❻ **colleague** [`kɑlig] 同事

❼ **co-worker**
[͵koˋwɝkɚ] 同事

❽ **hobby**
[ˋhɑbɪ] 愛好

❾ **attention**
[əˋtɛnʃən] 注意

❿ **aid**
[ed] 幫助

⓫ **team**
[tim] 團隊

⓬ **achieve**
[əˋtʃiv] 完成

⓭ **staff**
[stæf] 員工

⓮ **personnel**
[͵pɝsnˋɛl] 人員

⓯ **recruit**
[rɪˋkrut] 新成員

⓰ **guidance**
[ˋgaɪdns] 指導

⓱ **section**
[ˋsɛkʃən] 部門

⓲ **positive**
[ˋpɑzətɪv] 積極的

⓳ **energetic**
[͵ɛnɚˋdʒɛtɪk] 精力充沛的

⓴ **easy-going**
[͵izɪˋgoɪŋ] 隨和的

專業貼心便條

試用期其實是你與公司的磨合期，在積極踏實工作的同時，你也要知道有哪些事情是不該做的。

1. 不要對老員工表現出不屑，作為新人的你要虛心聽取老員工的意見，這樣才能跟同事相處融洽並贏得別人的尊重。
2. 不要跟同事抱怨，作為新人，抱怨公司不但不會引起眾人的共鳴，反而會讓大家懷疑你的工作態度。
3. 不要使用命令式的語言，這樣會很容易招致大家的反感。

SECTION 02

領取辦公用品

Getting Office Supplies

隨身應急情境句

Track 009

1	Excuse me, where can I get office supplies? 不好意思，請問在哪裡領取辦公用品？
2	May I ask where to get office supplies? 請問到哪裡領取辦公用品？
3	You can apply for office supplies in the administration department. 你可以到行政部申請辦公用品。
4	I'm running out of notebooks. 我的筆記本快用完了。
5	I'm out of staples for my stapler. 我釘書機的訂書針用完了。
6	May I have two ballpoint pens and a notebook? 給我兩支鋼珠筆和一本筆記本好嗎？
7	Could you find a pencil sharpener for me? 你能幫我找個削筆刀嗎？
8	I need some office paper. 我需要一些辦公用紙。

9	I am looking for a paper tray. 我在找紙盒。
10	We'll definitely need some filing cabinets and at least one desk unit. 我們肯定需要一些新的檔案櫃和至少一套組合辦公桌。
11	You need to fill this form before receiving the office supplies. 在領辦公用品前，你需要填一下這張表格。
12	Here are some necessities for you to have in the office. 這裡有些你需要用到的辦公室必需品。
13	This is your access card. 這是你的門禁卡。
14	You need to swipe your access card on the sensor of the door when entering the building. 你在進大樓的時候，要在門上的感應器上刷一下門禁卡。
15	Be sure to clock in and out before and after you work. 上下班一定要打卡。
16	Don't forget to punch your time card. 不要忘記打出勤卡。
17	I don't know how to use the punch clock. 我不知道怎麼打卡。

18 Your payroll card will be ready this Friday.
這個禮拜五前會把你的工資卡發給你。

萬能好用句型

- May I ask where to get office supplies?
  請問到哪裡領取辦公用品？
- You can apply for office supplies in the administration department.
  你可以到行政部申請辦公用品。
- I am running out of …. 我的……快用完了。
- Could you find … for me? 能幫我找……嗎？
- This is your access card. 這是你的門禁卡。
- Don't forget to punch your time card. 不要忘記打出勤卡。

職場應答對話

✦ 換台電腦 Change a Computer ✦

Tom My office computer is dying; I think it's time for a replacement. Do we have any contracts with specific suppliers for computers?

湯姆 我的辦公電腦快壞了。我想是時候換台新的了。我們有跟哪家電腦供應商簽合約嗎？

Lisa I think we order all of ours through Dell. Are you talking about your laptop, or the desktop?

麗莎 我想我們都是跟戴爾訂的。你說的是筆記型電腦，還是桌上型電腦？

Tom	The desktop. Can I replace it with a laptop?
湯姆	桌上型電腦。我能換一台筆記型電腦嗎？
Lisa	Maybe, I don't see why not. I'll ask our boss.
麗莎	也許吧，我看也沒有不行的理由。我會問問看我們的主管。
Tom	Thanks. A work laptop would also make my life much easier; it's more convenient than switching files from my personal laptop to the desktop here.
湯姆	謝謝。辦公用的筆記型電腦會讓我的生活比較輕鬆；這比我把檔案從我的個人筆記型電腦複製到這裡的桌上型電腦上方便多了。
Lisa	That's true.
麗莎	是這樣沒錯。
Tom	So if I can get a laptop instead, that would be great. It's probably cheaper, too.
湯姆	所以如果我能換台筆記型電腦就太好了。筆記型電腦可能還會比較便宜。
Lisa	I'll look into it.
麗莎	我會處理這件事的。

- replacement [rɪˋplesmənt] n 代替物，更換
- supplier [səˋplaɪɚ] n 供應商
- laptop [ˋlæptɑp] n 筆記型電腦
- desktop [ˋdɛsktɑp] n 桌上型電腦
- file [faɪl] n 檔案

關聯必備單字

❶ **stationery**
[ˋsteʃən͵ɛrɪ] 文具

❷ **equipment**
[ɪˋkwɪpmənt] 設備

❸ **necessity**
[nəˋsɛsətɪ] 必需品

❹ **notebook**
[ˋnot͵bʊk] 筆記本

❺ **pen**
[pɛn] 筆

❻ **calculator**
[ˋkælkjə͵letɚ] 計算機

❼ **stapler**
[ˋsteplɚ] 釘書機

❽ **staple**
[ˋstepl̩] 訂書釘

❾ **desk**
[dɛsk] 辦公桌

❿ **chair**
[tʃɛr] 椅子

⓫ **memo**
[ˋmɛmo] 備忘錄

⓬ **eraser**
[ɪˋresɚ] 橡皮

⓭ **glue**
[glu] 膠水

⓮ **ruler**
[ˋrulɚ] 尺子

⓯ **pencil**
[ˋpɛnsl̩] 鉛筆

⓰ **pen holder**
筆筒

⓱ **ballpoint**
[ˋbɔl͵pɔɪnt] 鋼珠筆

⓲ **swipe**
[swaɪp] 刷卡

⓳ **sensor**
[ˋsɛnsɚ] 感應器

專業貼心便條

常用辦公設備詞彙與用語：

1. 電源插座 electric outlets/sockets
2. 桌上型電腦 desktop
3. 筆記型電腦 laptop
4. 電腦當機了。The computer just crashed/froze/died.
5. 電腦壞了。The computer is down.
6. 影印存檔。Make a set of copies for your files.
7. 掃描 scan
8. 紙張尺寸 paper size
9. 出故障 be out of order
10. 叫維修工 call/contact a repairman/service man
11. 用完了 run/be out of
12. 發傳真 fax sth. to sb.
13. 傳真格式 fax template
14. 傳真很模糊。The fax comes through blurred.
15. 傳真機沒墨水了。The fax machine is out of toner.
16. 文件櫃 cabinet
17. 鎖櫃 locker
18. 碎紙機 paper shredder
19. 文件盒 tray
20. 磁片 floppy disk
21. 便利貼 adhesive notes
22. 透明膠 cellophane tape
23. 印泥 inkpad
24. 吸墨紙 blotter
25. 搭扣信封 clasp envelope

SECTION

03 熟悉工作環境

Getting Familiar with the Work Environment

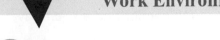

隨身應急情境句

Track 010

1 Welcome to our team. We could have a walk around.
歡迎加入我們團隊。我們可以四處走走。

2 I'll show you around. Please come with me.
我帶你四處看看。請跟我來。

3 Let's meet some of the others in the office.
我們來認識一下辦公室的其他人。

4 Excuse me, where is my desk?
不好意思，請問我的辦公桌在哪裡？

5 Sorry to bother you, where is the copy room?
很抱歉打擾您，請問影印室在哪裡？

6 Let me show you to your desk.
我帶你去你的辦公桌吧。

7 Welcome to the marketing department. Your desk is over there.
歡迎來到行銷部。你的辦公桌在那邊。

8 That is your desk, just near the window.
那是你的辦公桌，靠近窗戶那張。

9	I got a seat for you right here, so come over. 我把你的位置安排在這裡了，請過來。
10	There is a break room in the second floor with a water dispenser, a refrigerator and a microwave oven. 在二樓有一個休息室，裡面有飲水機、冰箱和微波爐。
11	Have you seen the exhibition hall? 你看過展示廳了嗎？
12	Our reception area is right over there. 那邊是我們的接待室。
13	The break room is the third room on the left. 休息室是靠左第三個房間。
14	You can have a cup of coffee in the pantry. 你可以在茶水間來杯咖啡。
15	We can have a break in the pantry. It's a place to make friends. 我們可以在茶水間休息一下。在這裡可以交到很多朋友。
16	We can sit down at tea time and enjoy a cup of coffee. 我們可以在下午茶時間坐下來，享受一杯咖啡。
17	Teatime is from 3:00 p.m. to 3:30 p.m. 下午茶時間是下午 3：00～3：30。

萬能好用句型

- Welcome to our team.
  歡迎加入我們團隊。
- I'll show you around. Please come with me.
  我帶你到處看看吧。請跟我來。
- Excuse me, where is my desk?
  不好意思，請問我的辦公桌在哪裡？
- Sorry to bother you, where is ….
  很抱歉打擾您，請問……在哪裡？
- Welcome to 1 department.
  歡迎來到……部。
- Have you seen …?
  你看過……了嗎？
- … is right over there.
  ……就在那裡。

職場應答對話

✦ 參觀辦公室 Visit the Office ✦

Kevin Can you show me around the office? I still don't know where everything is located.

凱文 妳能帶我參觀一下辦公室嗎？我還是搞不清楚各個地方的位置。

Jane Of course. So in the front is the main reception area, and behind it a few offices. If we go downstairs, you'll find the cafeteria and mailroom, as well as a locker room with showers.

珍 當然。前面的是主接待室，在它後面是一些辦公室。如果我們下樓，你會看到自助餐廳、郵件收發室以及附淋浴的更衣室。

Kevin A locker room?

凱文 更衣室？

Jane Yes, many employees run or ride their bikes to work in the morning or have a short workout during lunch.

珍 是的，很多員工都會早上跑步或騎自行車來上班，或者在午餐時間進行短時間的鍛鍊。

Kevin I see. What is on the second and third floors?

凱文 我知道了。二樓和三樓有什麼？

Jane On the second floor is your office, as well as others in various departments. And the third floor is our conference room and the CEO's office.

珍 你的辦公室在二樓，還有其他部門的同事。我們的會議室和首席執行長的辦公室在三樓。

- cafeteria [ˌkæfəˋtɪrɪə] n 自助餐廳
- locker room 更衣室
- workout [ˋwɝkaʊt] n 鍛鍊

關聯必備單字

❶ **orientation**
[ˏorɪən`teʃən] 方向

❷ **environment**
[ɪn`vaɪrənmənt] 環境

❸ **familiar**
[fə`mɪljɚ] 熟悉的

❹ **area**
[`erɪə] 區域

❺ **bulletin**
[`bʊlətɪn] 公告

❻ **cubicle**
[`kjubɪkḷ] 小隔間

❼ **seat**
[sit] 座位

❽ **condition**
[kən`dɪʃən] 條件

❾ **reception**
[rɪ`sɛpʃən] 接待

❿ **bathroom**
[`bæθˏrum] 衛生間

⓫ **hall**
[hɔl] 大廳

⓬ **stair**
[ster] 樓梯

⓭ **teatime**
[`titaɪm] 下午茶時間

⓮ **elevator**
[`ɛləˏvetɚ] 電梯

⓯ **break room**
休息室

⓰ **water dispenser**
飲水機

⓱ **microwave oven**
微波爐

⓲ **pantry**
[`pæntrɪ] 茶水間

⓳ **exhibition hall**
展示廳

⓴ **reception area**
接待處，接待室

㉑ **facility**
[fə`sɪlətɪ] 設施，設備

㉒ **complex**
[`kɑmplɛks] 綜合大樓

專業貼心便條

下面是世界首富比爾•蓋茲的十句經典名言，一起來學習吧！

1. 人生是不公平的，習慣去接受它吧。
2. 這個世界不會在乎你的自尊，這個世界期望你先作出成績，再去強調自己的感受。
3. 你不會一離開學校就有百萬年薪，你不會馬上就是副總裁，兩者你都必須靠努力賺來。
4. 如果你覺得你的老闆很凶，等你當了老闆就知道了，老闆是沒有工作任期保障的。
5. 在速食店煎個漢堡並不是作踐自己，你的祖父母對煎漢堡有完全不同的定義。
6. 如果你一事無成，不是你父母的錯，所以不要只會對自己犯的錯發牢騷，要從錯誤中學習。
7. 在你出生前，你的父母並不像現在這般無趣，他們變成這樣是因為忙著付你的開銷，洗你的衣服，聽你吹噓自己有多了不起，所以在你拯救被父母這代人破壞的熱帶雨林前，先整理一下自己的房間吧。
8. 在學校裡可能有贏家和輸家，在人生中卻還言之過早，學校可能會不斷給你機會找到正確的答案，現實人生中卻完全不是這麼回事。
9. 人生不是學期制，人生沒有寒假，沒有哪個雇主有興趣協助你尋找自我，請用自己的空暇做這件事吧。
10. 電視上演的並不是真實的人生，真實人生中每個人都要離開咖啡廳去上班。

SECTION 04

學習公司規章制度
Learning the Company Rules and Regulations

隨身應急情境句

Track 011

1 This is staff manual. Please read it carefully.
這是員工手冊。請仔細閱讀。

2 Please read this safety manual first.
請先讀一下這份安全手冊。

3 You will receive two weeks' paid vacation a year.
你每年有兩個禮拜的帶薪假期。

4 The company provides fringe benefits such as an annual bonus, two-week paid vacation a year, and health insurance.
公司提供附加福利，比如年終獎、每年兩個禮拜的帶薪假期和醫療保險。

5 Our working hours are 9 a.m. to 6 p.m.
我們的工作時間是早上 9 點到晚上 6 點。

6 Our working hours are flexible.
我們的工作時間是很有彈性的。

7 Can I make personal phone calls during office hours?
我可以在上班時間打私人電話嗎？

8	The company allows you to make personal phone calls during office hours, but don't chat over the phone. 公司允許你在上班時間打私人電話，但不要聊起天來。
9	You must arrive for work on time. 你必須準時上班。
10	Always remember to be punctual. Don't be late. 要記得準時。別遲到。
11	Don't take too long for lunch. 午餐不要用太久。
12	What's the dress code for our company? 我們公司有什麼衣著規定？
13	Never wear loose clothes or hair. 不要穿寬鬆的衣服或散著頭髮。
14	Are there any rules about dating co-workers? 辦公室戀情方面有什麼規定嗎？
15	Is it all right if I smoke here? 我可以在這裡吸煙嗎？
16	You cannot smoke here. It's non-smoking area. 你不可以在這裡吸煙。這裡是禁煙區。
17	Do we have a regular meeting? 我們有例會嗎？

18	We usually have a regular meeting every two weeks. 我們通常每兩個星期開一次例會。
19	Daily meeting will be hold at 3 p.m. every afternoon. 每天下午 3 點開例會。
20	It's very important for new members to know about the office rules. 瞭解辦公制度對新員工來說很重要。

萬能好用句型

- This is staff manual. Please read it carefully.
  這是員工手冊。請仔細閱讀。
- Please read the safety manual first.
  請先讀一下這份安全手冊。
- Our working hours are 9 a.m. to 6 p.m.
  我們的工作時間是早上 9 點到晚上 6 點。
- Can I make personal phone calls during officehours?
  我可以在上班時間打私人電話嗎？
- You must arrive for work on time.
  你必須準時上班。
- Are there any rules about … ?
  有關於……的規定嗎？
- Is it all right if I smoke here?
  我可以在這裡吸煙嗎？

職場應答對話

✦ 公司制度的調整 The Changes of Company Policies ✦

Mary Did you get the memo I sent to the new employees yesterday?

瑪莉 你有收到昨天我寄給新員工的備忘錄嗎？

Kevin No, I didn't. What was the memo about?

凱文 沒有，我沒收到。是關於什麼的？

Mary We have some company policies regarding the hours each employee works and also a change in the sick leave policy.

瑪莉 是關於每位員工工作時間的一些公司制度，以及病假制度的調整。

Kevin Oh? What are the changes?

凱文 噢？有哪些變動？

Mary Well, you are a salary worker, not hourly but you are still required to put in a minimum of thirty-five hours each week.

瑪莉 嗯，你是正式員工，雖然不是按時薪算，但還是要求你每週的工作時間不得少於 35 小時。

Kevin Okay, that sounds pretty typical. What about the sick leave policy?

凱文 好的，這聽起來滿典型的。那病假制度呢？

Mary Well, the previous policy was three sick days per month for salary employees, but the company has changed this to four weeks annually. So it is a bit shortened.

瑪莉 嗯，先前的制度規定正式員工每個月享有三天病假，但現在公司改成了每年享有四個禮拜的病假，所以稍微減少了一點。

Kevin That's fine.
凱文 沒關係。

- minimum [ˋmɪnɪməm] n 最小值，最低限度
- previous [ˋpriviəs] adj 早先的，以前的
- annually [ˋænjʊəlɪ] adv 每年

關聯必備單字

❶ **rule**
[rul] 規則

❷ **regulation**
[͵rɛgjəˋleʃən] 規章

❸ **policy**
[ˋpɑləsɪ] 政策

❹ **duty**
[ˋdjutɪ] 責任

❺ **personal**
[ˋpɝsn̩l] 個人的

❻ **practice**
[ˋpræktɪs] 慣例

❼ **right**
[raɪt] 權利

❽ **privilege**
[ˋprɪvl̩ɪdʒ] 優待

❾ **private**
[ˋpraɪvɪt] 私人的

❿ **compulsory**
[kəmˋpʌlsərɪ] 義務的

⓫ **manual**
[ˋmænjʊəl] 手冊

⓬ **require**
[rɪˋkwaɪr] 要求

⓭ **flexible**
[ˋflɛksəbl̩] 靈活的

⓮ **punctual**
[ˋpʌŋktʃʊəl] 準時的

⓯ **staff manual**
員工手冊

⓰ **safety manual**
安全手冊

⓱ **paid vacation**
有薪假

⓲ **fringe benefit**
附加福利

SECTION
05 參加培訓
Attending Training Courses

隨身應急情境句

Track 012

1 Do we have any training programs for the new hire?
我們有針對新員工的培訓計劃嗎？

2 Every new hire should take part in the training.
每一位新員工都要參加培訓。

3 We have a whole set of training program. That was specially designed for our company.
我們有一整套培訓項目，這是專門為我們公司設計的。

4 There will be a training session for new employees today.
今天會開一個新員工培訓會。

5 The manager will give you a training workshop next Tuesday.
經理下禮拜二會替你們開培訓會。

6 There will be a training course that you must attend on time.
有一個培訓課程，你一定要準時參加。

7	Your training period can vary widely. 你們的培訓時間可能不太一樣。
8	Training time depends solely on your duties. 培訓時間的長短只取決於你的職責。
9	There is a two-week training program for new staff. 新員工要接受兩個禮拜的培訓。
10	This training session mainly focuses on sales skills. 這次培訓會主要是講述銷售技巧。
11	I'll be training you today. 今天由我來培訓你們。
12	For the first day of training, you need to watch this video. 今天是培訓的第一天，你們需要看一下這段影片。
13	Please watch this video. It broadly covers your duties and safety procedures. 請看一下這段影片，基本上它涵蓋了你們的工作職責和安全程式。
14	I want you to spare some time to scan the training manual. 我希望你們能抽空看一下培訓手冊。
15	Do you think companies should provide training for all their staff? 你覺得公司應該為全體員工提供培訓嗎？

16

Training new members is really necessary, and we need to make a workable plan for staff training.

培訓新員工是十分的必要。我們需要制定一個可行的員工培訓方案。

萬能好用句型

- There will be a training course that you must attend on time.
  有一個培訓課程，你一定要準時參加。
- There is a two-week training program for new staff.
  新員工要接受兩個禮拜的培訓。
- I'll be training you today. 今天由我來培訓你們。
- This training session mainly focuses on ….
  這次培訓會主要講……。
- Please watch this video.　請看這段影片。
- In today's training session, we'll be getting to know ….
  在今天的培訓課中，我們將要瞭解……。

職場應答對話

✦ 三場研討會 Three Workshops ✦

Greg In today's training session, we'll be getting to know the company's most important clientele and etiquette on interacting with them, and other clients. Any questions?

格雷 在今天的培訓課中，我們將要瞭解公司最重要的客戶及同他們來往的禮節，還要瞭解其他一些客戶。有什麼疑問嗎？

Tina	Will there be workshops?
蒂娜	會有研討會嗎？
Greg	Yes, three in all.
格雷	會的，總共三場。
Tina	What will they cover?
蒂娜	它們是關於什麼事項？
Greg	One will be a detailed overview of the company, and the other two will focus on clientele and doing business.
格雷	其中一場是對公司的詳細介紹，另外兩場主要針對客戶及業務拓展。
Tina	We will be split up into groups then?
蒂娜	那我們將會進行分組了？
Greg	Yes, three groups of about thirty people.
格雷	是的，分成三組，大約三十個人一組。
Tina	One more question, who will be leading the workshops?
蒂娜	還有一個問題，誰要來主持研討會？
Greg	We have three of our best managers here to hold the workshops.
格雷	由我們的非常出色的三位經理來主持研討會。
Tina	Okay, thank you.
蒂娜	好的，謝謝。

- clientele [ˋklaɪənˌtɛl] n 客戶
- etiquette [ˋɛtɪkɛt] n 禮節， 規矩

關聯必備單字

❶ **training**
[ˋtrenɪŋ] 培訓

❷ **improvement**
[ɪmˋpruvmənt] 改善

❸ **examination**
[ɪgˏzæməˋneʃən] 考查

❹ **welfare**
[ˋwɛlˏfer] 福利

❺ **acquire**
[əˋkwaɪr] 獲得

❻ **efficient**
[ɪˋfɪʃənt] 有效率的

❼ **attend**
[əˋtɛnd] 參加

❽ **course**
[kɔrs] 課程

❾ **precaution**
[prɪˋkɔʃən] 預防

❿ **focus**
[ˋfokəs] 集中

⓫ **procedure**
[prəˋsidʒɚ] 程式

⓬ **group**
[grup] 組

⓭ **divide**
[dɪˋvaɪd] 劃分

⓮ **workshop**
[ˋwɝkˏʃɑp] 研討會

⓯ **scan**
[skæn] 流覽

⓰ **workable**
[ˋwɝkəbl̩] 行得通的

專業貼心便條

企業對新員工的培訓主要包括以下兩個方面：

1. 基礎教育培訓：即為新員工講解企業發展歷史、企業文化、規章制度，以及與本企業相關的新知識和新觀念等。
2. 行為培訓：即為新員工講解企業現狀及發展目標，讓新員工熟悉工作流程等。

入職培訓是十分重要的，通過這些培訓，不僅能夠提高員工的綜合素質，還可以幫助員工儘快適應新環境，融入企業文化，並使員工產生一種歸屬感。

CHAPTER 03

日常事務 Daily Affairs

1. 日常文件整理 Filing Documents
2. 收發傳真 Sending and Receiving Faxes
3. 影印、列印資料 Copying and Printing
4. 公司內部郵件往來 Communicating with Co-Workers via Email
5. 發函聯絡客戶 Contacting Clients Using Business Emails
6. 遇到了問題，尋求幫助 Asking for Help
7. 面對失誤，不要氣餒 Facing Mistakes

SECTION 01

日常文件整理
Filing Documents

隨身應急情境句

Track 013

1 I'd like you to take over the filing work.
我想讓你接手文件歸檔的工作。

2 This is your filing cabinet. You are responsible for keeping all files in order.
這是你的檔案櫃。你負責整理所有的檔案。

3 My boss asked me to manage these documents.
我的上司讓我處理這些檔案。

4 Can you help me file these documents in chronological order?
你能幫我把這些檔案照時間順序歸檔嗎？

5 You need to classify the files.
你需要把這些檔案歸類。

6 You need to sort methodically through the papers.
你需要有條理地整理這些檔案。

7 These forms should be filed alphabetically.
這些表格應該要照字母順序整理。

8	The documents should be ordered alphabetically by subject. 這些檔案應該要根據主題的字母順序整理。
9	Please file these reports according to their company names. 請將這些報告按照公司名稱歸檔。
10	All the documents are arranged chronologically. 所有的檔案都是按時間順序排列的。
11	It isn't that difficult to sort out the materials. You need patience. 整理這些要素並沒有那麼難。你要有耐心。
12	Did you look up the documents I requested? 我要的文件你查了嗎？
13	Do you have those files that I asked for? 你那裡有我要的那些檔案嗎？
14	I'd like to check again under a different heading. 我想在別的標題下再查一下。
15	Here are the files you were just looking for. 這是您剛才要找的檔案。
16	The confidential files are kept in the safe. 機密檔案都存放在保險櫃裡。
17	You can find these letters in the top drawer of my desk. 你可以在我辦公桌最上面的抽屜裡找到那些信件。

萬能好用句型

- I'd like you to take over the filing work.
  我想讓你接手文件歸檔工作。
- You are responsible for .... 你負責……。
- Can you help me ...? 你能幫我……嗎？
- You need to classify the files. 你需要把這些檔案歸類。
- The documents should be ordered by ....
  這些檔案應該要根據……整理。
- You need patience. 你需要有耐心。
- Here are the files you were just looking for.
  這是您剛才要找的檔案。

職場應答對話

✦ 按照日期歸檔 File Documents Under the Date ✦

Mary I found those documents. I had filed them, but the system wasn't very good, so I've now changed it.

瑪麗 我找到那些檔案了。我把它們歸檔了，但系統不太好用，現在我已經進行更改了。

Oliver Thank you. What was wrong with the filing system?

奧利佛 謝謝。歸檔系統出了什麼問題？

Mary They were filed alphabetically according to the client's family name, which is good, and makes sense. Only quite often the names on the files are written the other way, with the forenames first. That means even if they are filed in the right place, when you're looking for them, you can't see them.

瑪麗　檔案是根據客戶姓氏的字母順序歸檔的，這沒什麼問題，也有一定的道理，只不過很多時候檔案裡的名字並不是這樣記錄的，都是名字在前。這就意味著即使你放對了位置，但要找它們的時候，還是會找不到。

Oliver So what have you done?

奧利佛 那妳是怎麼做的？

Mary I've filed them under the date the client filed the case. The dates are available on the computers, so a simple search will show where the paper files are.

瑪麗 我根據登記客戶檔案的日期來進行歸檔。資料可以在電腦裡面找到，所以只需簡單搜索就能找到檔案。

Oliver Sounds good to me. Thank you.

奧利佛 這聽起來不錯。謝謝。

- client [ˋklaɪənt] n 顧客，客人
- make sense 有道理
- forename [ˋfɔrˏnem] n 名字

關聯必備單字

❶ **document** [ˋdɑkjəmənt] 文件

❷ **file** [faɪl] 把……歸檔

❸ **classify** [ˋklæsəˏfaɪ] 把……分類

❹ **folder** [ˋfoldɚ] 資料夾

❺ **form** [fɔrm] 表格

❻ **order** [ˋɔrdɚ] 順序

❼ **heading** [ˋhɛdɪŋ] 標題

❽ **drawer** [drɔɚ] 抽屜

❾ **relevant**
[ˋrɛləvənt] 有關的

❿ **pile**
[paɪl] 堆，大量

⓫ **archive**
[ˋɑrkaɪv] 檔案，資料庫

⓬ **alphabetically**
[ˏælfəˋbɛtɪklɪ] 按字母順序

⓭ **chronological**
[ˏkrɑnəˋlɑdʒɪkḷ] 按時間順序的

⓮ **subject**
[ˋsʌbdʒɛkt] 主題

⓯ **filing cabinet**
檔案案櫃

⓰ **methodically**
[mɪˋθɑdɪkəlɪ] 有條理地

⓱ **confidential**
[ˏkɑnfəˋdɛnʃəl] 機密的

⓲ **safe**
[sef] 保險櫃，保險箱

⓳ **sort out**
整理

專業貼心便條

工作雖然十分繁忙，但也要記住笑臉迎人，微笑不僅能夠拉近彼此之間的距離，也是你自身修養的一種表現。在職場中，有時就需要練就完美的職業笑容，你知道怎麼做到嗎？

1. 初級微笑：拿一根筷子，用牙齒輕輕橫咬住它，對著鏡子記住此時你的面部和嘴部的形狀，而這個口形就是合適的「微笑」。
2. 高級微笑：這是發自內心的微笑，當用紙擋住鼻子以下的部位時，還可以看到眼中的笑意。

SECTION 02

收發傳真
Sending and Receiving Faxes

隨身應急情境句

Track 014

1	Can you send it to me by fax? 你能把它傳真給我嗎？
2	Could you fax it to me now? 你能不能現在把它傳真給我？
3	Please fax me the catalogue of your new items. 請把你們新產品的目錄傳真給我。
4	Would you send this fax for me, please? 你能幫我把這份傳真發出去嗎？
5	Can you teach me how to use the fax machine? I need to send a fax. 你能教我如何使用傳真機嗎？我要發一份傳真。
6	Press the button “start” after you get through. 撥通時按「開始」鍵。
7	I'd like to send a fax to Paris, please. 我想發一份傳真到巴黎。
8	Kate asked me to send a fax to Mr. Brown. 凱特要我發傳真給布朗先生。

9	How many pages are you sending? 你要發多少頁？
10	What's your fax number? 你的傳真號碼是多少？
11	Can you tell me your fax number? 能告訴我你的傳真號碼嗎？
12	Where do you want to fax it to? 請問你想傳真到哪裡？
13	I just got an error message. 我剛剛收到一個錯誤資訊。
14	Your fax didn't go through. 你的傳真沒有發出去。
15	Our fax machine is under repair now. 我們的傳真機現在在維修。
16	I was on vacation last week and didn't receive your fax. 我上個禮拜在度假，沒收到你們的傳真。

萬能好用句型

- Could you fax it to …? 你能不能把它傳真給……？
- Please fax me …. 請把……傳真給我。
- I need to send a fax. 我要發一份傳真。
- What's your fax number? 你的傳真號碼是多少？

- Where do you want to fax it to? 請問你想傳真到哪裡？
- Your fax didn't go through. 你的傳真沒發出去。
- I've never sent a fax before. 我之前沒發過傳真

職場應答對話

✦ 如何發傳真 How to Send a Fax ✦

Emma Hey, Tommy, can you help me to do this? I've never sent a fax before.

艾瑪 嘿，湯米，你能幫我弄一下這個嗎？我之前沒發過傳真。

Tommy Of course. Do you have the details of the person you are sending the fax to?

湯米 當然。妳有收件人的資訊嗎？

Emma Yes. The number is written down here.

艾瑪 有。號碼寫在這裡了。

Tommy Have you contacted the company to tell them that you are sending them a fax?

湯米 妳有聯繫收件公司跟他們說妳要發一份傳真過去了嗎？

Emma Yes. I just spoke with them on the phone. They are expecting it.

艾瑪 有啊。我剛剛有打過去跟他們說。他們正在等。

Tommy OK. So what you do is to punch their number into this dial on the right. Next, you have to feed the first sheet of paper into this section here — it will be sucked into the machine quite slowly. Then you feed each sheet one by one after. Simple as that.

湯米 好的。那妳要做的就是在右邊的面板上輸入他們的傳真號碼。然後，妳把紙張的第一頁放在這裡——紙會慢慢被捲入機器。然後妳再一張一張地放紙。就這麼簡單。

Emma Thanks very much.

艾瑪 非常謝謝你。

- punch [pʌntʃ] v 敲打，猛擊
- sheet [ʃit] n （紙）薄片，張
- suck [sʌk] v 把……捲入，吸

關聯必備單字

❶ **fax**
[fæks] 傳真

❷ **fax machine**
傳真機

❸ **sheet of paper**
紙張

❹ **transmission**
[træns`mɪʃən] 傳送

❺ **temperature**
[`tɛmprətʃɚ] 溫度

❻ **confirmation**
[ˌkɑnfɚ`meʃən] 確認

❼ **prompt**
[prɑmpt] 立刻的

❽ **template**
[`tɛmplɪt] 範本

❾ **bitmap**
[`bɪtmæp] 點陣圖

❿ **format**
[`fɔrmæt] 格式

⓫ **error**
[`ɛrɚ] 錯誤

⓬ **error page**
錯誤頁面

⓭ **catalog**
[`kætəlɔg] 目錄

⓮ **button**
[`bʌtn] 按鈕

SECTION 03

影印、列印資料
Copying and Printing

隨身應急情境句

Track 015

1 Do you know how to add ink to the photocopier?
你知道怎麼給影印機加墨嗎？

2 I'm afraid it's out of paper. You have to add paper to the copier.
紙恐怕用完了。你要加一些紙到影印機裡面。

3 Please copy this report for me.
請幫我影印這份文件。

4 The copy machine is over there.
影印機在那邊。

5 How many copies would you like?
您要影印多少份？

6 Please make five copies of the document.
請把這份文件影印五份。

7 Do you want color copies or black and white copies?
你想要印彩色的還是黑白的？

8 You can do double-sided copying.
你可以雙面影印。

9	What's the paper size that you want? 你想要什麼紙型？
10	Which size should I use? 我應該用哪種尺寸的紙？
11	The A4 paper is fine. A4 紙就可以了。
12	I'm printing a copy of the document for you. 我正在替您列印這份檔案。
13	I need to bind these copies. 我需要裝訂這些影印資料。
14	You can find the print papers in the paper tray over there. 你能在那邊的紙盒裡找到列印紙。
15	The printer is out of order. 這個印表機故障了。
16	I think we need a new photocopier. This one is so easy to get a paper jam. 我覺得我們需要一台新的影印機。這台很容易卡紙。

萬能好用句型

- It's out of paper. 紙用完了。
- How many copies would you like? 您要影印多少份？
- Please make … copies of the document.
  請把這份文件影印……份。

- You can do double-sided copying. 你可以雙面影印。
- What's the paper size that you want? 你想要什麼紙型？
- … is out of order. ……故障了。
- I need to make prints of these documents
  我需要列印這些檔案。

職場應答對話

✦ 要找影印店來完成 Need a Print Shop to Finish ✦

Jessica I need to make prints of these documents.
潔西卡 我需要列印這些檔案。

Steve Just use the printer down the hall.
史蒂夫 就用走廊那邊的印表機吧。

Jessica I've got to print out five hundred and fifty copies. They can't be photocopied, because we don't have a color copy machine, and I need color prints.
潔西卡 我要列印 550 份。但不能影印，因為我們沒有彩色影印機，而我需要彩色列印。

Steve Wow! That is a lot. Maybe it would be a better idea to send them to a print shop?
史蒂夫 哇！那很多耶。或許去影印店列印會比較好？

Jessica Right. They'll be able to handle the large volume, and it would probably work out cheaper than using our small machine here. Do you know where a good print shop is?
潔西卡 對。他們可以應付大需求量，而且可能比使用我們這裡的小型印表機更省錢。你知道哪裡有好的影印店嗎？

Steve	Honestly, no, I don't. But I'm sure if you ask reception they'll find you one.
史蒂夫	老實說，我不知道。但我想如果妳去櫃台問一下，他們能幫妳找到吧。
Jessica	Thanks, Steve.
潔西卡	謝謝，史蒂夫。

- volume [ˋvaljum] n 量
- reception [rɪˋsɛpʃən] n 接待

關聯必備單字

❶ **photocopier**
[ˋfotə͵kɑpɪɚ] 影印機

❷ **printer**
[ˋprɪntɚ] 印表機

❸ **color printer**
彩色印表機

❹ **laser printer**
雷射印表機

❺ **copy**
[ˋkɑpɪ] 影印

❻ **print**
[prɪnt] 列印

❼ **type**
[taɪp] 打字

❽ **filename**
[ˋfaɪlnem] 檔案名稱

❾ **ink**
[ɪŋk] 油墨

❿ **flash**
[flæʃ] 閃光

⓫ **bind**
[baɪnd] 裝訂

⓬ **stapler**
[ˋsteplɚ] 訂書器

⓭ **double-sided**
兩面的，雙面的

⓮ **paper size**
紙型，紙張尺寸

⓯ **paper jam**
卡紙

SECTION 04

公司內部郵件往來
Communicating with Co-Workers via Email

隨身應急情境句

Track 016

1. Can you send me an email with more details?
能不能寄一封信給我跟我說一下更多細節？

2. I haven't got an email box.
我還沒有電子信箱。

3. Can you help me set up an email account?
你能幫我創建一個電子郵件帳戶嗎？

4. I need to apply for a free mailbox.
我要申請一個免費信箱。

5. What's your email address?
你的電子信箱位址是？

6. Let's exchange our email addresses.
讓我們交換一下電子信箱地址吧。

7. You can send it to my email.
你可以寄電子郵件給我。

8. Please send a copy of this email to Mike.
請寄一份這封信的副本給邁克。

9	Please send email to Mr. Parker directly and CC to Jason meanwhile. 請直接給寄信派克先生，同時發副本給給傑生。
10	I just got an email from Mr. Parker. 我剛收到一封來自派克先生的郵件。
11	I emailed you these information yesterday. 這些資訊我昨天有用郵件寄給你了。
12	Please check your email. 請查看你的信件。
13	I need to delete these junk emails. 我要刪除這些垃圾信件。
14	I have a stack of emails in my inbox. 我的收件箱裡有一堆信件。
15	There must be something wrong with my email. 我的電子郵件一定有問題。
16	The email I sent to Mary was returned as undeliverable. 我寄給瑪麗的信件被退了回來，寄不出去。

萬能好用句型

- What's your email address?　你的電子信箱位址是？
- You can send … to my email.　你可以把……用郵件寄給我。

Chapter 01
Chapter 02
Chapter 03
Chapter 04
Chapter 05
Chapter 06
Chapter 07
Chapter 08
Chapter 09
Chapter 10
Chapter 11

- Please send a copy of this email to …
  請寄一份這封信的副本給……。
- Please send email to … directly and CC to … meanwhile.
  請直接寄信給……，同時寄副本給……
- I just got an email from …　我剛收到一封來自……的信。
- Please check your email.　請查看你的郵件。
- I need to delete these junk emails.　我要刪除這些垃圾信件。

職場應答對話

✦ 設置郵件主題 Give Every Email a Subject ✦

Susan So I emailed you those instructions yesterday, Adam. Did you not see them? Because the conclusion to the report isn't the same as what I asked for.

蘇珊 亞當，我昨天把那些說明寄給你了。你沒有看到是嗎？因為這個報告的結論跟我要求的不一樣。

Adam Actually, no, I didn't see them. Are you sure you sent it to me?

亞當 事實上，沒有，我沒看到。妳確定寄給我了嗎？

Susan Yes. I sent them yesterday afternoon.

蘇珊 是的。我昨天下午寄的。

Adam Can you tell me the subject of the email, so I can search through my inbox?

亞當 你能告訴我信件的主題嗎，這樣我可以在收件箱裡進行搜索？

Susan Subject? I don't think I gave the email a subject.

蘇珊 主題？我應該沒有寫郵件的主題。

Adam That's the problem then. You must give every email a subject. The company email system will remove all emails without subjects, and place them in "spam" to make sure we don't get junk emails from outside.

亞當 那這就是問題所在了。妳一定要在每一封信件裡都設主題。公司的郵件系統會移除沒有主題的信件，把它丟到「垃圾郵件」裡，確保我們不會收到來自外部的垃圾郵件。

Susan Oh, no. I had no idea. Next time, I'll be sure to write one.

蘇珊 噢，不會吧。我不知道。下次我一定會寫一個。

- instruction [ɪn`strʌkʃn] n 用法說明
- conclusion [kən`kluʒən] n 結論
- remove [rɪ`muv] v 移動，移開
- spam [spæm] n 垃圾郵件

關聯必備單字

1. **account** [ə`kaʊnt] 帳戶
2. **username** [`juzɚ͵nem] 用戶名
3. **password** [`pæs͵wɝd] 密碼
4. **inbox** [`ɪnbɑks] 收件箱
5. **outbox** [`aʊtbɑks] 寄件匣
6. **draft** [dræft] 草稿
7. **send** [sɛnd] 寄送
8. **receive** [rɪ`siv] 接受
9. **delete** [dɪ`lit] 刪除
10. **enclosure** [ɪn`kloʒɚ] 附件

⓫ **postscript**
[ˋpostˏskrɪpt] 附言

⓬ **subject**
[ˋsʌbdʒɪkt] 主題

⓭ **via**
[ˋvaɪə] 通過

⓮ **junk email**
垃圾信件

專業貼心便條

你知道電子郵件的由來嗎？對於世界上第一封電子郵件，現在有兩種說法：

1. 第一種說法是，據《互聯網世界》報導，世界上第一封電子郵件是 1969 年 10 月由電腦科學家 Leonard K. 教授發給他的同事的一條簡短消息。
2. 第二種說法是，1971 年由為阿帕網工作的麻省理工學院博士 Ray Tomlinson 測試軟體 SNDMSG 時發出的，並且首次使用「@」作為位址間隔標示。

SECTION 05

發函聯絡客戶

Contacting Clients Using Business Emails

隨身應急情境句

Track 017

1. If you have any questions, please feel free to contact us.
如果您有任何問題，請隨時跟我們聯繫。

2. Would you please reply to this email if you are interested in this project?
如果您對這個項目感興趣的話，請回信告知我們好嗎？

3. If you are interested in these new items, please contact us.
如果您對這些新產品感興趣的話，請聯繫我們。

4. If you plan to attend, let me know by email as soon as possible.
如果您計劃參加，請儘快寄郵件告知。

5. I'll email you a confirmation immediately.
我馬上寄一封確認函給您。

6. Any information on business cooperation will be much appreciated.
任何生意合作的訊息，我們都將非常感激。

7	Any comments will be highly appreciated. 對於您的任何建議，我們都將非常感激。
8	I would appreciate it if you could send me your reply by next Friday. 如果能在下週五前收到您的回覆，我將不勝感激。
9	We will be always at your service. 我們會隨時為您服務。
10	We look forward to your prompt reply. 我們期待您的及時回覆。
11	Thank you for your attention and we are looking forward to hearing from you soon. 謝謝您的關注，我們期待能很快收到您的回覆。
12	Hopefully I'll get a reply from him very soon. 希望我能很快收到他的回覆。
13	Let's keep in touch. We can correspond via email. 讓我們保持聯繫吧。我們可以用電子郵件通信。
14	Glad to receive your email. 很高興收到您的電子郵件。
15	Thank you for your reply. 謝謝您的回覆。
16	Please keep me informed on the matter. 請隨時讓我知道這件事的進展。

萬能好用句型

- If you have any questions, please feel free to contact us.
  如果您有任何問題，請隨時跟我們聯繫。
- If you are interested in …, please contact us.
  如果您對……感興趣的話，請聯繫我們。
- Would you please reply to this email if you are interested in …?
  如果您對……感興趣的話，請回覆郵件告知我們好嗎？
- … will be highly appreciated.　對於……我們將非常感激。
- I would appreciate it if you could send me your reply by ….
  如果能在……前收到您的回覆，我將不勝感激。
- We will be always at your service.　我們會隨時為您服務。
- We are looking forward to hearing from you soon.
  我們期待能很快得到您的回覆。

職場應答對話

✦ 與客戶的溝通方式 The Way of Contacting Clients ✦

Kevin Hey Jenny, thanks for coming. We need to have a talk today about the way you've been contacting some of the clients.

凱文 嘿，珍妮，謝謝妳過來。今天我們需要談一談妳跟一些客戶溝通的方式。

Jenny Oh. Is there a problem?

珍妮 噢。有什麼問題嗎？

Kevin Yes, I'm afraid, but only a small one. You see, most of the time you are writing to people through their company email address, correct?

凱文 恐怕是的，不過只是一個小問題。妳看，大部份時間妳都是寄郵件到他們的公司信箱，對嗎？

Jenny Yes, that's right.

珍妮 沒錯，就是這樣。

Kevin The problem is, your language is very informal when you write to them, and we've had one or two comments about it. You need to use much more formal, business-like language, not the same language you use to contact friends. Company emails can be read by anyone in the company, so please be sure to be more professional in company emails in the future.

凱文 問題是，妳寫郵件給他們時，使用的言語很不正式，在這點上我們有一些建議。妳要使用更為正式和商務化的言語，而不是跟朋友聯繫時所用的那種。辦公郵件可能會被轉發給公司其他人看，所以請確保今後辦公電子郵件的內容更加專業。

Jenny OK. Sorry for that.

珍妮 好的。我對此感到很抱歉。

關聯必備單字

❶ **succinct**
[sək`sɪŋkt] 簡潔的

❷ **concise**
[kən`saɪs] 簡明扼要的

❸ **equivalent**
[ɪ`kwɪvələnt] 相等的

❹ **informality**
[ˌɪnfɔr`mælətɪ] 非正式

❺ **formal**
[`fɔrml̩] 正式的

❻ **recipient**
[rɪ`sɪpɪənt] 接受者

❼ **contact**
[`kɑntækt] 聯繫

❽ **grammatical**
[grə`mætɪkl̩] 文法上的

❾ **grammar**
[ˋgræmɚ] 文法

❿ **punctuation**
[ˏpʌŋktʃʊˋeʃən] 標點

⓫ **sincerely**
[sɪnˋsɪrlɪ] 由衷地

⓬ **confirmation**
[ˏkɑnfɚˋmeʃən] 確認函，證實

⓭ **comment**
[ˋkɑmɛnt] 評論， 意見

⓮ **prompt**
[prɑmpt] 敏捷的，迅速的

⓯ **correspond**
[ˏkɔrɪˋspɑnd] 通信

⓰ **stumble**
[ˋstʌmbl̩] 出錯

專業貼心便條

電子郵件行銷是通過電子郵件的方式向目標使用者傳遞價值資訊的一種網路行銷手段。而在實施電子郵件行銷策略的時候，下面的這幾條禁忌是你必須要知道的：

1. 濫發郵件；
2. 郵件沒有主題，或主題不夠明確；
3. 隱藏寄件者姓名；
4. 郵件內容繁雜；
5. 郵件內容採用附件形式；
6. 發送頻率過高；
7. 沒有目標定位；
8. 郵件格式混亂；
9. 不及時回覆客戶郵件；
10. 對主動來信的客戶索取高額費用。

SECTION 06

遇到了問題，尋求幫助
Asking for Help

隨身應急情境句

Track 018

1 Could you give me a hand?
你能幫我個忙嗎？

2 I really need some help with this.
這件事我真的需要幫助。

3 I wonder if you could do me a favor.
我想知道你能不能幫我一個忙。

4 Could you do me a favor?
你能幫我個忙嗎？

5 Is there anything else I can do for you?
還有什麼我能幫你做的嗎？

6 Can I be of any assistance?
我能幫上什麼忙嗎？

7 Can you do me a favor by sending this fax to Mr. Smith?
你能幫我把這份傳真寄給史密斯先生嗎？

8 Will you help me make a decision?
你能幫我作個決定嗎？

9	What do you need to help decide on? 你需要幫忙做什麼決定？
10	Can you help me scan this photo? 你能幫我掃描這張照片嗎？
11	Can you show me how the scanner works? 你能示範給我看一下這台掃描器怎麼用嗎？
12	Thank you for taking the time to help. 謝謝你花時間來幫我。
13	I really appreciate your help. 非常感謝你的幫忙。
14	I am very grateful for your help. 我很感謝你的幫助。
15	I'm sorry to take up so much of your time. 佔用了你這麼多時間，不好意思。
16	I'm glad I could be of some help to you. 我很高興我能給你幫上忙。
17	I wish I could help you, but I can't. 我希望能幫你，但我幫不了。
18	I can do nothing about it. 我對此無能為力。
19	I'm sorry I can't help you. 抱歉，我幫不了你。

萬能好用句型

- I really need some help with this.
  這件事我真的需要幫助。
- Could you do me a favor?
  你能幫我個忙嗎？
- Can I be of any assistance?
  我能幫上什麼忙嗎？
- Will you help me …?
  你能幫我……嗎？
- I am very grateful for your help.
  我很感激你的幫助。
- I'm glad I could be of some help to you.
  我很高興我能幫上你的忙。
- I can do nothing about it.
  我對此無能為力。

職場應答對話

✦ 你應該找安妮幫忙 You Should Ask Annie for Help ✦

Roger Megan, can I speak with you for a moment?
羅傑 梅根，我能跟妳談一下嗎？

Megan Of course. What's wrong?
梅根 當然。怎麼了？

Roger Well, this task that you completed yesterday is completely wrong. From beginning to end, it is done in completely the wrong order, and two sections don't have all the required information. The thing is, you were going to ask Annie for help with this, but you didn't, did you?

羅傑 噢，昨天妳完成的這項任務完全做錯了。從頭到尾順序全弄錯了，而且有兩個部分要求要有的資訊不全。問題是，妳應該找安妮幫忙的，但妳沒有，是嗎？

Megan No, I didn't. She seemed busy, so I decided to try by myself.

梅根 是的，我沒有。她好像很忙，所以我決定自己試試看。

Roger It's perfectly fine to ask for help. You asked me. Why couldn't you ask her? In future, you can't make any more mistakes like this. Everyone gets it wrong in the beginning, but if you don't get help, you'll never get it right.

羅傑 請求幫助沒有什麼的。妳有問過我啊。為什麼不能問她呢？今後妳不能再犯這樣的錯誤了。剛開始時每個人都會犯錯，但如果妳不尋求幫助的話，妳永遠都會做不到。

Megan OK. I'll be sure to ask in future.

梅根 好的。我保證以後會問的。

關聯必備單字

❶ **assistance**
[əˋsɪstəns] 幫助

❷ **aid**
[ed] 援助

❸ **help**
[hɛlp] 幫助

❹ **helpful**
[ˋhɛlpfəl] 有幫助的

❺ **useful**
[ˋjusfəl] 有用的

❻ **problem**
[ˋprɑbləm] 問題

❼ **scanner**
[ˋskænɚ] 掃描器

❽ **scan**
[skæn] 掃描

❾ **bother**
[ˋbɑðɚ] 打擾

❿ **backup**
[ˋbækʌp] 支援

⓫ **puzzle**
[ˋpʌzl̩] 使……困惑

⓬ **confused**
[kənˋfjuzd] 困惑的

⓭ **beneficial**
[ˏbɛnəˋfɪʃəl] 有益的

⓮ **appreciate**
[əˋpriʃɪˏet] 感激

⓯ **grateful**
[ˋgretfəl] 感激的

⓰ **take up**
佔用（時間、空間或精力）

專業貼心便條

我們應該如何釋放壓力呢，下面幾點可供大家參考：

1. 通過溝通釋放壓力，敞開心扉，多與親朋好友聊天，必要時還可以與上司談心；
2. 學會勞逸結合，每工作一段時間就要休息一下，做一些可以娛樂精神和放鬆身體的活動；
3. 不要將責任都攬到自己身上，要設法學會和他人合作，與他人分擔責任；不要過分拘泥于成功， 有意義、有經驗的失敗要比簡單的成功獲益更大；
4. 有時候可以自我讚美一番，保持自我良好感覺；
5. 要著眼於全域，不拘泥於瑣碎之事。如果對每一件小事、每一個細節之處過分擔心，長此以往， 將被壓力壓垮。

SECTION 07

面對失誤，不要氣餒
Facing Mistakes

隨身應急情境句

Track 019

1	I screwed up. 我搞砸了。
2	I really messed up this time! 這次我真的是搞砸了！
3	It's all my fault. 這都是我的錯。
4	I should apologize for this. 我應該為這件事道歉。
5	All my efforts ended in failure. 我所有的努力都以失敗告終。
6	It's nobody's fault. You didn't do anything wrong. 這不是任何人的錯。你沒做錯任何事。
7	Don't worry. We all make mistakes. 別擔心了。我們都會犯錯。
8	Take it easy. Failure is the mother of success. 放輕鬆。失敗是成功之母。

9	We learn and grow through mistakes. 我們在錯誤中學習和成長。
10	One grows in defeat. 人在失敗中成長。
11	I promise that won't happen again. 我保證那樣的事再也不會發生了。
12	I'll never do it again. 我再也不會這麼做了。
13	You did a good job. It should be fine. 你做得很好。應該沒事的。
14	Keep on working and you'll be successful. 好好做，你會成功的。
15	Keep your chin up. 別灰心。
16	There's no reason to lose confidence in yourself. 你沒有理由對自己失去信心。
17	But I am always worrying about making mistakes. 但我總是擔心出錯。
18	Don't give up. I'm right behind you. 不要放棄。我支持你。
19	I appreciate your kind words. 我很感謝你友善的話語。

萬能好用句型

- I screwed up.　我搞砸了。
- I should apologize for this.　我應該為此事道歉。
- It's nobody's fault.　這不是任何人的錯。
- We all make mistakes.　我們都會犯錯。
- Failure is the mother of success.　失敗是成功之母。
- One grows in defeat.　人在失敗中成長。
- Keep your chin up.　別灰心。
- Don't give up. I'm right behind you.　不要放棄。我支持你。

職場應答對話

✦ 面對失誤 Facing Mistakes ✦

Will Helen. Can I have a word with you in my office, please?

威爾 海倫，能到我的辦公室來談一下嗎？

Helen Sure.

海倫 當然可以。

Will Great. Follow me. Take a seat, please. Now I've looked over the project you completed last month and to tell you the truth, it doesn't look very good at all. Not at all what we were looking for. What do you have to say about it?

威爾 很好。跟我來。請坐。現在我看完妳上個月完成的項目了，說實話，看起來做得很不好。完全不是我們想要的那樣。妳有什麼要說的嗎？

Helen I'm sorry. I tried to take it in a different direction, and I got it all confused and missed the point of the project entirely. It's all my fault, just using poor judgment, and in the future I'll know not to deviate too much from the outlines I'm given.

海倫 我很抱歉。我嘗試從另一個方面來做，可都搞亂了，而且完全忽視了專案的重點。這都是我的錯，判斷失誤，以後我就知道不要跟我得到的大綱偏離太多了。

Will Well. Thanks for facing your mistake. It seems like we're going to be able to avoid these mistakes in the future.

威爾 好吧。謝謝妳面對自己的失誤。看來今後我們就能避免這些錯誤了。

- deviate [ˋdivɪˏet] v 脫離，偏離
- outline [ˋaʊtlaɪn] n 大綱，輪廓

關聯必備單字

❶ **blame**
[blem] 責備

❷ **mistake**
[mɪˋstek] 錯誤

❸ **slip**
[slɪp] 差錯，疏漏

❹ **fault**
[fɔlt] 過錯

❺ **trouble**
[ˋtrʌbl̩] 麻煩

❻ **failure**
[ˋfeljɚ] 失敗

❼ **defeat**
[dɪˋfit] 挫敗

❽ **frustrated**
[frʌˋstretɪd] 受挫的

❾ **thwart**
[θwɔrt] 阻撓

❿ **apologize**
[əˋpɑləˏdʒaɪz] 道歉

⓫ **adversity**
[ədˋvɝsətɪ] 逆境

⓬ **faith**
[feθ] 信念

⓭ **setback**
[ˋsetˏbæk] 挫折

⓮ **lesson**
[ˋlɛsn] 教訓

⓯ **smooth**
[smuð] 順利的

⓰ **mess**
[mɛs] 弄亂，毀壞

專業貼心便條

心理資本指的是個體在成長和發展過程中表現出來的一種積極心理狀態，是企業除了財力、人力、社會三大資本以外的第四大資本。心理資本能夠促進個人的成長和績效的提升，它主要包含以下幾方面：

1. 希望：一個沒有希望、自暴自棄的人是不可能創造價值的。
2. 樂觀：樂觀者會將不好的事歸結為暫時的原因，而把好事歸結為持久的原因。
3. 韌性：從逆境、衝突及失敗中迅速恢復的心理能力。
4. 主觀幸福感： 自己心裡覺得幸福，才是真正的幸福。
5. 情商：進行自我激勵、有效地管理自己情緒的能力。
6. 組織公民行為：自覺、自發地了解組織，關心組織利益，並且維護組織效益的行為。

CHAPTER

04

工作進行時 Working Time

SECTION 01

主管分配任務
Taking on a Task

隨身應急情境句

Track 020

1 I'm going to assign today's work.
我要分配今天的工作了。

2 Your task today is to write an article about young fashion designers.
你今天的任務是撰寫一篇有關年輕時裝設計師的文章。

3 Let me tell you your duties here.
我要告訴你你在這裡的職責。

4 Your main duty is to answer the telephone and receive visitors.
你主要負責接聽電話和接待訪客。

5 I'll leave it to you to inform Jenny of her work.
我讓你通知珍妮告訴她工作內容吧。

6 My immediate superior is Mr. Black. I have run a lot of errands for him today.
布萊克先生是我的直屬上司。今天我為他做了很多跑腿的事。

7 Mary, can you run an errand for me?
瑪麗，你能幫我跑個腿嗎？

8	Kate is always asked to do all the legwork of gathering information. 凱特總是被叫去做搜集資料之類的跑腿差。
9	I'm the legman for the company. 我負責為公司搜集資料。
10	Matt, I want you to do the job. 麥特，我想讓你來做這項工作。
11	Either you do it, or I'll ask for someone else. 要嘛你來做，要嘛我請其他人來做。
12	Jim will hand over the rest of his work to you. 吉姆會把剩下的工作交給你。
13	Now it will devolve on you to manage these documents. 這些檔案現在就交給你處理了。
14	When do you need it? 您什麼時候需要呢？
15	Do you need it finished right away? 您現在就要嗎？
16	How soon will you finish that? 你多久能做完那個？
17	How long do you have to get all this stuff done? 你要多久能把所有的這些事情做完？
18	You have to get this done before you leave. 你必須在下班前做完這項工作。

萬能好用句型

- Your task today is to .... 你今天的任務是⋯⋯。
- Your main duty is to .... 你主要負責⋯⋯。
- Can you run an errand for me? 你能幫我跑個腿嗎？
- I want you to do the job. 我要讓你來做這項工作。
- When do you need it? 您什麼時候需要呢？
- How long do you have to get all this stuff done?
  你要多久能把所有的這些事情做完？
- I'd like to ask some questions about ....
  我想請教一下有關⋯⋯的一些問題。

職場應答對話

✦ 專題的視角 The Angle of the Feature ✦

Paula Richard, I'd like to ask some questions about how to get started on the feature.
寶拉 理查，我想請教一下有關如何著手這個專題的一些問題。

Richard OK. Shoot.
理查 好的。說吧。

Paula Well, firstly, what kind of angle would you like me to write?
寶拉 嗯，首先，您希望我從哪個視角來寫呢？

Richard That is something we're happy for you to choose yourself.
理查 對此我們很樂意由妳自己來選擇。

Paula OK. Do you want there to be plenty of interviews, or more of my own writing?

寶拉	好的。您希望裡面含有大量的採訪，還是多一點我自己的寫作呢？
Richard	You need to do lots of research, and I'd recommend the public library as they have a great section of historical books on the subject, but you don't need to do too many interviews. One or two should be enough.
理查	妳需要做很多調查，我推薦妳去公共圖書館，裡面有大量關於這個主題的歷史著作，但妳不需進行太多的採訪。一兩個應該就夠了。
Paula	OK then. And the deadline is midday on Friday?
寶拉	好的。截稿日期是星期五的中午？
Richard	As always. You have four more days, so you had better get moving!
理查	同往常一樣。妳還有四天的時間，所以趕快著手吧！

- feature [ˋfitʃɚ] n 特寫或專題節目
- angle [ˋæŋg!] n 角度
- deadline [ˋdɛdˌlaɪn] n 截止日期

關聯必備單字

❶ **task**
[tæsk] 任務

❷ **undertake**
[ˌʌndɚˋtek] 承擔

❸ **assign**
[əˋsaɪn] 分配

❹ **assignment**
[əˋsaɪnmənt] 任務

❺ **errand**
[ˋɛrənd] 差事

❻ **fairly**
[ˋfɛrlɪ] 公平地

❼ **carry out**
執行

❽ **president**
[ˋprɛzədənt] 總裁

❾ **vice-president**
[ˏvaɪsˋprɛzədənt] 副總裁

❿ **boss**
[bɔs] 老闆

⓫ **manager**
[ˋmænɪdʒɚ] 經理

⓬ **general manager**
總經理

⓭ **superior**
[səˋpɪrɪɚ] 上司

⓮ **subordinate**
[səˋbɔrdnɪt] 下屬

⓯ **article**
[ˋɑrtɪkl̩] 文章

⓰ **recommend**
[ˏrɛkəˋmɛnd] 推薦

專業貼心便條

當記下了重要工作時，可以將之寫在便條紙上，從而提醒自己及時處理。但你知道要怎麼寫便條才能讓工作效率得到提高嗎，下面幾點要記下：

1. 一張便條紙只記下一件事情，可以防止你遺漏掉某件重要的事情。
2. 字要寫得大些，這樣才更醒目，也才能更好地達到提醒的作用。
3. 可以根據事情的緊急和重要程度，使用不同顏色的便條紙。
4. 處理完的事情就撕掉吧，可以增加一些成就感。

SECTION 02

開始進行工作
Getting Started

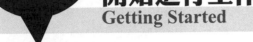

隨身應急情境句

Track 021

1. Let's get down to work.
我們開始工作吧。

2. Let's get to work, shall we?
我們開始工作吧，好嗎？

3. We must start to work.
我們得開始工作了。

4. Shall I begin my work?
我可以開始工作了嗎？

5. I must go back to my work.
我必須回去工作了。

6. I have to go back to work now.
現在我得回去工作了。

7. There is much work to be done.
還有很多工作要做。

8. Let's hurry up.
我們快點吧。

9. Let's get moving.
我們加快速度吧。

10	Let’s press on with our work. 我們抓緊時間工作吧。
11	Things are sticky and time is limited. 事情很棘手，時間又有限。
12	It is the first step that costs troublesome. 萬事開頭難。
13	A good beginning makes a good ending. 好的開始是成功的一半。
14	My boss asked me to apply for an enterprise email before I get to work. 老闆叫我開始工作之前先申請一個公司用電子信箱。
15	I’ll try my best to get used to my new job. 我會儘快適應我的新工作。
16	Don’t worry. Things will come out all right. 別擔心。一切都會好的。
17	I’m doing what I can, bit by bit. 我在一步一步做我能做的。
18	I believe you can do it well. 我相信你能把它做好。
19	Get going! And I’m sure you’ll be fine. 開始做吧！我相信你沒有問題的。

萬能好用句型

- Let's get down to work.
  我們開始工作吧。
- I have to go back to work now.
  現在我得回去工作了。
- There is much work to be done.
  還有很多工作要做。
- Let's get moving.
  我們加快速度吧。
- A good beginning makes a good ending.
  好的開始是成功的一半。
- I'll try my best to get used to my new job.
  我會儘快適應我的新工作。
- How did it go today?
  今天怎麼樣？

職場應答對話

✦ 我的計劃 My Plan ✦

Peter So, how did it go today? Did you get what you needed?
彼得 那麼，今天怎麼樣？妳要的東西到手了嗎？

Helen Yes, thanks. It went well. I took some great pictures, and they are being printed out tonight. I know what I need to write about. I just need to work out what order I'm going to do things in.

海倫 是的，謝謝。進行得很順利。我拍了一些很棒的照片，今晚都能洗出來。我知道我要寫什麼了。我只需要確定按照順序來處理這些事情就行了。

Peter So you're planning it out now?

彼得 那妳現在計劃好了嗎？

Helen Yes. This here is my plan. I've started, but I can't start writing until I've decided how the project will be structured. Here I have some diagrams and charts to help me decide the best way.

海倫 好了。這就是我的計劃。我已經開始做了，但要等到確定了專案的結構以後我才能動筆。這裡有些圖解和圖表來幫我判斷出最佳方法。

Peter Looks like you're organizing it very well.

彼得 看起來妳處理得不錯啊。

Helen It's tough, but it is a really important step. After this, I can really start to put the project together.

海倫 很難，但這是很重要的一步。在這之後，我就能真正開始把這個項目合併到一起了。

- structure [ˋstrʌktʃɚ] v 構成，組織
- tough [tʌf] adj 艱苦的，困難的

關聯必備單字

❶ **project**
[ˋprɑdʒɛkt] 項目

❷ **diagram**
[ˋdaɪə͵græm] 圖解， 圖表

❸ **chart**
[tʃɑrt] 圖表

❹ **troublesome**
[ˋtrʌbl̩səm] 麻煩的

❺ **beginning**
[bɪˋgɪnɪŋ] 開始

❻ **rush**
[rʌʃ] 匆忙

❼ **speed**
[spid] 速度

❽ **limited**
[ˋlɪmɪtɪd] 有限的

❾ **immediately**
[ɪˋmidɪɪtlɪ] 馬上

❿ **schedule**
[ˋskɛdʒʊl] 計劃

⓫ **hurry**
[ˋhɝɪ] 急忙，匆忙

⓬ **sticky**
[ˋstɪkɪ] 棘手的

專業貼心便條

為了提高工作效率，可以將你所有的工作劃分為「事務型」和「思考型」兩類：

1.「事務型」工作

是指那些無需動腦、能夠按照所熟悉的流程做下去的工作。這類工作不怕干擾和中斷，可按照自己的計劃在任何情況下順利完成。

2.「思考型」工作

是指那些必須集中精力進行腦力勞動才能完成的工作。此類工作集中進行處理更有成效。

SECTION 03

與同事溝通交流
Communicating with Your Co-Workers

隨身應急情境句

Track 022

1	May I call you Bella? 我可以叫你貝拉嗎？
2	Could I call you by your first name? 我可以叫你的名字嗎？
3	It's a pleasure working with you, Jason. 跟你一起工作很愉快，傑森。
4	Where shall we start? 我們從哪裡開始？
5	If you have any problem, please turn to Kate. 如果有任何問題，請向凱特請教。
6	You may turn to Vicky, if there is any problem. 如果有什麼問題，你可以去問薇姬。
7	It isn't that easy. You may come across many problems. 這沒那麼簡單。你們可能會遇到很多問題。
8	It's not an easy job, but worth it. 這不是一件容易的工作，但辛苦終將值得。

9	This job is getting really tough. 工作真的越來越艱難了。
10	There's something wrong. 出問題了。
11	Just look on the bright side. 要往好的一面看。
12	Can you do me a favor to operate the computer? 你可以幫我弄一下電腦嗎？
13	Thanks for everything you did for me. 謝謝你為我做的一切。
14	I'm here if you need me. 我隨傳隨到。
15	Why not pour out your troubles? 你為什麼不把你的煩惱說出來呢？
16	Why not talk to your boss about your concerns to make him know exactly how you feel? 為什麼不和你的上司說一下你的憂慮，讓他瞭解你的感受呢？
17	Now just relax. Take some deep breaths. 現在只要放鬆下來。深呼吸。
18	Sports can help us relax. 運動能讓我們放鬆。

19 Listening to music is an excellent means of relaxation.
聽音樂是一種非常好的放鬆方式。

20 Getting a run in the garden, at times, is necessary for clearing one's head from the stress of life.
有時候，在公園裡跑步有助於放鬆心情，擺脫沉重的生活壓力。

萬能好用句型

- May I call you ...? 我可以叫你……嗎？
- It's a pleasure working with you.
  跟你一起工作很愉快。
- If you have any problem, please turn to ...
  如果有任何問題，請向……請教。
- You may turn to ... if there is any problem.
  如果有什麼問題，你可以去問……。
- There's something wrong.
  出問題了。
- Just look on the bright side.
  要往好的一面看。
- I'm here if you need me.
  我隨傳隨到。
- ... is an excellent means of relaxation .
  ……是一種非常好的放鬆方式。

職場應答對話

✦ 與上司溝通 Communicate with the Boss ✦

Lucy I think there needs to be a better way for us to communicate with the bosses. It's fine when we want to talk to each other, but only to get to talk to them once a month in the meeting, and that's not enough.

露西 我覺得我們需要一個更好的方式跟主管們進行溝通。我們想彼此溝通是沒問題的，但只有在每月的例會上才能跟他們交流，那不夠。

Bill I know. Nothing ever gets changed.

比爾 我明白。可一直都沒什麼變化。

Lucy What could we suggest?

露西 我們要提出什麼建議呢？

Bill Firstly, we could have meetings once a week instead of once a month.

比爾 首先，我們可以把每月一次的會議改為每週一次。

Lucy OK. And perhaps we could have a direct Internet line to them, that need to check every few days to know about problems.

露西 好的。或許我們還可以在網路上直接跟主管聯絡，那就需要每隔幾天查看一下問題。

Bill Right. A special email address, only for intra-company emails.

比爾 沒錯。一個特殊的電子信箱，只供公司內部交流使用。

Lucy That would certainly speed up communication, and make the workers feel like they were being heard.

露西 這樣肯定能加強溝通，讓員工們感到他們的心聲有被傾聽。

Bill We should suggest it.

比爾 我們應該提出這個建議。

- intra-company [ˌɪntrəˋkʌmpənɪ] adj 公司內部的
- speed up（使）加速

關聯必備單字

❶ **communication**
[kəˌmjunɪˋkeʃən] 溝通

❷ **communication skills**
溝通技巧

❸ **courteous**
[ˋkɝtɪəs] 謙遜的

❹ **upcoming**
[ˋʌpkʌmɪŋ] 即將到來的

❺ **pressure**
[ˋprɛʃɚ] 壓力

❻ **obstacle**
[ˋɑbstəkl̩] 障礙

❼ **side**
[saɪd] 方面

❽ **motto**
[ˋmɑto] 格言

❾ **worth**
[wɝθ] 值得

❿ **enjoyable**
[ɪnˋdʒɔɪəbl̩] 令人愉快的

⓫ **thoroughly**
[ˋθɝolɪ] 徹底地

⓬ **hesitate**
[ˋhɛzəˌtet] 猶豫

⓭ **operate**
[ˋɑpəret] 操作，運轉

⓮ **concern**
[kənˋsɝn] 擔心，憂慮

⓯ **relaxation**
[ˌrilækˋseʃən] 放鬆，消遣

⓰ **stress**
[strɛs] 壓力

SECTION 04

彙報工作進度
Reporting Your Progress

隨身應急情境句

Track 023

1 What are you getting done today?
今天你完成了什麼任務？

2 Are you done with these documents?
你處理完這些檔案了嗎？

3 Did you get everything done today?
今天的事情都處理好了嗎？

4 Can I see your papers?
我可以看一下你的報告嗎？

5 I need to go over the financial reports.
我要看一下財務報告。

6 How's the project going?
項目進展得怎麼樣了？

7 How's the report coming along?
報告進展得如何？

8 Everything is under control.
一切都在掌握中。

9 I'm afraid there's gonna be a change in plans.
恐怕計劃會有些改變。

10	Please inform the sales manager of the change immediately. 請立刻通知業務部經理計劃有變。
11	Just go ahead as planned. 按照原計劃進行吧。
12	I stick to the original plan. 我堅持按照原計劃執行。
13	Things will go on as scheduled. 事情會按照原計劃進行。
14	How much longer do you need to get the project done? 你還要多久能把項目做完？
15	How soon will you finish this report? 這份報告你還要多久能做完？
16	We need to submit our progress report today. 我們今天需要繳交進度報告。
17	We must have it done by tomorrow. 我們明天之前必須做完。
18	We're halfway there. 我們已經完成一半了。
19	It's 80% done. 這個已經完成 80%了。
20	We're ahead of schedule. 我們要提前完工了。

萬能好用句型

- Are you done with …? 你處理完……了嗎？
- How's … going? ……進展得怎麼樣了？
- Everything is under control. 一切都在掌握中。
- There's gonna be a change in plans. 計劃有變。
- Just go ahead as planned. 按原計劃進行吧。
- How much longer do you need to get … done?
  你還要多久能把……做完？
- We need to submit our progress report today.
  我們今天需要繳交進度報告。
- We're ahead of schedule. 我們要提前完工了。
- The deadline is …. 截止日期是……。

職場應答對話

✦ 週報的截止日期 The Deadline of Weekly Reports ✦

David OK, everyone. We need to have a quick word about the weekly reports. As you know, we require weekly reports every Friday, but there have been lots of problems with these.

大衛 好吧，各位，我們得簡單說一下週報的事情。你們知道，我們要求每週五繳交週報，但這些週報仍然存在很多問題。

Annie There have been conflicting orders coming out of the offices!

安妮 辦公室週報的情況很混亂啊！

David OK, Annie, that's true, which is why we're having this meeting now.

大衛	是的，安妮，的確如此，這也是現在我們召開這次會議的原因。
Annie	So what you're about to say is how the reports should actually be written?
安妮	所以您要講的是該怎麼寫報告對嗎？
David	That's right. So listen carefully. Make sure that both this week's figures and last week's figures are included at the end. And the deadline is five o'clock on Friday, not Monday morning.
大衛	是的。所以請仔細聽一下。要確保上個禮拜及這個禮拜的資料最後都能包含在內。還有，截止日期是週五的五點，不是星期一早上。
Annie	Alright.
安妮	好的。

關聯必備單字

❶ **demand**
[dɪˋmænd] 要求

❷ **report**
[rɪˋpɔrt] 報告

❸ **submit**
[səbˋmɪt] 繳交

❹ **progress**
[ˋprogrɛs] 進展

❺ **satisfy**
[ˋsætɪsˏfaɪ] 使滿意

❻ **steady**
[ˋstɛdɪ] 穩定的

❼ **rapid**
[ˋræpɪd] 迅速的

❽ **include**
[ɪnˋklud] 包含

❾ **quick**
[kwɪk] 迅速的

❿ **ahead**
[əˋhɛd] 領先的

⓫ **run behind**
落後，延誤

⓬ **come up with**
提出

⓭ **otherwise**
[`ʌðɚ͵waɪz] 否則

⓮ **preparation**
[͵prɛpə`reʃən] 準備

⓯ **original**
[ə`rɪdʒənḷ] 原先的

⓰ **halfway**
[͵hæf`we] 半路地

⓱ **instead**
[ɪn`stɛd] 代替

⓲ **embark**
[ɪm`bɑrk] 從事或開始

⓳ **initiative**
[ɪ`nɪʃətɪv] 主動性

⓴ **enterprise**
[`ɛntɚ͵praɪz] 企業

㉑ **under control**
處於控制之下

㉒ **come along**
進行，進展

事業貼心便條

你知道「二八法則」嗎？其核心內容是生活中 80% 的結果幾乎源於 20%的努力，所以要把你的注意力放在 20% 的關鍵事情上。根據這個原則，你對要做的事情應分清楚輕重緩急：

1. 重要且緊急的事情必須立刻做。
2. 緊急而不重要的事情，要先考慮了重要事情後，再考慮它們，不要誤認為「緊急」就是優先。
3. 重要但不緊急的事情，應該當成緊急的事去做，切記千萬不能拖延。
4. 既不緊急也不重要的事情，等有空了再做。

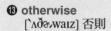

SECTION 05

團隊合作力量大
Being a Team Player

隨身應急情境句

Track 024

1	Do you enjoy working in teams? 你喜歡團隊合作嗎？
2	Mr. Black is our team leader. 我們團隊的領導人是布萊克先生。
3	Helen is in charge of our team. 我們團隊由海倫負責。
4	I always confer with my subordinates before making decisions. 我總是跟下屬們討論完再作決定。
5	I may make fast decisions at times, but this could be balanced by teamwork. 我有時候會過快地作出決定，不過團隊合作可以彌補這個問題。
6	We are in a team now, and we must trust each other. 現在我們在一個團隊裡，我們必須要彼此信任。
7	It's going to take a real team effort. 這需要團隊的努力。

8	I'm a team player and I love working with others. 我是團隊的一員，我喜歡跟其他人一起工作。
9	I really appreciate your team-working spirit. 我十分欣賞你的團隊精神。
10	Let's go for it! 我們一起加油吧！
11	Come on. Don't give up. You can do it.v 加油。別放棄。你可以的。
12	You have our backing. 我們支持你。
13	We made it! 我們成功了！
14	We went through a whole year for it. Now it's really happened. 我們為此奮鬥了整整一年。現在終於如願以償了。
15	We've got the order from ABC company! 我們得到 ABC 公司的訂單了！
16	I cannot believe it. That's really thrilling. 我簡直不敢相信。好興奮。
17	Only if we trust each other can we work together. 我們只有彼此信任才能一起工作。
18	I hope we can have confidence in each other. 我希望我們能相互信任。

Chapter 01
Chapter 02
Chapter 03
Chapter 04
Chapter 05
Chapter 06
Chapter 07
Chapter 08
Chapter 09
Chapter 10
Chapter 11

萬能好用句型

- … is our team leader.　我們的團隊的領導人是……。
- That problem could be balanced by teamwork.
  團隊合作可以彌補那個問題。
- I love working with others.　我喜歡跟其他人一起工作。
- Let's go for it!　我們一起加油吧！
- You have our backing.　我們支持你。
- Only if we trust each other can we work together.
  我們只有彼此信任才能一起工作。
- In order to …, it's going to take a real team effort.
  為了……，需要發揮團隊的作用。

職場應答對話

✦ 團隊合作 Team Cooperation ✦

Martin　OK, everyone. In order to finish this work on time, it's going to take a real team effort. We're going to need to delegate sections to each person. Any ideas?

馬汀　好吧，各位。為了按時完成工作，需要發揮團隊的作用。每個人都會負責一個區塊。有什麼意見嗎？

Ella　I'd be happy to carry on the number section. I've done most of it already, and I know it better than everyone else. Maureen should focus on the layout. She's good at that. Paul is the best man for the art, and I think Thomas should carry out the last of research, while you focus on the rewrites.

艾拉　我願意負責資料這塊。我已經做完大部分了，而且我比任何人都更熟悉這項內容。莫琳應該負責版面設計，她擅長這方面。保羅是負責圖片部分的最佳人選，還有，我認為

	湯瑪斯應該進行剩下的調查，而你主要負責修寫工作。
Martin	Sounds good to me. If there are no objections, we should get started.
馬汀	我覺得可以。如果沒有異議，我們就開始吧。
Ella	Remember, if anyone doesn't do their job, the whole team will suffer.
艾拉	記住，如果任何一個人沒有做好自己的工作，整個團隊都要遭殃。
Martin	Right. Let's all get to it.
馬汀	對。我們開始吧。

- delegate [ˋdɛlə͵get] v 委託
- carry on 繼續
- layout [ˋle͵aʊt] n 佈局，設計
- objection [əbˋdʒɛkʃən] n 異議，反對

關聯必備單字

❶ **team**
[tim] 團隊

❷ **teamwork**
[ˋtim͵wɝk] 團隊合作

❸ **team building**
團隊建設

❹ **characteristic**
[͵kærəktəˋrɪstɪk] 特徵

❺ **rely on**
依靠，依賴

❻ **support**
[səˋpɔrt] 支持

❼ **supporter**
[səˋpɔrtɚ] 支持者

❽ **loyal**
[ˋlɔɪəl] 忠誠的

❾ **spirit**
[ˋspɪrɪt] 精神

❿ **kindred**
[ˋkɪndrəd] 同類的

⓫ **mutual**
[ˋmjutʃʊəl] 相互的

⓬ **mutual understanding**
相互理解

⓭ **mutual trust**
相互信任

⓮ **cooperate**
[koˋɑpəret] 合作，配合

⓯ **cooperation**
[ko͵ɑpəˋreʃən] 合作，配合

⓰ **implement**
[ˋɪmpləment] 貫徹，執行

專業貼心便條

團隊有五個重要的構成要素，總結為 5P：

1. 目標 (Purpose)：

團隊必須要有一個既定目標，來為團隊成員們導航。

2. 人 (People)：

這是構成團隊最核心的力量。

3. 定位 (Place)：

要明確該團隊在企業中所處的位置，團隊成員由誰選擇和決定，以及團隊最終應對誰負責等。

4. 許可權 (Power)：

團隊中領導者的權力大小是跟團隊的發展階段相關聯的。通常，團隊發展初期，領導權相對較集中；而團隊越成熟，領導者所擁有的權力越小。

5. 計劃 (Plan)：

為了實現目標，要制定一系列具體的行動方案，團隊按照計劃行進，一步一步接近目標。

SECTION 06

受到讚賞
Receiving a Compliment

隨身應急情境句

Track 025

1	Well done! 做得好！
2	Good for you. 好樣的。
3	You're so awesome! Congratulations! 你太棒了！恭喜！
4	You're such a quick learner. 你學東西真快啊。
5	You're a hard worker. 你工作很努力。
6	You are so good at learning. 你很善於學習。
7	The report you did yesterday was really fantastic, and the manager was so impressed. 昨天你做的報告真的很棒，經理留下了很深刻的印象。
8	I love your ideas. They're very creative. 我喜歡你的想法。很有創意。

9	I appreciate your large inventory of ways to manage the ups and downs. 我很欣賞你有很多應對各種情況的方法。
10	Please keep up the good work! 再接再厲！
11	Please continue! 再接再厲！
12	It seems that the world is your oyster. 好像事情都在你的掌控之中。
13	You have withstood the crisis well. 你很好地應對了危機。
14	Thanks for having faith in me. 謝謝您對我的信任。
15	Thank you for your confidence in me. 謝謝您對我的信任。
16	Thank you for your reliance. 謝謝您的信任。

萬能好用句型

- Well done!
  做得好！
- Congratulations!
  恭喜！

➲ You're such a quick learner.
你學東西真快啊。

➲ You're a hard worker.
你工作很努力。

➲ Please continue!
再接再厲！

➲ Thank you for your confidence in me.
謝謝您對我的信任。

➲ Thanks for the encouragement.
謝謝鼓勵。

職場應答對話

✦ 報告做得不錯 Good Job on Reports ✦

Lisa Good job on those reports last week. You really impressed everyone with those.

麗莎 上個禮拜的報告做得很不錯。你讓每個人都留下了十分深刻的印象。

Peter Me? No! I hardly did anything. I just wrote them the way I always do.

彼得 我？不會吧！我也沒做什麼。我只是像往常一樣寫這些東西。

Lisa Take a compliment, will you! The bosses are really happy with you. You always file the report, for sure, but this time the writing was spectacular and it has helped them to win a few extra contracts.

麗莎 接受讚美吧，好吧！主管們對你非常滿意。當然，你總是會交報告，但這次的內容太棒了，這報告幫他們多簽了幾份合約。

Peter Well, thank you. I had no idea they were going to be important.

彼得 好吧，謝謝。我不知道報告會有這麼重要。

Lisa No. Thank you. If you keep working like that, I'm sure that the bosses will promote you really quickly.

麗莎 不。要感謝你。如果你一直這麼下去，我相信主管們會很快提拔你的。

Peter Really? That would be great. Thanks for the encouragement. I really appreciate it.

彼得 真的嗎？那太好了。謝謝鼓勵。我真的很感謝。

- spectacular [spɛkˋtækjələ˞] adj 壯觀的
- extra [ˋɛkstrə] adj 額外的
- contract [ˋkɑntrækt] n 合約

關聯必備單字

❶ **compliment** [ˋkɑmplɪmənt] 稱讚

❷ **praise** [prez] 讚美

❸ **encouragement** [ɪnˋkɝɪdʒmənt] 鼓勵

❹ **extraordinary** [ɪkˋstrɔrdnˏɛrɪ] 非同尋常的

❺ **remarkable** [rɪˋmɑrkəbl̩] 卓越的

❻ **excellent** [ˋeksələnt] 極好的

❼ **thrilling** [ˋθrɪlɪŋ] 令人興奮的

❽ **positively** [ˋpɑzətɪvlɪ] 積極地

9 **creative**
[krɪ`etɪv] 有創造力的

10 **smart**
[smɑrt] 聰明的

11 **hard-working**
[`hardˏwɝkɪŋ] 勤勉的

12 **impressive**
[ɪm`prɛsɪv] 令人敬佩的

13 **diligent**
[`dɪlədʒənt] 勤勉的

14 **independent**
[ˏɪndɪ`pɛndənt] 獨立的

15 **earnest**
[`ɝnɪst] 真誠的

16 **devote**
[dɪ`vot] 奉獻

17 **cooperative**
[ko`ɑpərətɪv] 有合作精神的

18 **selfless**
[`sɛlflɪs] 無私的

19 **honest**
[`ɑnɪst] 誠實的

20 **impressed**
[ɪm`prɛst] 印象深刻的

專業貼心便條

有時行動更勝言辭，如果想要給別人留下不錯的印象，就一定要十分重視自己的身體語言。有研究顯示，外表、聲音和語調能夠占到全部印象的 90%以上。

其中，視覺占 55%，身體語言、手勢和視線的接觸，以及整體的儀態與行為舉止等都有助於立即產生印象；聲音占 38%，使用不同的語調、音高和語速，會在一定程度上影響他人理解你所說的話；語言占 7%，儘管所占比例不高，但當視覺和聲音的效果消減時，就只剩下所要傳達的資訊了，所以這也要予以重視。

SECTION 07

保證如期完成
Finishing on Time

隨身應急情境句

Track 026

1	Will you finish on time? 你能準時完成嗎？
2	Can you speed up? 你能加快速度嗎？
3	Please make sure you finish it on time. It's very important. 請確保準時完成。這非常重要。
4	It's only two hours to go. 只剩下兩個小時了。
5	It's due tomorrow. 明天是最後期限。
6	We're really pressed for time. 我們確實時間緊迫。
7	We're in a hurry. 我們趕時間。
8	You have no time to lose. 你沒有時間可以浪費。

9	We must get the report done by six. Let's hurry up, guys. 我們必須在六點之前完成報告。大家，我們趕快吧。
10	We have to make every minute count. 我們必須分秒必爭。
11	We worked against the clock all day to get the report done by six. 為了在六點之前完成報告，我們一整天都在分秒必爭地工作。
12	We are working like hell to meet next Tuesday's deadline. 我們拼命工作，希望在下週二最後期限之前完成。
13	It's due next Wednesday. 下週三就是最後的期限了。
14	When you decide to do something, stick to it. 當你決定做什麼的時候，一定要堅持到底。
15	Tough people stick it out. 堅強的人能夠堅持到底。
16	Persistence is victory. Let's get moving. 堅持就是勝利。我們加快速度吧。
17	People who persist will finally win the day. 堅持到底的人將會取得最後的勝利。
18	Be persistent and you will get the last chance. 堅持到底，你會贏得最後的機會。

萬能好用句型

- Can you speed up?
  你能加快速度嗎？
- Please make sure you finish it on time.
  請確保準時完成。
- It's only … minutes / hours to go.
  只剩下……分鐘／小時了。
- We're in a hurry.
  我們趕時間。
- We have to make every minute count.
  我們必須分秒必爭。
- Persistence is victory. Let's get moving.
  堅持就是勝利。我們加快速度吧。

職場應答對話

✦ 確保今晚準時完成 Make Sure to Finish on Time Tonight ✦

Alice Are you free today? It would be great if we could hang out at lunch.

愛莉絲 你今天有空嗎？如果我們能一起吃午餐，就太好了。

Mike Actually, I'm pretty busy. I have to make sure I can finish on time tonight. I have plans.

麥克 事實上，我很忙。我必須保證今天晚上能準時完成。我有安排。

Alice OK. Maybe later in the week.

愛莉絲 好吧。也許這個禮拜晚一點吧。

Mike Don't you also have to finish your work by tonight? Isn't it due then?

麥克 妳不是也要在今天晚上處理完工作嗎？這不是最後期限嗎？

Alice It is due tonight, but I'm not worried. I'll make sure I get it done in the afternoon when I get back.

愛莉絲 今晚是最後期限，但我不擔心。等我回來後我保證下午都會處理好。

Mike OK. But you had better make sure you finish it on time. They will be really upset if it's not.

麥克 好的。但妳最好確保能準時完成啊。如果妳沒有，他們會很失望的。

Alice I will, don't worry. Enjoy working through lunch, and I'll see you when I get back.

愛莉絲 我會的，別擔心。在午餐時間你就享受工作吧。等我回來，我們再見吧。

關聯必備單字

❶ **deadline**
[ˋdɛd͵laɪn] 截止日期

❷ **stressful**
[ˋstrɛsfəl] 壓力大的

❸ **overload**ˋ
[͵ovəˋlod] 使負荷過多

❹ **anxiety**
[æŋˋzaɪətɪ] 焦慮

❺ **acute**
[əˋkjut] 嚴重的

❻ **urgency**
[ˋɝdʒənsɪ] 緊迫

❼ **tension**
[ˋtɛnʃən] 緊張

❽ **release**
[rɪˋlis] 釋放

❾ **victory**
[ˋvɪktərɪ] 勝利

❿ **overcome**
[ˏovɚˋkʌm] 克服

⓫ **fussy**
[ˋfʌsɪ] 愛挑剔的

⓬ **persistence**
[pɚˋsɪstəns] 堅持

⓭ **finally**
[ˋfaɪnəlɪ] 最終

⓮ **due**
[dju] 到期的，預期的

專業貼心便條

如果你工作沒有次序，總是會處於混亂狀態，這樣會嚴重影響你的工作效率。因此，有次序的工作是十分必要的，而如何讓自己擁有一個比較好的工作次序呢，可以參考下面的建議：

1. 要明確自己的工作及所肩負的責任是什麼，然後將自己所有的工作記在筆記本上，再根據其重要程度進行排序。
2. 在每項工作後，都標註上最有效的解決方法以及可能會遇到的問題，從而確保自己對將要執行的每項事務都很清楚，並且能夠十分有條理地進行處理。

CHAPTER 05

跟同事相處 Getting Along with Your Co-Workers

SECTION 01

跟同事聊天
Small Talk

隨身應急情境句

Track 027

1. Fancy meeting you here.
沒想到會在這裡碰到你。
2. What brings you here?
什麼風把你吹到這裡來啦？
3. What are you chatting about?
你們在聊什麼啊？
4. Tell me all the latest gossip!
跟我説最新的八卦！
5. Don’t believe all the gossip that you hear.
別相信你聽到的那些流言蜚語。
6. Why the long face?
為什麼臭臉？
7. Is anything bothering you?
有什麼事讓你很煩嗎？
8. Her flattery really sickens me.
她的諂媚讓我覺得很噁心。
9. The flattery made her expand.
那些奉承讓她心花怒放。

10	Ellen is always chewing gum. 艾倫總是在吃口香糖。
11	If it's not time for a snack, I will drink tea or chew gum. 如果還沒到吃點心的時間，我就喝茶或是吃口香糖。
12	That book was a turn-off. 那本書讓我倒盡胃口。
13	I really love reading Wuthering Heights. 我真的很喜歡看《咆嘯山莊》。
14	Hey, did you see the new Tom Hanks movie? 嘿，你看過湯姆・漢克新拍的那部影片嗎？
15	I want to go see the new Spiderman movie. I heard it was fantastic! 我想去看新的《蜘蛛人》電影，聽説很棒！
16	This movie has been ruling the box office for weeks. 這部電影已經雄踞票房榜首好幾個星期了。
17	That film created a sensation. 那部電影引起了轟動。
18	Are there any interesting programs on TV? 電視上有什麼有趣的節目嗎？
19	Did you hear the new rumor about Johnny Depp? 你聽説過強尼・戴普的新傳聞嗎？

20	I heard Ronald and Kate were dating. 我聽說羅納多和凱特在約會。
21	No way! We have to find out for sure! 不可能吧！我們得查明是否是真的！
22	I don't want to be this heavy anymore. I'll try and lose weight. 我不想再這麼胖了。我要試著減肥。
23	I feel like I've been gaining weight recently. 我覺得我最近一直在變胖。
24	I'm going on a diet. 我正在節食。

萬能好用句型

- What are you chatting about?
  你們在聊些什麼呢？
- Tell me all the latest gossip!
  跟我說最新的八卦！
- Is anything bothering you?
  有什麼事讓你很煩嗎？
- … was a turn-off.
  ……讓我倒盡胃口。
- … created a sensation.
  ……引起了轟動。

- Did you hear the new rumor about …?
  你聽說過……的新傳聞嗎？
- How are you doing today?
  你今天過得怎麼樣？
- Sounds great.
  聽起來很棒。

職場應答對話

✦ 關於週末的計劃 About the Weekend Plan ✦

Kate Hi Sam, how are you doing today?
凱特 嗨，山姆，今天過得怎麼樣？

Sam I am doing well. Thank you. How about you?
山姆 我很好，謝謝。妳呢？

Kate Glad to hear! I'm doing good as well. Thank you. Do you have any plans this weekend?
凱特 很高興聽到你這麼說！我也很好，謝謝。這個週末你有什麼安排嗎？

Sam Not much was planned really, aside from catching up on some sleep.
山姆 老實說，除了補眠之外沒什麼安排。

Kate Oh, really? Well, I am having a barbecue this Saturday with some friends and you are more than welcome to join us.
凱特 欸，真的嗎？這禮拜六我跟一些朋友要烤肉，非常歡迎你加入我們哦。

Sam The weather sure is nice, so it probably is for the best to spend some time outdoors. I appreciate the invite. I think I remember where you live, so I won't need directions. What time should I arrive?

山姆 天氣滿好的，所以花一些時間在戶外應該會很不錯。謝謝妳的邀請。我想我記得妳住哪裡，所以不用替我指路。我應該幾點到？

Kate Any time between 6 and 7 p.m. and it will be going on until about 11.

凱特 晚上 6 點到 7 點之間的任何時候都可以，烤肉會一直進行到 11 點左右。

Sam Sounds great. I will see you then.

山姆 聽起來很棒。到時候見。

- catch up on 彌補，趕上
- barbecue [ˋbɑrbɪkju] n 燒烤

關聯必備單字

❶ **gossip** [ˋgɑsɪp] 流言蜚語

❷ **flattery** [ˋflætərɪ] 諂媚

❸ **sicken** [ˋsɪkən] 使厭惡

❹ **amuse** [əˋmjuz] 逗（某人）笑

❺ **giggle** [ˋgɪgḷ] 咯咯地笑

❻ **chew** [tʃu] 咀嚼

❼ **gum** [gʌm] 口香糖

❽ **celebrity** [səˋlɛbrətɪ] 名人

❾ **hit** [hɪt] 紅極一時的人或事物

❿ **sociable** [ˋsoʃəbḷ] 好交際的

⓫ **chat**
[tʃæt] 閒聊

⓬ **intimacy**
[ˋɪntəməsɪ] 親密

⓭ **snack**
[snæk] 小吃，點心

⓮ **turn-off**
[tɝn,ɑf] 掃興的事物

⓯ **trailer**
[ˋtrelɚ] 預告片

⓰ **rumor**
[ˋrumɚ] 傳聞

⓱ **sensation**
[sɛnˋseʃən] 轟動

⓲ **sitcom**
[ˋsɪt,kɑm] 情境喜劇

專業貼心便條

聊天達人是如何練成的呢？

1. 在交際場中，最好往人群聚集的地方去，聽聽他們在談些什麼，這樣你也會有機會發表意見。等到有趣的話題談得差不多的時候，找個藉口離開。這樣你可以找到真正可以聊天的內容，也可以認識更多的朋友。
2. 聊天時不要冷落任何一個人，邀請沉默的人加入到談話中來。
3. 聊天的話題最好是大家熟悉的，避免冷場。平日裡可以多積累一些談話的小素材。
4. 不要輕易發表對一個人的不滿，也許身邊就有他的朋友。如果發覺聽眾已經不耐煩了，最好趕快閉嘴，聽聽別人的高論。
5. 每一位男士都喜歡聽到別人說他很風趣，每一位女士都喜歡別人稱讚她很漂亮。

SECTION 02

跟同事共進午餐
Having Lunch with Your Co-Workers

隨身應急情境句

Track 028

1	Let's do lunch today. 今天我們一起吃午餐吧。
2	Where do you wanna eat? 你想去哪裡吃？
3	What shall we have for lunch? 我們中午吃什麼呢？
4	Let's go somewhere nice. I'm tired of fast food. 我們去個好一點的地方吧，我不想吃速食了。
5	What are your specials today? 你們今天的特餐是什麼？
6	Are there any specials going on? 有什麼特餐嗎？
7	What's on the menu today? 今天的菜單上有什麼？
8	What do you have to drink here? 你們有什麼喝的？
9	Pizza sounds good but I've been eating it a lot lately. How about a steak? 披薩聽起來不錯，但我最近吃得太多了，吃牛排怎麼樣？

10	I'd like to order the chicken salad as an appetizer. 我想點雞肉沙拉當開胃菜。
11	I'm really in the mood for some fish. 我很想吃魚。
12	I'd like a steak, but could you get this cooked medium well? 我想要牛排，但是我想要七分熟的，可以嗎？
13	I think I'll just get the cheeseburger. 我想我就來一個起司漢堡吧。
14	I'm not picky. 我不挑食。
15	Don't be so fussy about your food. 你別那麼挑食。
16	This is pretty good, but it's a little spicy for me. 這個滿不錯的，但對我來說有點辣。
17	This is great, but it could use some more salt. 這很不錯，但可以再加點鹽。
18	She's a vegetarian. 她是一個素食主義者。
19	I can eat an ox. 我餓的要命。
20	I have a wolf in the stomach. 我超級餓的。

21	I'm very hungry. I can eat anything. 我現在很餓，我什麼都能吃。
22	You eat like a horse. 你真能吃。
23	I'm stuffed. 我吃飽了。
24	I'm full. That was really good. 我吃飽了。那個真的很不錯。

萬能好用句型

- Let's do lunch today.　今天我們一起吃午餐吧。
- Where do you wanna eat?　你想去哪裡吃？
- What's on the menu today?　今天的菜單上有什麼？
- I'd like to order ....　我想點……。
- I'm not picky.　我不挑食。
- I can eat an ox.　我餓得要命。
- You eat like a horse.　你真能吃。

職場應答對話

✦ 吃午餐閒聊 Eat Their Lunch and Chat ✦

Jack　The weather is pretty bad today, isn't it?
傑克　今天的天氣真糟糕，是吧？

Bill Yeah, it sure is. I heard there might be a thunderstorm tonight.

比爾 是的，的確如此。我聽說今晚可能有雷陣雨。

Jack Oh really? I didn't know that. Thank you for the warning. I will be sure to bring an umbrella home tonight just in case it starts raining on my way home.

傑克 噢，真的嗎？我不知道。謝謝你的提醒。晚上回家我會帶把傘，以免在回家的路上開始下雨。

Bill Good plan. I will bring mine with me too.

比爾 好主意。我也要帶我的傘。

Jack Are you still planning on going to the movies to see the new Spiderman?

傑克 你還有要去電影院看新的《蜘蛛人》電影嗎？

Bill I probably will. I heard that it got great reviews so I think it's worth it to see in theatres.

比爾 我可能會去。我聽說評價很不錯，所以我覺得值得到影院去看。

Jack My wife is out of town on a business trip this weekend, so she asked me to wait until next weekend to see it with her.

傑克 這週末我太太在外面出差，她要我等到下個週末跟她一起去看。

Bill l Oh, OK, yeah, girls can be pretty fussy about those kind of things, hey?

比爾 噢，好吧，女人對這種事情都很挑，對吧？

Jack Yes, they sure can. But I don't mind waiting. It's nice to go on dates sometimes instead of always only eating at home.

傑克 是的，她們都這樣啊。但我不介意等她。有時候出去約會的感覺不錯，不用總是在家吃飯。

Bill	l Okay. I will try my best not to spoil the movie for you in the next week.
比爾	好吧，下個禮拜我儘量不劇透，以免破壞你看電影的興致。
Jack	Thank you, I'd appreciate that. Hope you have fun this week-end!
傑克	謝謝，我很感激。希望你這週末玩得愉快！

關聯必備單字

❶ **cafeteria**
[ˏkæfəˋtɪrɪə] 自助餐廳

❷ **lunch**
[lʌntʃ] 午餐

❸ **menu**
[ˋmɛnju] 菜單

❹ **cook**
[kʊk] 廚師

❺ **gourmet**
[ˋgʊrme] 美食家

❻ **appetite**
[ˋæpəˏtaɪt] 胃口

❼ **stuffed**
[stʌft] 飽的

❽ **soup**
[sup] 湯

❾ **spoon**
[spun] 勺子

❿ **chopstick**
[ˋtʃɑpˏstɪk] 筷子

⓫ **tasty**
[ˋtestɪ] 美味的

⓬ **cheeseburger**
[ˋtʃizˏbɝgɚ] 起司漢堡

⓭ **yummy**
[ˋjʌmɪ] 好吃的

⓮ **dish**
[dɪʃ] 一道菜

⓯ **salty**
[ˋsɔltɪ] 鹹的

⓰ **spicy**
[ˋspaɪsɪ] 辛辣的

⓱ **fast food**
速食

⓲ **special**
[ˋspɛʃəl] 特色菜，特價菜

⑲ **steak**
[stɛk] 牛排

⑳ **appetizer**
[ˋæpəˏtaɪzɚ] 開胃菜

㉑ **pasta**
[ˋpæstə] 義大利面

㉒ **recipe**
[ˋrɛsəpɪ] 食譜

㉓ **picky**
[ˋpɪkɪ] 挑剔的

㉔ **fussy**
[ˋfʌsɪ] 愛挑剔的

㉕ **vegetarian**
[ˏvɛdʒəˋtɛərɪən] 素食主義者

㉖ **leftover**
[ˋlɛftˏovɚ] 吃剩的

專業貼心便條

西方進食的餐具主要是刀和叉，那麼刀叉的用法你知道嗎？

1. 進餐時，餐盤在中間，刀子和勺子放置在盤子的右邊，叉子放在左邊。一般右手寫字的人，享用西餐時，很自然地用右手拿刀或勺，左手拿叉，杯子也用右手來端。
2. 在桌子上擺放刀叉，一般最多不能超過三副。三道菜以上的套餐，必須在擺放的刀叉用完後隨上菜再放置新的刀叉。刀叉是從外側向裡側按順序使用。
3. 進餐時，通常都是左右手互相配合，也就是一刀一叉成雙成對使用的。
4. 刀叉有不同規格，因為用途不同所以其尺寸也有區別。吃肉時要使用大號的刀。吃沙拉、甜食或一些開胃小菜時，要用中號刀。叉或勺一般隨刀的大小而變。喝湯時，要用大號勺，而喝咖啡和吃冰淇淋時，則用小號為宜。
5. 如果食用某道菜不需要用刀，也可用右手握叉，例如義大利人在吃麵條時，只使用一把叉子，不需要其他餐具，那麼用右手來握叉子倒是簡易方便的。
6. 叉子和勺子可入口，但刀子不能放入口中，不管它上面是否有食物。除了禮儀上的要求，刀子入口也是危險的。

SECTION 03

虛心向同事學習
Learning from Your Co-Workers

隨身應急情境句

Track 029

1	Will you show me how to use this software? 你能示範一下怎麼使用這個軟體給我看嗎？
2	Would you mind telling me how to order things on-line? 你能告訴我怎麼在網上路訂購東西嗎？
3	What do you usually put on your blog? 你通常都在部落格上寫什麼？
4	Could you be more specific? 你能説得更具體一點嗎？
5	I came up with a good idea. 我想到一個好點子。
6	Do you know anyone who could help me out with HTML? I need it for my blog layout. 你知道有誰能幫我解決 HTML 問題嗎？我需要用它來設計部落格的版型。
7	Let me give you a piece of advice. 我來給你一點建議。

8	Can I offer you some advice? 我能提一些建議給你嗎？
9	Could I suggest something to you? 我能建議你一些事嗎？
10	Can I suggest something? 我能提一些建議嗎？
11	What kind of suggestion? 什麼建議？
12	Why couldn't you go for it? 你為什麼不努力去做呢？
13	You should at least try. It's not like it would hurt anything. 至少你應該試一下，又不會有什麼損失。
14	Just try. It couldn't hurt. 就試一下吧，不會有什麼損失的。
15	Why not try again? 為什麼不再試一下呢？
16	You should finish what you start. 你應該有始有終。
17	It always works out. Don't think too much. 事情總會解決的。別想太多了。
18	A fall into a pit, a gain in your wit. 不經一事，不長一智。

19	There you go! 你說得沒錯！
20	I'll get back to you if I have some questions. 如果有什麼問題的話，我再回來找你。

萬能好用句型

- Will you show me how to ...?
  你能示範一下怎麼……給我看嗎？
- Would you mind telling me how to ...?
  你能告訴我怎麼……嗎？
- Could you be more specific?
  你能說得更具體一點嗎？
- It always works out.
  事情總會解決的。
- There you go!
  你說得沒錯！
- What are you having trouble with?
  你遇到什麼麻煩了？
- Was there anything else you wanted help with?
  你還有什麼需要幫忙的嗎？

職場應答對話

✦ 幫助同事操作 PPT 軟體 Help a Co-Worker to Operate the PPT ✦

Jim Hi Selina, can you please come over here?
吉姆 嗨，瑟琳娜，請妳過來一下好嗎？

Selina Sure, what do you need?
瑟琳娜 好的，你需要什麼？

Jim I would like some help with this PowerPoint presentation.
吉姆 我需要一些關於這個 PPT 簡報的協助。

Selina Okay, what are you having trouble with?
瑟琳娜 好的，你遇到什麼麻煩了？

Jim I need to increase the speed of the slides transitioning but I can't find the proper section to do that.
吉姆 我要加快幻燈片切換的速度，但是我找不到可以在哪裡操作。

Selina That part is a little tricky to find, but I remember where it is. Take a look at the second toolbar here, and it is the fourth option in the drop-down menu.
瑟琳娜 那個是不太好找，但我記得在哪裡。看一下這裡的第二個工具列，下拉式功能表的第四個選項就是。

Jim Oooh, that's right. I remember learning that before. It was just hiding from me.
吉姆 噢，是的。我記得之前學過。只是一時之間想不起來。

Selina	Glad that worked out! Was there anything else you wanted help with?
瑟琳娜	真高興成功了！你還有什麼需要幫忙的嗎？
Jim	Would you be able to wait and double check that this works before leaving?
吉姆	妳能不能等一下，在走之前再次確認一下這個可以嗎？
Selina	Not a problem. OK, let's see if it works. Press「play」now.
瑟琳娜	沒問題。好吧，我們看看能不能用。現在按「播放」吧。
Jim	Okay here it goes... and it is a success! Thanks again for your help.
吉姆	好的，開始吧……成功了！再次感謝妳的幫助！

- tricky [ˋtrɪkɪ] adj 棘手的
- toolbar [ˋtul͵bɑr] n 工具列
- drop-down [ˋdrɑp͵daʊn] n 下拉

關聯必備單字

❶ **update**
[͵ʌpˋdet] 更新

❷ **logo**
[ˋlogo] 標誌

❸ **online**
[͵ɑnˋlaɪn] 線上的

❹ **specific**
[spəˋsɪfɪk] 具體的

❺ **practice**
[ˋpræktɪs] 練習

❻ **halt**
[hɔlt] 暫停

❼ **triumph**
[ˋtraɪəmf] 勝利

❽ **transition**
[trænˋzɪʃən] 過渡

❾ **humble**
[ˋhʌmbl̩] 謙虛的

❿ **microblog**
[ˋmaɪkro͵blɑg] 部落格

⓫ **come up with**
提出，想出

⓬ **layout**
[ˋle͵aʊt] 編排，設計

專業貼心便條

在剛入職場的時候，如何給同事和上司留下較好的印象，並獲取他們的信任呢？

1. 當工作遇到困難與挫折時，隨時運用你的智慧，或許只要一點創意或靈感便能解決困難；
2. 注意形象，並學會施展你的人格魅力，在辦公室可以幽默活潑，善解人意；
3. 要勇於面對問題，有辦法解決的問題全力以赴去解決，無法解決的問題先尋求公司支持；
4. 突出的工作成績最有說服力，最能讓人信賴和敬佩。

SECTION 04

不吝惜讚美
Giving Compliments

隨身應急情境句

Track 030

1. I like your new hairstyle.
我喜歡你的新髮型。

2. Your hairstyle reveals a lot about your personality and style!
你的髮型會顯示你個性和風格方面的很多東西！

3. I adore your bracelet. It's very classy!
我喜歡你的手鐲，非常漂亮！

4. What a cute necklace!
多漂亮的項鍊啊！

5. You look fantastic in this dress.
你穿這條裙子很好看。

6. This style is all the rage at the moment.
現在最流行這個款式了。

7. This style is very popular this year.
今年很流行這個款式。

8. That colour matches your eyes perfectly.
那個顏色和你的眼睛真是完美的搭配。

9	Orange is definitely your color. 橙色真的很適合你。
10	That color suits you very well. 那種顏色很適合你。
11	You look pretty sharp today. 你今天看起來很有精神。
12	I think you are so stunning. 我覺得你太有魅力了。
13	You look absolutely gorgeous! 你看起來真是美極了！
14	You have a lovely complexion. 你的膚色太美了。
15	You are quite a beauty. 你真是個大美人。
16	You really are a vision. 你好美噢。
17	You sure can speak English well. 你的英文說得真好啊。
18	You do have a flair for languages. 你真的很有語言天分。
19	Honestly, I really admire your courage. 說實話，我真的很佩服你的勇氣。

20	You're flattering me. 您真是過獎了。
21	I'm overjoyed. 我非常高興。
22	That's cool. It makes me happy. 那太好了，這讓我很高興。
23	Nothing would please me more. 沒有比這更讓人高興的了。
24	I couldn't be happier. 我特別高興。
25	I'm glad to see you so happy. 看到你這麼高興我也很高興。

萬能好用句型

- I like / adore your …. 我喜歡你的……。
- You look sharp today. 你今天看起來很有精神。
- You look absolutely gorgeous! 你看起來真是美極了！
- You sure can speak English well. 你的英文說得真好啊。
- You're flattering me. 您真是過獎了。
- Thanks for the tip! 多謝你的建議！

職場應答對話

✦ 你打字真快 You Type So Fast ✦

Ann Hi Peter, how are you doing today?

安 嗨，彼得，今天感覺怎麼樣啊？

Peter Pretty good. Thank you. How about yourself?

彼得 還不錯，謝謝。妳自己呢？

Ann Oh I'm fine. Thanks. Just typing up this report for the boss.

安 噢，我很好，謝謝。就只是在替主管打這份報告。

Peter You sure are typing fast! Much faster than I can type.

彼得 妳打字速度真快啊！比我打字快多了。

Ann Thank you. It took a lot of practice and I actually took a few typing classes as well.

安 謝謝。我花很多時間練習過，其實我也上了一些打字課。

Peter Really? That sounds like something that I should look into. I actually only use my index and middle fingers to type, so I am pretty sure that's why it takes so much longer for me.

彼得 真的嗎？聽起來我應該去看一下。事實上我只用食指和中指打字，所以我想這就是我打字慢很多的原因。

Ann Yes, that is probably why. The courses are offered every month, so next week you can register for one if you'd like.

安 是的，可能就是這個原因。每個月都有這些課程，所以如果你想的話，可以下個禮拜去報一個。

Peter Thanks for the tip! I will be sure to look into that.

彼得 謝謝妳的建議！我一定會去看看的。

- index [ˋɪndɛks] n 食指
- register [ˋrɛdʒɪstɚ] v 登記，註冊

關聯必備單字

❶ **hairstyle** [ˋhɛr͵staɪl] 髮型

❷ **jewellery** [ˋdʒuəlrɪ] 珠寶

❸ **necklace** [ˋnɛklɪs] 項鍊

❹ **sweater** [ˋswɛtɚ] 毛衣

❺ **clothing** [ˋkloðɪŋ] 衣服

❻ **compliment** [ˋkɑmpləmənt] 稱讚

❼ **classy** [ˋklæsɪ] 漂亮的

❽ **French** [frɛntʃ] 法語

❾ **stunning** [ˋstʌnɪŋ] 極好的

❿ **combination** [͵kɑmbəˋneʃən] 結合

⓫ **fashionable** [ˋfæʃənəbl̩] 時尚的

⓬ **type** [taɪp] 打字

⓭ **gorgeous** [ˋgɔrdʒəs] 非常漂亮的

⓮ **bracelet** [ˋbreslɪt] 手鐲

⓯ **complexion** [kəmˋplɛkʃən] 面貌

⓰ **vision** [ˋvɪʒən] 異常漂亮的人

⓱ **flair** [flɛr] 天資，天分

⓲ **overjoyed** [͵ovɚˋdʒɔɪd] 狂喜的

專業貼心便條

在職場中，要善於找到對方真正的優點，並真心讚美。讚美也是需要細心經營的：

1. 記住一個要領：逢物加價，遇人減歲。
2. 第一次見面要讚美對方的顯著特徵，熟人就要讚美他們身上發生的變化。
3. 第一時間送上讚美，過期無效。
4. 讓對方獲得認同感。
5. 讚美希望對方做的一切，領導對下屬更應如此。
6. 背後讚美別人會有意想不到的效果，也可以引用別人的讚美。

SECTION

05

及時解決矛盾與衝突
Solving Contradictions and Conflicts

隨身應急情境句

Track 031

1	Does it bother you? 這妨礙你了嗎？
2	Why are you always picking on me? 你為什麼總是挑我的毛病？
3	You're to blame. 這是你的錯。
4	You shouldn't blame him. It wasn't his fault. 你不應該怪他，那並不是他的錯。
5	Stop beating around the bush. Just to the point. 別再繞圈子了。直接說重點吧。
6	I had a terrible quarrel with one of my co-workers yesterday. 我昨天我跟我的一個同事大吵了一架。
7	They had a quarrel about that report. 他們因為那份報告吵了起來。
8	He always comes into conflict with his boss. 他總是跟他的主管起衝突。

9	Her attitude really pissed me off. 她的態度真讓我生氣。
10	I know you're angry, but don't get aggressive. 我知道你很生氣，但是別咄咄逼人。
11	How can we resolve this apparent contradiction? 我們怎麼來解決這個明顯的矛盾呢？
12	Let's find a way to resolve this contradiction. 讓我們找個方法來解決這個矛盾吧。
13	I didn't think it would be a big deal. 我覺得這沒什麼大不了的。
14	Don't be so quick-tempered. 別那麼性急。
15	You have to calm down right now. 你現在必須冷靜下來。
16	Please calm down a bit. 請冷靜一點兒。
17	I'm sorry I got angry. 對不起，我發火了。
18	I feel a lot better now that you talked me out of that. 你跟我把話講開了，所以我現在感覺好多了。
19	I feel better now that you talked to me. 你和我聊了之後我感覺好一點了。

20 I really cooled off once you talked to me.
你和我一說我就平靜下來了。

萬能好用句型

- Why are you always picking on me? 你為什麼總是挑我的毛病？
- It wasn't … fault. 這不是……的錯。
- I had a terrible quarrel with … 我跟……大吵了一架。
- They had a quarrel about … 他們因為……吵了起來。
- He always comes into conflict with … 他總是跟……起衝突。
- Let's find a way to resolve this contradiction.
  讓我們找個方法來解決這個矛盾吧。
- Please calm down a bit. 請冷靜一點。

職場應答對話

✦ 請把餐具放到水槽 Please Put the Dishes in the Sink ✦

Ella Hey, Bill, there is something I have been meaning to ask you.
艾拉 嗨，比爾，有件事我要問你一下。

Bill Okay, what is it?
比爾 好的。什麼事？

Ella It is one of my jobs to do the dishes in the office, but lately the cupboard has been empty. I found out that you have been leaving the dirty dishes in your office and not bringing them to the sink for me to clean. I keep hearing people complain about not having a mug for their morning coffee, and it seems like they

	think it's my fault. From now on could you please just put the dishes in the sink like everyone else?
艾拉	清洗辦公室的餐具是我的工作之一，但最近碗櫃都是空的。我發現你把髒的餐具留在你的辦公室，而不把它們拿到水槽來讓我清洗。我總是聽到有人抱怨早上沒有杯子來沖咖啡，而且他們好像認為是我的錯。從現在起，你能跟別人一樣把餐具放在水槽裡嗎？
Bill	Well, I can't help my hectic schedule. If I am rushing to a meeting, I wouldn't think of doing something as small as that. Why not just buy more dishes so this won't happen?
比爾	可是我控制不了忙碌的日程啊。如果我急著去開會，我就不會記得去做這樣一件小事。為什麼不多買些餐具來避免發生這樣的事呢？
Ella	We don't have extra money in our budget for that, so we can't do that.
艾拉	我們的預算裡並沒有額外的錢，所以我們不能這麼做。
Bill	Okay, fine. I will try to take care of my dishes.
比爾	好吧，我會試著處理好我的餐具的。
Ella	Thank you very much.
艾拉	非常感謝。

- sink [sɪŋk] n 洗滌槽，水槽
- mug [mʌg] n 馬克杯，杯子
- hectic [ˋhɛktɪk] adj 緊張忙碌的

關聯必備單字

❶ **blame**
[blem] 責備

❷ **contradiction**
[ˏkɑntrəˋdɪkʃən] 矛盾

❸ **conflict**
[ˋkɑnflɪkt] 衝突

❹ **incompatibility**
[ˏɪnkəmˏpætəˋbɪlətɪ] 不相容

❺ **vex**
[vɛks] 使惱火

❻ **enemy**
[ˋɛnəmɪ] 敵人

❼ **hostile**
[ˋhɑstɪl] 有敵意的

❽ **frustrated**
[frʌˋstretɪd] 沮喪的

❾ **unfriendly**
[ʌnˋfrɛndlɪ] 不友好的

❿ **controversial**
[ˏkɑntrəˋvɝʃḷ] 有爭議的

⓫ **quarrel**
[ˋkwɔrəl] 爭吵

⓬ **complaint**
[kəmˋplent] 抱怨

⓭ **aggressive**
[əˋgrɛsɪv] 好鬥的

⓮ **quick-tempered**
[ˏkwɪkˋtɛmpɚd] 易怒的

CHAPTER

06

辦公電話 Telephone Communications

SECTION 01

接聽電話，禮貌得體
Answering the Phone

隨身應急情境句

Track 032

1	Hello. JP company. 您好，JP 公司。
2	Good morning, HR department. 早安，人力資源部。
3	Good afternoon, this is Mr. Cruz's office. 午安，這裡是克魯茲先生的辦公室。
4	Hello, is this YM company? 你好，請問是 YM 公司嗎？
5	Good afternoon. YM Jack speaking. 午安，這裡是 YM 公司，我是傑克。
6	Hello, this is Kate from YM company. 你好，我是 YM 公司的凱特。
7	Who are you calling, please? 請問您找哪位？
8	Hello. Who would you like to talk to? 您好。您找哪位？

9	Anyone in particular? 您要找哪位？
10	May I speak to Mr. Wang? 可以請王先生接電話嗎？
11	Is Mr. Wang there? 王先生在嗎？
12	I'd like to speak to Lisa. 我想跟麗莎說話。
13	Who's calling, please? 請問您是哪位？
14	It's Jim from I.T. Magazine calling. 我是《I.T.雜誌》的吉姆。
15	Hello. Jessica speaking. 你好。我是潔西卡。
16	I'm sorry, he is not in right now. 很抱歉，他現在不在。
17	He's not on duty now. 他現在沒有在上班。
18	Thank you for calling JP company. 感謝您致電 JP 公司。
19	Thank you for calling us. Goodbye. 謝謝您給我們打電話。再見。

萬能好用句型

- Who would you like to talk to? 您找哪一位？
- May I speak to …? 能請……接電話嗎？
- Is … there? ……在嗎？
- Who's calling, please? 請問您是哪位？
- It's … from … calling. 我是……的……。
- … speaking. 我是……。
- I'm sorry, he is not in right now. 很抱歉，他現在不在。
- Thank you for calling …. 感謝您致電……。

職場應答對話

✦ 請薇姬接電話 May I Speak to Vicky ✦

Vicky Good afternoon. Johnson Motors.
薇姬 午安，詹森汽車公司。

Adam May I speak to Vicky?
亞當 能請薇姬接一下電話嗎？

Vicky Yes, speaking.
薇姬 我就是，請說。

Adam Hi, Vicky. I saw your ad in the newspaper about used cars.
亞當 嗨，薇姬。我在報紙上看到了你們刊登的有關二手汽車的廣告。

Vicky Yes. In which car are you interested?
薇姬 是的。那您對哪輛車有興趣呢？

Adam The 2006 Chevy truck.

亞當	2006 年產的雪佛蘭卡車。
Vicky	Oh. That truck was sold yesterday.
薇姬	噢，那輛卡車昨天已經賣出去了。
Adam	OK. Thanks anyway.
亞當	好吧。還是謝謝你。
Vicky	Can I interest you in another one of our trucks?
薇姬	我跟您推薦一下我們其他款卡車好嗎？
Adam	No, thanks.
亞當	不用了，謝謝。
Vicky	Thank you for calling Johnson Motors. Bye.
薇姬	感謝您致電詹森汽車公司。再見。
Adam	Goodbye.
亞當	再見。

- motor [ˋmotɚ] n 汽車
- ad [æd] n 廣告
- truck [trʌk] n 卡車
- interest [ˋɪntərɪst] v 引起某人做某事的興趣

關聯必備單字

1. **dial** [ˋdaɪəl] 撥打
2. **speak** [spik] 說
3. **number** [ˋnʌmbɚ] 號碼
4. **call** [kɔl] 打電話

❺ **talk**
[tɔk] 交談

❻ **answer**
[ˋænsɚ] 應答

❼ **telephone**
[ˋtɛlə͵fon] 電話

❽ **mobile**
[ˋmobɪl] 可移動的

❾ **signal**
[ˋsɪgnḷ] 信號

❿ **hear**
[hɪr] 聽

⓫ **loud**
[laʊd] 大聲的

⓬ **connection**
[kəˋnɛkʃən] 連接

專業貼心便條

接聽電話時，要注意以下三點噢：

1. 接聽電話必須要及時，鈴聲響起應不超過三次，若鈴響三次後才接，應向對方表示道歉。儘快接電話會給對方留下比較好的印象，也是向對方表示尊重。
2. 接聽電話時，要注意嘴和聽筒應保持 4 公分左右的距離，將耳朵貼近聽筒，做到仔細傾聽。
3. 應讓對方自己結束通話，然後輕輕地將聽筒放好，千萬不可「啪」的一下扔回原處，這是非常不禮貌的做法。

SECTION 02

轉接電話
Transferring a Call

隨身應急情境句

Track 033

1	Could you transfer me to Tom? 你可以幫我轉接給湯姆嗎？
2	Could you put me through to sales department? 你能幫我接一下業務部嗎？
3	Could you put me through to extension 817? 你能幫我轉接分機 817 嗎？
4	How may I direct your call? 您想轉接到哪裡？
5	I will put you through. 我幫你轉接過去。
6	Hold on, please. 請不要掛斷。
7	Please hold one moment while I transfer your call. 請稍等一下，我幫你轉接。
8	I'll just find out if she is in her office. 我去看看她在不在辦公室。

9	Mr. Brown is in conference and cannot come to the telephone. 布朗先生在開會，不能接電話。
10	I'll fetch her up. 我去找她過來。
11	She'll pick up the phone soon. 她馬上就來接電話了。
12	The line is busy / engaged. 線路正忙／占線。
13	Please stay on the line. 請保持通話。
14	I'll switch you over to Miss Lin. 我會將您的電話轉給林小姐。
15	Mr. Cruz, there is a call for you. 克魯茲先生，有你的一通電話。
16	Jane, you are wanted on the phone. 珍，有你的電話。
17	Please tell her I'll call her right back. 請告訴她我會馬上回電話給她的。
18	If the phone rings, could you please answer it for me? 如果電話響了，你能幫我接一下嗎？
19	Could you take my calls? 你可以幫我接一下電話嗎？

萬能好用句型

- Could you transfer me to …?
  你可以幫我轉接給……嗎？
- Could you put me through to …?
  你能幫我接一下……嗎？
- Can I have extension …?
  你能幫我轉接分機……嗎？
- How may I direct your call?
  您想轉接到哪裡？
- Please stay on the line.
  請保持通話。
- I'll switch you over to ….
  我會將您的電話轉給……。
- …, there is a call for you.
  ……，有你的一通電話。

職場應答對話

✦ 請別掛斷電話 Please Hold ✦

Jessica Good morning. AET company. How may I direct your call?
潔西卡 早安。AET 公司。您想轉接到哪裡？

Mike Sales department, please.
麥克 請轉到業務部。

Jessica	Would you like to speak to someone in charge?
潔西卡	您要找負責人嗎？
Mike	Yes. Mr. Smith, please.
麥克	是的。請接史密斯先生。
Jessica	OK. Let me see if Mr. Smith is available. Please hold.
潔西卡	好的。讓我看看史密斯先生在不在。請不要掛斷電話。
Mike	OK.
麥克	好的。
Jessica	Mr. Smith is having a meeting. Would you like to speak to someone else?
潔西卡	史密斯先生在開會。您要找其他人嗎？
Mike	OK. I'd like to talk to Mr. Smith's assistant.
麥克	好的。我想跟史密斯先生的助理通話。
Jessica	I will put you through to Miss Lin. Please hold.
潔西卡	我幫您轉給林小姐。請不要掛斷。
Mike	OK. Thank you.
麥克	好的。謝謝妳。

關聯必備單字

❶ **transfer**
[træns`fɝ] 轉接

❷ **extension**
[ɪk`stɛnʃən] 電話分機

❼ **continue**
[kən`tɪnjʊ] 繼續

❽ **switch**
[swɪtʃ] 轉換

❸ **repeat**
[rɪ`pit] 重複

❹ **caller**
[`kɔlɚ] 打電話者

❺ **engaged**
[ɪn`gedʒd] 忙碌的

❻ **charge**
[tʃardʒ] 負責

❾ **connect**
[kə`nɛkt] 連接

❿ **again**
[ə`gen] 再次

⓫ **put…through**
把……接通

⓬ **fetch**
[fɛtʃ] 拿來，取過

專業貼心便條

打電話的過程中一定不能喝東西、吃零食或吸煙，同時要注意保持端正的姿態。在打電話的時候，你若是悠閒地躺在椅子上，對方聽你的聲音便是懶散的，甚至無精打采的；你若坐姿十分端正，傳遞到對方耳中的聲音則會格外清楚，而且親切悅耳。

此外，打電話時要注意保持愉悅的心情，即使對方看不見你，也可以從歡快的語調中受到感染，這樣你就容易給對方留下較好的印象。面部表情是會影響聲音變化的，因此打電話的時候，要抱著對方在看著我的心態來應對。

SECTION 03

留言
Leaving a Message

隨身應急情境句

Track 034

1	Could I leave a message? 我能留個言嗎？
2	May I leave her a message? 我能留言給她嗎？
3	Would you like to leave a message? 您要留個言嗎？
4	Shall I take a message? 需要我傳話嗎？
5	Please tell her to call me back. 請叫她回個電話給我。
6	Please give me a call when you are free. 有空請回電話給我。
7	Would you let him call me back later, please? 你能叫他過等一下回個電話給我嗎？
8	Will you please have him call me back? 你能叫他回電話給我嗎？

9	Could you ask him to call me tomorrow? 你能讓他明天打個電話給我嗎？
10	I'll have her call back as soon as she gets in. 她一到我就請她回電話給您。
11	Let me repeat your message to see if I've got it all. 我重複一遍您的留言，看看我是不是記清楚了。
12	Would you please spell your full name? 您能不能拼一下您的全名呢？
13	Can you spell that for me, please? 能請您拼一下嗎？
14	May I trouble you to repeat? 可以麻煩您重複一遍嗎？
15	I beg your pardon? 您能再說一遍嗎？
16	I'll make sure she gets your message. 我會確保她收到您的留言的。
17	There's a message for you. 有人留言給你。
18	Kate called you during the meeting. 您開會的時候凱特打電話來了。
19	Mr. Brown called you this morning. 今天上午布朗先生打電話給你了。

萬能好用句型

- Could I leave a message? 我能留個言嗎？
- Would you like to leave a message? 您要留個言嗎？
- Shall I take a message? 需要我傳話嗎？
- Please tell … to call me back. 請叫……回電話給我。
- Please give me a call when you are free. 有空請回電話給我。
- Will you please have…call me back?
  你能請……回個電話給我嗎？
- I'll make sure … gets your message.
  我會確保……收到您的留言的。

職場應答對話

✦ 留言訂花 Leave a Message to Order a Flower ✦

Rebeca Good morning. Julie's Flowers and Gifts.
蕾貝卡 早安，茱莉鮮花禮品店。

Dennis Good morning. Is Julie there?
丹尼斯 早安。茱莉在嗎？

Rebeca I'm afraid she's not in today.
蕾貝卡 她今天恐怕不在店裡。

Dennis Could I leave a message for her?
丹尼斯 我能留個言給她嗎？

Rebeca Certainly. Whenever you are ready.
蕾貝卡 當然。隨時都可以。

Dennis	Please tell her this is Dennis Smith. I was in the shop yesterday. I'm sure she remembers me.
丹尼斯	請告訴她我是丹尼斯．史密斯。昨天我來過店裡。我肯定她記得我。
Rebeca	OK. Go on.
蕾貝卡	好的。請繼續說。
Dennis	I would like her to make a flower arrange-ment for my wife. It's her birthday next week.
丹尼斯	我希望她替我太太做一盆插花。下個禮拜是我太太的生日。
Rebeca	And what kind of flowers?
蕾貝卡	那您要用哪種花呢？
Dennis	I will leave that up to Julie.
丹尼斯	這讓茱莉決定吧。
Rebeca	And when will you be in to pick up the flowers?
蕾貝卡	那您什麼時候會過來拿花呢？
Dennis	Next Monday.
丹尼斯	下個禮拜一。
Rebeca	OK. I will leave her the message. Please call next Monday before you come in.
蕾貝卡	好的。我會轉告她的。麻煩您下個禮拜一過來之前先打個電話。
Dennis	OK. I will.
丹尼斯	好，我會的。
Rebeca	Thank you. And have a great day!
蕾貝卡	謝謝。祝您有個愉快的一天！
Dennis	You too. Bye.
丹尼斯	妳也是。再見。

➲ flower arrangement 插花

關聯必備單字

❶ **message**
[ˋmɛsɪdʒ] 留言

❷ **urgent**
[ˋɝdʒənt] 緊急的

❸ **emergency**
[ɪˋmɝdʒənsɪ] 緊急情況

❹ **overseas**
[ˏovɚˋsiz] 海外的

❺ **suppose**
[səˋpoz] 猜想

❻ **repeat**
[rɪˋpit] 重複

❼ **spell**
[spɛl] 拼寫

❽ **slowly**
[ˋslolɪ] 慢慢地

❾ **ring**
[rɪŋ] 鈴聲

❿ **check**
[tʃɛk] 查看

⓫ **convenient**
[kənˋvinjənt] 方便的

⓬ **answering machine**
答錄機

專業貼心便條

處理電話留言時，可參照考以下的流程：

1. 如果對方想要找的人不在，應主動請對方留言或詢問是否需要轉告。
2. 記錄留言時，運用 5W1H 技巧，即按 When（何時）、Who（何人）、Where（何地）、What（何事）、Why（為什麼）、How（如何進行）來詢問並記錄。
3. 記錄完成後，記得再向對方複述一遍內容，以確保所記資訊的準確性。

SECTION 04

應對電話諮詢
Responding to Enquiries

隨身應急情境句

Track 035

1	Can I help you? 能為您效勞嗎？
2	What can I do for you? 有什麼可以為您效勞的嗎？
3	I am calling to enquire about your new product. 我打電話來是想諮詢下你們的新產品。
4	I am calling to check my order status. 我打電話來是想詢問一下我的訂單狀況。
5	I am calling about an order I placed three weeks ago. 我打電話是為了三個禮拜前我訂的物品。
6	I was referred to you by Tom. 湯姆叫我找你的。
7	How can I pay for these flowers? 我要怎麼付這些花？
8	Can I pay by credit card? 我能用信用卡付款嗎？

9	Can you send me your catalog and a sample of your newest product? 你能不能寄一份目錄和你們最新產品的樣品給我？
10	Could you please tell me how to make an international call? 你能告訴我怎麼打國際長途電話嗎？
11	First, you should know the codes and numbers. 首先你要知道區號和電話號碼。
12	If you want to call abroad, you need to dial the country code, the city code and the number in turn. 如果你想打國際長途電話，你需要照順序撥打國家代碼、城市區號和電話號碼。
13	Could you please tell me the country code for Canada? 能不能告訴我加拿大的國家代碼？
14	How about the charges? 要怎麼收費呢？
15	How much should I pay for it? 我要付多少錢？

萬能好用句型

- Can I help you? 能為您效勞嗎？
- What can I do for you? 有什麼可以為您效勞的嗎？

- I am calling to enquire about .... 我打電話是想諮詢一下……。
- I was referred to you by .... ……叫我來找你。
- How can I pay for ...? 我要怎麼付……？
- Could you please tell me how to make an international call? 你能告訴我怎麼打國際長途電話嗎？
- How about the charges? 要怎麼收費呢？

職場應答對話

✦ 電話諮詢新電影 A Call to Enquire About the New Movie ✦

Rachel	Hello. J&P Cinema. Can I help you?
瑞秋	您好，J&P 電影院。有什麼能為您服務的？
Nate	I am calling to enquire about your new movies this weekend.
奈特	我打電話來是想詢問一下你們這個週末上映的新電影。
Rachel	We only have one new movie coming out this Friday.
瑞秋	只有本週五有一部新片上映。
Nate	And which one is that?
奈特	是哪部電影呢？
Rachel	It's the new Spiderman movie.
瑞秋	是新的《蜘蛛人》電影。
Nate	Great! I have been looking forward to seeing it!
奈特	太好了！我一直都想看這部電影！
Rachel	Yes. It is sure to be a true blockbuster!
瑞秋	是的。它肯定會是一部真正的大片！

Nate Could you give me the show times for Friday?

奈特 妳可以告訴我週五的放映時間嗎？

Rachel No problem. There is a matinee at 1 p.m. And there are three shows in the evening. One at 6 p.m., one at 8 p.m. and one at 10 p.m.

瑞秋 沒問題。日場在下午 1 點。晚上有三場，分別是晚上 6 點、8 點和 10 點。

Nate Very good! Thanks for your help.

奈特 好的！謝謝妳的幫忙。

Rachel My pleasure. And thank you for calling J&P Cinema. Bye.

瑞秋 不客氣。感謝您致電 J&P 電影院。再見。

Nate Bye.

奈特 再見。

- blockbuster [ˋblɑkˏbʌstɚ] n 大片
- matinee [ˏmætənˋe] n 日場

關聯必備單字

1. **enquire** [ɪnˋkwaɪɚ] 詢問
2. **newspaper** [ˋnjuzˏpepɚ] 報紙
3. **customer** [ˋkʌstəmɚ] 顧客
4. **manual telephone** 人工電話
5. **bother** [ˋbɑðɚ] 打擾
6. **feedback** [ˋfidˏbæk] 回饋
7. **respond** [rɪˋspɑnd] 回復
8. **receiver** [rɪˋsivɚ] 聽筒

❾ **line**
[laɪn] 電話線

❿ **status**
[ˋstetəs] 狀況

⓫ **place**
[ples] 訂購

⓬ **catalog**
[ˋkætəlɔg] 目錄

⓭ **sample**
[ˋsæmpḷ] 樣品，樣本

⓮ **ticket**
[ˋtɪkɪt] 票

專業貼心便條

如何撥打國際長途電話呢？

國際長途電話包括國際直撥電話和國際人工、半自動電話。國際直撥電話是一種已被各國廣泛採用的現代化通訊方式，需要事先到電信公司申請開通國際直撥功能，成為國際直撥授權使用者。撥叫時要連續撥號，中途不要停頓，撥完後稍等片刻，即可聽到回鈴音。

國際人工電話包括叫人電話、叫號電話、對方付費電話和信用卡電話等。撥叫國際人工、半自動電話時，先向「115」人工或半自動國際台掛號，掛號時應將自己的電話號碼、姓名、帳號及對方國家的城市地名、電話號碼和受話人的姓名告訴話務員。撥叫人工電話時，需掛機等候，待話務員接通電話後才能通話。

Chapter 01
Chapter 02
Chapter 03
Chapter 04
Chapter 05
Chapter 06
Chapter 07
Chapter 08
Chapter 09
Chapter 10
Chapter 11

SECTION

05 處理客戶投訴

Responding to Customer's Complaints

隨身應急情境句

Track 036

1	I'm here to make a complaint. 我是來這裡投訴的。
2	The magazine you sent to me is not what I ordered. 你們送來的雜誌不是我訂的那本。
3	The product that I ordered three weeks ago hasn't arrived yet. 三個禮拜前我訂的產品到現在都還沒到。
4	The camera I bought last month is always breaking down. 我上個月買的照相機老是出問題。
5	The phone I bought yesterday at one of your stores is already broken. 昨天我在你們的一家店裡買的電話已經壞了。
6	I'm sorry to hear that, sir. 聽到這個消息我感到很抱歉，先生。
7	I'm very sorry you feel that way. 讓您有那樣的感受我很抱歉。

8	We apologize for our mistake. 我們對所犯的錯誤表示歉意。
9	You can bring the camera to our repair center. They will repair it for free. 您可以把照相機拿到我們的維修中心。他們會免費為您維修。
10	If your MP4 player doesn't work, then we can give you a replacement or refund. 如果您的 MP4 播放機無法使用的話，我們可以換貨或退款給您。
11	We'll deal with the problem as soon as possible. 我們會儘快處理這個問題。
12	You can return your purchase at no extra charge. 您可以免費退貨。
13	If you can't get this straightened out, I'm going to a different firm. 如果你們解決不了這個問題，我要去找另一家公司了。
14	If you still delay delivery, I'll have to cancel the order. 如果你們仍然延遲交付，我們就不得不取消訂單。
15	If the shipment is too late, we'll be forced to withdraw the contract. 如果太晚出貨的話，我們就不得不撤銷合約了。

16	If you could just give us a few more days, we should be able to get this problem ironed out. 如果您能再多給我們幾天時間，我們應該能把這個問題解決好。
17	Terribly sorry. We will try our best. 十分抱歉。我們會盡力的。
18	We are doing everything in our power to work this out. 我們正在竭盡全力解決這個問題。
19	We prefer to resolve disputes by amicable conciliation between two parties. 我們願意透過友善的和談來解決雙方的爭端。
20	We should settle the dispute through negotiations without resorting to legal proceeding. 我們應該透過談判來解決糾紛，而不是訴諸法律。

萬能好用句型

- I'm sorry to hear that.　聽到這個消息我感到很抱歉。
- We apologize for our mistake.　我們為所犯的錯誤表示歉意。
- You can bring … to the repair center.
  您可以把……拿到維修中心。
- If … doesn't work, then we can give you areplacement or refund.
  如果……無法使用的話，我們可以換貨或退款給您。

➲ We'll deal with the problem as soon as possible.
我們會儘快處理這個問題。

➲ And again, my apologies.　還有，再次表達我的歉意。

職場應答對話

✦ 三明治弄錯了 The Wrong Sandwich ✦

Tracy Hello. Jenny's Deli. What can I do for you?
翠西 你好。珍妮熟食店。有什麼可以為您服務的嗎？

Ronald Hi. I was just at your deli. You gave me the wrong sandwich!
雷諾 嗨。我剛才在你們的熟食店，你們把我的三明治弄錯了！

Tracy Oh! I am so sorry about that! What did you order?
翠西 噢！十分抱歉！您點的是什麼？

Ronald I ordered a roast beef, but you gave me a pastrami.
雷諾 我點的是烤牛肉三明治，你們給我的是醃燻牛肉的。

Tracy I see. When you come in next time, I will give you a free sandwich of your choice.
翠西 我知道了。您下次光臨時，我們會免費送您一個由您自己挑選的三明治。

Ronald Great! I appreciate that.
雷諾 太好了！那就謝謝妳了。

Tracy Just ask for Tracy. That's me…I'm the manager.
翠西 您過來找翠西就可以了。就是我……我是這裡的經理。

Ronald OK. I will come in tomorrow at lunchtime.
雷諾 好的。我就明天午餐時間過來吧。

Tracy	Good. I will be here all day tomorrow. And may I have your name, sir?
翠西	好的。明天我整天都在這裡。還有，先生，請問您叫什麼名字？
Ronald	It's Ronald Davis.
雷諾	我叫雷諾．戴維斯。
Tracy	OK. See you tomorrow, Mr. Davis. And again, my apologies.
翠西	好的。明天見，戴維斯先生。還有，再次表達我的歉意。
Ronald	Don't worry about it, Tracy. See you.
雷諾	沒關係，翠西。再見。
Tracy	Bye.
翠西	再見。

- deli [ˋdɛlɪ] n （= delicatessen）熟食店
- roast beef 烤牛肉
- pastrami [pəˋstrɑmɪ] n 燻牛肉

關聯必備單字

❶ **complaint**
[kəmˋplent] 投訴

❷ **solve**
[sɑlv] 解決

❸ **problem**
[ˋprɑbləm] 問題

❹ **replacement**
[rɪˋplesmənt] 更換

❺ **repair**
[rɪˋpɛr] 修理

❻ **service**
[ˋsɝvɪs] 服務

❼ **apology**
[əˋpɑlədʒɪ] 道歉

❽ **refund**
[ˋrɪfʌnd] 退款

❾ **claim**
[klem] 理賠

❿ **damage**
[ˋdæmɪdʒ] 損壞

⓫ **defective**
[dɪˋfɛktɪv] 有瑕疵的

⓬ **dispute**
[dɪˋspjut] 爭端

⓭ **purchase**
[ˋpɝtʃəs] 購買的東西

⓮ **straighten out**
理清，糾正錯誤

⓯ **withdraw**
[wɪðˋdrɔ] 撤銷

⓰ **iron out**
解決，消除

⓱ **amicable**
[ˋæmɪkəbl̩] 友好的

⓲ **conciliation**
[kənˏsɪlɪˋeʃən] 調解

專業貼心便條

面對客戶投訴時，要虛心接受，耐心傾聽對方訴說，並對客戶表示理解。客戶敘述完後，先重複說一次對方所講的主要內容，然後徵詢客戶的意見。對於比較小的投訴，如果自己可以解決，應立即給客戶答覆；如果當時無法解答，則要作出時間承諾，在承諾的時間之內答覆客戶，將問題解決。當接到客戶的投訴時，要具有換位思考的意識。若是己方的失誤，要代表公司致歉，並站在客戶的立場上提供解決方案。同時，要準備三到四套解決方案，首先將自己認為的最佳方案提供給客戶，若客戶提出異議，可另換一套。在解決完問題後，要徵求客戶對該問題的處理意見，爭取再一次的合作機會。

SECTION 06

進行電話預約

Telephone Appointments

隨身應急情境句

Track 037

1	I'd like to make an appointment with Miss Lin. 我想和林小姐預約會面。
2	I was wondering if I could schedule an appointment to see Mr. Collins? 我想知道能不能預約與柯林斯先生會面？
3	Can I have an appointment with Mr. Brown next week? 我可以預約下個禮拜跟布朗先生會面嗎？
4	Could we arrange a specific time to meet? 我們可以安排一個具體的時間見面嗎？
5	Can you suggest a time when it will be con-venient to meet? 您訂一個方便見面的時間好嗎？
6	He won't see anyone at short notice. 他不會接待任何臨時預約的客人。
7	When do you think suit you most? 哪個時間對您來說最合適？

8	When are you available? 您什麼時候有空？
9	When will it be convenient for you? 您什麼時候方便呢？
10	Let me check the schedule. 讓我看一下行程。
11	I need to check my schedule for next week. 我要看一下下個禮拜的行程。
12	How is next Tuesday? 下個禮拜二怎麼樣？
13	How about this Friday at 3 p.m.? 這個禮拜五下午 3 點怎麼樣？
14	Shall we make it 11 a.m.? 我們把時間定在上午 11 點好嗎？
15	His schedule is filled up throughout the week. 他這個禮拜的行程排滿了。
16	She'll have a tight schedule this Thursday. 她這個禮拜四的行程很緊湊了。
17	Could I postpone my appointment with Mr. Brown? 我跟布朗先生的預約能不能往後延呢？
18	I want to cancel the appointment with Mr. Davis. 我想取消和戴維斯先生的預約。

19 If you don't mind, I want to postpone the appointment to next Thursday.
如果您不介意，我想把見面時間延到下週四。

20 I wonder if you could change the date of our appointment.
我想知道你能否改一下我們見面的時間。

21 You've missed your last appointment. Please call to reschedule.
您錯過了上次的預約。請打電話重新預約時間。

萬能好用句型

- I'd like to make an appointment with ….
  我想預約與……會面。
- … won't see anyone at short notice.
  ……不會接待任何臨時預約的客人。
- When are you available?
  您什麼時候有空？
- I need to check my schedule.
  我要看一下我的行程。
- How about … ?
  ……怎麼樣？
- Could I postpone my appointment with …?
  我跟……的預約能不能往後延呢？
- I want to cancel the appointment with ….
  我想取消和……的預約。

職場應答對話

✦ 預約換機油 Make an Appointment for Oil Changes ✦

Ella	Good afternoon. Dave's Auto Repair. What can I do for you?
艾拉	午安。戴夫汽車維修店。有什麼能為您效勞嗎？
Bill	Good afternoon. My car needs an oil change. Could I make an appointment to bring it in?
比爾	午安。我的汽車需要更換機油。我能預約一下時間把車開過來嗎？
Ella	OK. First let me check which days we have open for oil changes.
艾拉	好的。先讓我看一下都有哪幾天可以更換機油。
Bill	Fine.
比爾	好的。
Ella	How about this Tuesday at 8:30 a.m.?
艾拉	這個禮拜二早上 8:30 可以嗎？
Bill	Sorry, but I have to take my son to school at that time.
比爾	抱歉，但那個時間我要送我兒子上學。
Ella	Then, how about Thursday at 11 a.m.?
艾拉	那禮拜四早上 11 點呢？
Bill	That won't work either. I have to take my wife shopping.
比爾	也不行。我要陪我太太買東西。
Ella	These are the only two available times that I have for this week. Why don't you call again on Friday and schedule an appointment for next week?
艾拉	我們這個禮拜只有這兩個時間可以。不然您禮拜五再打電話過來，預約下個禮拜的時間？

Bill	OK. That's fine. Bye.
比爾	好的，可以。再見。
Ella	Thanks for calling Dave's Auto Repair. Bye.
艾拉	謝謝您致電戴夫汽車維修店。再見。

➲ oil change 更換機油

關聯必備單字

❶ **appointment**
[ə`pɔɪntmənt] 預約

❷ **schedule**
[`skɛdjʊl] 排程

❸ **calendar**
[`kæləndɚ] 日程表

❹ **available**
[ə`veləbl̩] 有時間的

❺ **inconvenience**
[ˌɪnkən`vɪnɪəns] 不方便

❻ **prompt**
[prɑmpt] 準時的

❼ **cancel**
[`kænsl̩] 取消

❽ **tight**
[taɪt] 緊湊的

❾ **postpone**
[post`pon] 延遲

❿ **agenda**
[ə`dʒɛndə] 議程

⓫ **arrange**
[ə`rendʒ] 安排

⓬ **recently**
[`risntlɪ] 最近

⓭ **clarity**
[`klærətɪ] 清晰，清楚

⓮ **reschedule**
[ˌri`skɛdjʊl] 重新安排時間

專業貼心便條

電話約訪的技巧，你知道嗎？下面這幾項就是你需掌握的：

1. 要微笑著說話，讓自己處於微笑狀態。
2. 讓自己的音量和語速跟對方的相協調。
3. 判斷對方的形象，增進彼此的互動——可通過對方的語調進行判斷，一般說話快的人屬於視覺型，說話速度中等的人屬於聽覺型，說話慢的人屬於感覺型。
4. 向對方表明不會佔用對方太多時間。
5. 要善用電話開場白，引起對方的興趣。
6. 談話中，要適當地暫停，讓對方表達自己的想法。

SECTION 07

與客戶在電話裡溝通
Communicating with Customers over the Phone

隨身應急情境句

Track 038

1	This is customer service for ABC company. 這裡是 ABC 公司的客服部。
2	I'd like to hear your feedback regarding this product. 我想聽聽您對這個產品的回饋意見。
3	Can you give me some suggestions about our new product? 您能對我們的新產品提些建議嗎？
4	I'm having trouble hearing you. 我聽不太清楚。
5	Sorry, I didn't catch you. 抱歉，我沒有聽清楚。
6	There's a bad connection. 這裡訊號不好。
7	This is Annie returning your call. 我是安妮，您打過電話給我。
8	I'm sorry. I missed your call. 很抱歉，我沒接到您的電話。

9	I'm calling from another line. 我在用另一個電話和你通話。
10	It took me a long time to get to you. 我花了很長一段時間才打通給你。
11	I want to ask if you've had any problems so far. 我想問一下您到目前為止有沒有遇到什麼問題。
12	Would you tell me what you have been trying to find out? 您能告訴我您一直想試著瞭解什麼嗎?
13	Something goes wrong with the delivery procedure. 出貨程式上出了問題。
14	We prefer a definite date. 我們想要更確切的日期。
15	It's now more than three months since we sent in the order for air conditioners. Yet we are still awaiting delivery. 我們訂購你們的空調現在已經三個多月了。但是我們還在等待出貨。
16	Your failure to deliver the goods within the stipulated time has greatly inconvenienced us. 你們沒有在規定的時間內出貨，給我們帶來了極大的麻煩。

17 Any delay in shipment would be detrimental to our future business.

延遲出貨會對我們往後的業務很不利。

萬能好用句型

- This is customer service for .... 這裡是……的客服部。
- I'd like to hear your feedback regarding ....
  我想聽聽您對……的回饋意見。
- I'm having trouble hearing you. 我聽不太清楚。
- Sorry, I didn't catch you. 很抱歉，我沒有聽清楚。
- This is ... returning your call. 我是……您打過電話給我。
- I'm sorry. I missed your call. 很抱歉，我沒接到您的電話。
- I want to ask if you've had any problems so far.
  我想問一下您到目前為止有沒有遇到什麼問題。

職場應答對話

✦ 獲得回饋 Obtain Feedback ✦

Jenny Hello. Is this Mr. Parker?
珍妮 您好。請問是派克先生嗎？

Mr. Parker Hello. Yes. Who is this?
派克先生 你好，是的。請問你是哪位？

Jenny This is customer service for A&B Electronics. You bought one of our cameras recently, right?

珍妮	這裡是 A&B 電子的客服部。您最近購買了我們的一台照相機，對嗎？
Mr. Parker	Yes. That's right.
派克先生	對，沒錯。
Jenny	I'm just calling today to make sure everything is fine with your camera and that you are completely satisfied.
珍妮	我今天打電話來只是想確認下您的照相機有沒有問題，以及您是否對它完全滿意。
Mr. Parker	Yes. Everything seems to be working fine with it. I have no complaints. 派克先生 是的。看起來一切都很好。我沒什麼好抱怨的。
Jenny	OK, Mr. Parker. I am very glad to hear that. If you have any problems with it in the future, then please don't hesitate to call us.
珍妮	好的，派克先生。很高興聽到您這麼說。如果您日後有任何問題，請隨時來電。
Mr. Parker	OK. Thank you.
派克先生	好的。謝謝。
Jenny	Thank you for your time and business. We really appreciate it. Have a nice day. Bye.
珍妮	感謝您抽空回答我的提問以及購買我們的產品。我們不勝感激。祝您有愉快的一天。再見。
Mr. Parker	Bye.
派克先生	再見。

關聯必備單字

❶ **confirm**
[kənˋfɝm] 確認

❷ **purchase**
[ˋpɝtʃəs] 購買

❸ **improve**
[ɪmˋpruv] 改善

❹ **overload**
[ˏovɚˋlod] 超載

❺ **trouble**
[ˋtrʌbl̩] 麻煩

❻ **visit**
[ˋvɪzɪt] 拜訪

❼ **interested**
[ˋɪntərɪstɪd] 感興趣的

❽ **retail**
[ˋritel] 零售

❾ **retailer**
[ˋritelɚ] 零售商

❿ **electronic**
[ɪˏlɛkˋtrɑnɪk] 電子的

⓫ **wish**
[wɪʃ] 希望

⓬ **feedback**
[ˋfidˏbæk] 回饋

⓭ **connection**
[kəˋnɛkʃən] 連接

⓮ **delivery**
[dɪˋlɪvərɪ] 交付（貨物）

⓯ **procedure**
[prəˋsidʒɚ] 程式

⓰ **air conditioner**
冷氣

⓱ **stipulated**
[ˋstɪpjəˏletɪd] 規定的

⓲ **detrimental**
[ˏdɛtrəˋmɛntl̩] 不利的

專業貼心便條

電話行銷是指透過使用電話來實現有計劃、有組織並且高效率地擴大顧客群、提高顧客滿意度、維護老顧客等市場行為的方法。而在打電話給客戶前，以下這些訊息是你需要準備的：

1. 記下潛在客戶的姓名、職位、性別，公司名稱及營業性質。
2. 想好打電話給潛在客戶的理由，並準備好要聊的內容。
3. 想好潛在客戶可能會提出的問題，以及如何應對客戶的拒絕。

CHAPTER 07

舉行會議 Holding a Meeting

1. 會議的籌備 Preparing for a Meeting
2. 會議開始了 Opening a Meeting
3. 共同討論議題 Discussing Items
4. 徵求別人意見 Asking for Suggestions
5. 表達贊同或反對 Agreeing and Disagreeing
6. 做好會議總結 Drawing a Conclusion

SECTION 01

會議的籌備
Preparing for a Meeting

隨身應急情境句

Track 039

1 The meeting is scheduled for 9 a.m. this Thursday.
會議被安排在這個禮拜四的上午 9 點進行。

2 The meeting will be held on Friday morning.
會議將在禮拜五上午舉行。

3 Mr. Brown will chair the meeting.
會議將由布朗先生主持。

4 How long will the conference last?
這次會議要持續多久的時間？

5 The conference will have lasted a full week.
會議將持續整整一個禮拜的時間。

6 The meeting is going to last four hours.
會議將持續四個小時。

7 Where do you think we will have the meeting?
你認為我們會在哪裡開會？

8 We'll reserve the main conference room for tomorrow and Friday.
我們預訂了主會議室，明天和禮拜五使用。

9	We have already sent out all the invitations. 我們已經寄出所有的邀請函了。
10	We didn't plan for providing the delegates' lunch. 我們並沒有計劃為與會代表提供午餐。
11	There are 20 participants here today. 今天有 20 人參加議會。
12	The delegation arrived in Beijing last Sunday. 代表團已經於上個禮拜日抵達北京。
13	Is there any chance to change the schedule? 有沒有可能更改日程？
14	Would it bother you if we changed the time? 如果我們更改時間，會造成你的不便嗎？
15	I would rather not change the time. 我寧願不要更改時間。
16	Any changes of the conference event will be notified to you in the first place. 有關會議的任何事項如有變更，將第一時間通知你。
17	Make sure all the delegates get informed in time. 確保所有的代表都及時得到通知。
18	The date for the meeting has been altered from Monday to Wednesday. 會議日期已從星期一改為星期三。

19 We want to change our meeting from this Wednesday to next Tuesday.
我們想把會議由本週三改為下週二。

20 The conference has changed to May 15th.
會議已改為 5 月 15 日舉行。

萬能好用句型

- The meeting is scheduled for ….
  會議被安排在……進行。
- … will chair the meeting.
  會議將由……主持。
- How long will the conference last?
  這次會議會持續多久的時間？
- The meeting is going to last ….
  會議將持續……。
- We've already sent out all the invitations.
  我們已經寄出所有的邀請函了。
- There are … participants here today.
  今天有……人參加會議。
- The date for the meeting has been altered from … to ….
  會議日期已從……改為……。

職場應答對話

✦ 明天的會議 Tomorrow's Meeting ✦

Regina	We're having a meeting tomorrow. Can you make it?
瑞吉娜	明天我們會有一個會議。你可以參加嗎？
Kyle	When is it taking place?
凱爾	什麼時候舉行？
Regina	We're planning on 11 a.m. Is that OK?
瑞吉娜	我們計劃在上午 11 點進行。可以嗎？
Kyle	Yes, that will be fine.
凱爾	好的，沒問題。
Regina	We're going to go over last quarter's sales figures.
瑞吉娜	我們要討論上一季度的銷售數字。
Kyle	Good. I have some input I'd like to make.
凱爾	很好。我有一些意見要提出來。
Regina	Jim also has some ideas about improving the bottom line.
瑞吉娜	吉姆也有一些有關提升收益的想法。
Kyle	That would be interesting. He always has good insight.
凱爾	那會很有趣。他一直擁有不錯的洞察力。
Regina	Yes, he's going to outline some new sales strategies.
瑞吉娜	是的。他將要概述一些新的銷售策略。
Kyle	Is Rick attending?
凱爾	里克會參加嗎？

Regina	No, he's flying to Los Angeles and won't be able to make it.
瑞吉娜	不會。他要飛往洛杉磯，不能參加了。
Kyle	Oh well, maybe he will phone in.
凱爾	哦，好吧，他也許會打電話過來。

- input [ˋɪn͵pʊt] n （想法、建議等的）投入
- bottom line 利潤，盈利，收益
- insight [ˋɪn͵saɪt] n 洞察力
- outline [ˋaʊt͵laɪn] v 概述，描述要點

關聯必備單字

❶ **conference**
[ˋkɑnfərəns] 會議

❷ **organize**
[ˋɔrgə͵naɪz] 組織

❸ **organizer**
[ˋɔrgə͵naɪzɚ] 組織者

❹ **delegation**
[͵dɛləˋgeʃən] 代表團

❺ **delegate**
[ˋdɛlə͵get] 會議代表

❻ **notify**
[ˋnotə͵faɪ] 通知

❼ **reserve**
[rɪˋzɝv] 預訂

❽ **hold**
[hold] 舉行

❾ **last**
[læst] 持續

❿ **invitation**
[͵ɪnvəˋteʃən] 邀請（函）

⓫ **arrive**
[əˋraɪv] 抵達

⓬ **attend**
[əˋtɛnd] 出席

⓭ **formal**
[ˋfɔrml̩] 正式的

⓮ **informal**
[ɪnˋfɔrml̩] 非正式的

⓯ **checklist**
[ˋtʃɛk͵lɪst] 核對清單

⓰ **meeting notice**
開會通知

⑰ **projector**
[prə`dʒɛktɚ] 投影儀

⑱ **whiteboard**
[`waɪt͵bord] 白板

⑲ **audio equipment**
音響設備

⑳ **network**
[`nɛt͵wɝk] 網路

專業貼心便條

倘若想要成為一名出色的會議籌畫者，首先要清楚自己的工作任務，可不要糊里糊塗地做些無用功。以下便是會議籌畫者的工作任務：

- 制訂計劃，確定必須要做的事項以滿足會議的需要並達到會議確定的目標。
- 制定會議議程。
- 選擇或提議合適的場所。
- 瞭解可供使用的場所和設施情況。
- 檢查並比較各項設施。
- 安排交通事宜。
- 協調會務工作人員的活動。
- 招收、培訓會務人員和廣告人員。
- 制定可行的預算或按既定預算安排有關工作。
- 確定各項工作的時間安排。
- 視察選定的場所和設施。
- 與各有關方面進行接洽（如運輸公司、旅行社、音響設備公司等）。
- 確定印刷公司。
- 安排食品、飲料相關事宜。
- 進行價格方面的談判。
- 跟會議發言人和各位貴賓進行聯繫。

SECTION 02

會議開始了
Opening a Meeting

隨身應急情境句

Track 040

1	I'd like to thank you all for attending today's meeting. 我想感謝各位參加今天的會議。
2	Welcome everyone to this meeting and thank you for coming. 歡迎各位參加這次會議，謝謝大家的到來。
3	Thanks again for joining us today. 再次感謝各位今天能夠加入我們。
4	We will have two presentations from 9:00 to 11:00 with a 10-minute break at halftime. 9 點到 11 點我們將有兩場簡報，中間休息 10 分鐘。
5	If you look at the agenda, you will find that we'll have two round-table discussions this afternoon. 如果您看一下議程表，您會發現今天下午我們有兩場圓桌討論會。
6	Shall we begin? 我們可以開始了嗎？

7	Let's call the meeting to order. 我們就開始開會吧。
8	The meeting will now come to order. 會議現在正式開始。
9	Let's take a look at today's agenda. 讓我們一起看看今天的議程。
10	Later I will brief you about the agenda. 等一下我會向大家簡單介紹一下議程。
11	Our goal is to provide chances for information exchanging. 我們的目的是給大家提供交流的機會。
12	Let's get to the point directly. 我們直接進入正題吧。
13	We aim to further cement our trade relations. Please feel free to express your ideas and seek for cooperation. 我們的目的是進一步鞏固彼此的貿易關係。請大家暢所欲言，尋求合作機會。
14	Miss Lin would be our first speaker. 首先發言的是林小姐。
15	Now I'm honored to introduce the two distinguished guests to you. 現在我非常榮幸地向大家介紹兩位尊貴的客人。

16	It gives me great pleasure to introduce our guests. 我很高興向大家介紹一下我們的客人。
17	I'd like to extend a warm welcome to Mr. Brown. 熱烈歡迎布朗先生參會。
18	Let's give him a big hand. 讓我們熱烈鼓掌歡迎他。

萬能好用句型

- Welcome everyone to this meeting and thank you for coming.
  歡迎各位參加這次會議，感謝大家的到來。
- Shall we begin?
  我們可以開始了嗎？
- The meeting will now come to order.
  會議現在正式開始。
- Let's take a look at today's agenda.
  讓我們一起看看今天的議程。
- Let's get to the point directly.
  我們直接進入正題吧。
- … would be our first speaker.
  首先發言的是……。
- It gives me great pleasure to introduce ….
  很高興向大家介紹……。
- I'd like to extend a warm welcome to ….
  熱烈歡迎……參與會議。

職場應答對話

✦ The Meeting Begins 會議開始✦

Chairman I think we'll begin now. First, I'd like to welcome you all and thank everyone for coming, especially at such short notice. I know you are all very busy and it's difficult to take time away from your daily tasks for meetings.

主席 我想現在我們可以開始了。首先，我要歡迎大家，並特別感謝各位在這麼倉促通知的情況下前來參加會議。我知道你們都很忙，很難從日常工作中抽出時間來開會。

Helen Sir, should I ...

海倫 先生，我應該……

Chairman I almost forgot. We have a new face here today. Helen, please stand up and introduce yourself.

主席 我差點忘了。今天我們有位新面孔。海倫，請站起來介紹一下自己。

Helen Hi everybody. I'm Helen. I will be taking over John's position while he is on sick leave.

海倫 大家好，我是海倫。在約翰休病假的期間，我將接替他的工作。

Chairman Thank you, Helen. And welcome. Now let's take a look at today's agenda.

主席 謝謝妳，海倫。歡迎妳的到來。現在讓我們一起看看今天的議程。

- take over 接管
- task [tæsk] n 任務，工作

關聯必備單字

❶ **host**
[host] 主持

❷ **announce**
[əˋnaʊns] 宣佈

❸ **agenda**
[əˋdʒendə] 議程

❹ **item**
[ˋaɪtəm] 議題

❺ **review**
[rɪˋvju] 回顧

❻ **record**
[rɪˋkɔrd] 記錄

❼ **material**
[məˋtɪrɪəl] 資料

❽ **chairperson**
[ˋtʃɛr͵pɝsn] 主席

❾ **mainly**
[ˋmenlɪ] 主要地

❿ **distinguished**
[dɪˋstɪŋgwɪʃt] 尊貴的

⓫ **cement**
[sɪˋmɛnt] 鞏固

⓬ **conference room**
會議室

⓭ **conference centre**
會議中心

⓮ **conference hall**
會議廳

⓯ **committee meeting**
委員會會議

⓰ **staff meeting**
員工會議

⓱ **project meeting**
專案會議

⓲ **budget meeting**
預算會議

⓳ **board meeting**
董事會會議

⓴ **round-table discussion**
圓桌會議

專業貼心便條

如何選擇最合適的會議場所，你知道嗎？

首先，製作一個會議場所清單表，在表上列出會議要求的所有重要條件，進而進行各個場所的比較和選擇；然後，根據會議的類型來挑選適合的場所，例如新產品展示會則需要選擇有展示空間的場所，而且交通要十分便利；最後，一定要到現場進行實地考察，這是至關重要的。

SECTION 03

共同討論議題
Discussing Items

隨身應急情境句

Track 041

1. Let's start with the issue of last month's sales figures.
讓我們從上個月的銷售數字說起吧。

2. The first item on the agenda today is about our new product.
今天議程的第一個議題是有關我們的新產品的。

3. The next thing on the agenda is about the marketing strategy of our latest product.
議程的下一個議題是關於我們最新產品的行銷策略。

4. The other talk of the day is about the promotion campaign we started two weeks ago. 今天討論的另一個議題是關於兩個禮拜前我們開展的促銷活動。

5. Let's move on to the next item.
讓我們進入到下一個議題吧。

6. It's time we get back to business.
我們該回到正題上了。

7. I'd like to put a question to the first speaker.
我想向第一個發言者提問。

8	I have something to say. 我有話要說。
9	I would like to speak. 我想說幾句。
10	Please go ahead. 請說。
11	We've already discussed this matter. 這個問題我們已經討論過了。
12	This matter has been covered. 這個問題已經討論過了。
13	Why don't we leave this issue open and go to the next part? 我們何不保留這個問題，先進行下個部分？
14	What is it that you want to say? 您想說什麼？
15	Can you make the point clear? 可以講得清楚一點嗎？
16	Could you please repeat that explanation? 可以重複一下你的解釋嗎？
17	Can you please say that again? 你能重複一遍嗎？
18	Shall I repeat the question? 需要我重複一遍問題嗎？

Chapter 01
Chapter 02
Chapter 03
Chapter 04
Chapter 05
Chapter 06
Chapter 07
Chapter 08
Chapter 09
Chapter 10
Chapter 11

萬能好用句型

- Let's start with ....　讓我們從……說起吧。
- The first item on the agenda today is about ....
  今天議程的第一個議題是有關……。
- The other talk of the day is about ....
  今天討論的另一個議題是關於……。
- It's time we get back to business.　我們該回到正題上了。
- I'd like to put a question to ....　我想向……提問。
- This matter has been covered.　這個問題已經討論過了。

職場應答對話

✦ 出差總結會 Trip Summaries Meeting ✦

Chairman Does anyone have anything to say about last week's business trip?
主席 關於上個禮拜的出差，大家有什麼要說的嗎？

Jane Yes, sir, I do.
珍 有的，先生，我有。

Chairman Go ahead, Jane.
主席 請說，珍。

Jane Well, it seems our counterparts in Japan are on a different page.
珍 嗯，我們在日本的公司似乎跟我們這邊的節奏不同。

Chairman What do you mean?
主席 妳的意思是？

Jane	They are working at a much slower pace than our team here in the States. And I don't think that they are taking the project as seriously as we are.
珍	他們的進度遠比我們美國這裡的團隊慢很多。而且我認為他們並沒有像我們一樣認真地對待這個項目。
Chairman	Yes. That does seem like a problem.
主席	是的。這看起來確實是個問題。
Jane	It might just be an issue of miscommuni-cation.
珍	也許這只是溝通不當的問題。
Chairman	Thank you for bringing this to our attention, Jane. I will call the project manager in Japan this afternoon.
主席	珍，謝謝妳讓我們注意到這個問題。今天下午我會打電話給日本那邊的專案經理。
Jane	No problem, sir. Yes, please call him as soon as possible.
珍	不用客氣，先生。是的，請儘快打電話給他。

- counterpart [ˋkaʊntɚ͵pɑrt] n 對應物，職務相當的人
- miscommunication [͵mɪskəmjunəˋkeʃən] n 錯誤傳達

關聯必備單字

❶ **topic**
[ˋtɑpɪk] 話題

❷ **theme**
[θim] 主題

❸ **view**
[vju] 意見

❹ **point of view**
觀點

❺ **opinion**
[əˋpɪnjən] 看法

❻ **notion**
[ˋnoʃən] 見解

❼ **discussion**
[dɪˋskʌʃən] 討論

❽ **debate**
[dɪˋbet] 辯論

❾ **argument**
[ˋɑrgjəmənt] 論據

❿ **idea**
[aɪˋdɪə] 想法

⓫ **express**
[ɪkˋsprɛs] 表達

⓬ **group**
[grup] 組

⓭ **pass out**
分發

⓮ **underlying**
[ˏʌndɚˋlaɪɪŋ] 潛在的

⓯ **fundamental**
[ˏfʌndəˋmɛntl̩] 根本的

⓰ **elementary**
[ˏɛləˋmɛntərɪ] 基本的

⓱ **essential**
[ɪˋsɛnʃəl] 必要的

⓲ **speaker**
[ˋspikɚ] 發言者

專業貼心便條

一位優秀的會議籌畫者都具備哪些素質呢？

1. 協商、溝通能力強，善於與人共事。
2. 注意細節，善於解決問題。
3. 行事果斷、執著。
4. 能夠處理會議財務事宜。
5. 能夠熟練操作電腦。
6. 熟悉酒店的運作，可安排恰到好處的功能表。
7. 能夠熟練地同視聽公司等各方面打交道。
8. 熟知各種禮儀，可妥善接待貴賓和外國客人。

SECTION 04

徵求別人意見
Asking for Suggestions

隨身應急情境句

Track 042

1. What's your opinion about this plan?
你怎麼看這個計劃？
2. Kate, what do you think?
凱特，妳怎麼看？
3. Now it's time for today's questions.
現在是今天的提問時間。
4. There will be a few minutes for questions.
將會有幾分鐘的提問時間。
5. And then everyone can express his point of view.
之後是自由發言時間。
6. Are there any suggestions?
有什麼建議嗎？
7. Anything unclear?
還有什麼不清楚的嗎？
8. Do you have any comments on this item?
你對這個議題有什麼看法嗎？
9. Do you think that is a good idea?
你認為那是個好主意嗎？

10	Shall we take a vote? 我們是否要投票決定？
11	Let's put it to the vote. 讓我們投票決定吧。
12	I'm open to any reasonable suggestions. Please feel free to express your views! 我樂意接受任何合理的建議。請大家暢所欲言！
13	We welcome any suggestions on the project. 我們歡迎針對這個項目的任何建議。
14	Are there any suggestions about how to tackle the problem? 針對如何解決這個問題，各位有什麼建議嗎？
15	Are you suggesting we should employ a spokes-man? 你是否建議我們聘請一位代言人呢？
16	Anything else you want to add? 還有什麼要補充的嗎？
17	Is there anything you'd like to add? 您還有什麼要補充的嗎？
18	What would you add to this list? 您還有什麼要補充的嗎？
19	Are there any other comments you want to add on? 還有什麼需要補充的嗎？

20	What does anyone else think? 其他人怎麼認為呢？
21	Does anyone else have any thoughts before I comment on that? 在我提出意見之前，其他人還有什麼想法嗎？

萬能好用句型

- What's your opinion about ...?
  你怎麼看……？
- What do you think?
  你怎麼看？
- Are there any suggestions about ...?
  針對……，有什麼建議嗎？
- Shall we take a vote?
  我們是否要投票決定？
- Please feel free to express your views!
  請大家暢所欲言！
- Do you have any comments on ...?
  你對……有什麼看法嗎？
- Anything else you want to add?
  還有什麼要補充的嗎？

職場應答對話

✦ 南美市場戰略 South America Strategy ✦

Chairman We have finished talking about our South America strategy. Does anyone have any suggestions on implementation? Yes, Roger.

主席 我們結束了針對南美市場戰略的討論。大家對執行方面有什麼建議嗎？好的，羅傑。

Roger It's a good plan, but I don't think we have really considered the language aspect.

羅傑 這是一個很好的計劃，但我認為我們並沒有真正考慮到語言方面的問題。

Chairman What do you mean?

主席 你的意思是？

Roger I mean, our colleagues in Southern California have a really good grasp on the Spanish language. They could help us quickly get our operations up and running.

羅傑 我的意思是，我們在加州南部的同事都很順利地掌握了西班牙語。他們能夠幫助我們迅速開展業務，進行運作。

Chairman Great suggestion!

主席 很好的建議！

Roger Yes, I think so. I think we should schedule a meeting with them right away.

羅傑 是的，我也這麼認為。我認為我們應該立刻安排一次跟他們的會議。

Chairman Of course. I will phone them this afternoon and we can plan a meeting together with them next week.

主席 當然。今天下午我會打電話給他們，我們可以安排下個禮拜跟他們開會。

Roger Excellent!

羅傑 太好了！

- implementation [ˏɪmpləmɛnˋteʃən] n 實施，執行
- aspect [ˋæspɛkt] n 方面
- colleague [kɑˋlɪg] n 同事
- Spanish [ˋspænɪʃ] n 西班牙語

關聯必備單字

❶ **suggestion**
[səˋdʒɛstʃən] 建議

❷ **comment**
[ˋkɑmɛnt] 評論，意見

❸ **criticism**
[ˋkrɪtəˏsɪzəm] 批評

❹ **evaluation**
[ɪˏvæljʊˋeʃən] 評估

❺ **regard**
[rɪˋgɑrd] 認為

❻ **consider**
[kənˋsɪdɚ] 考慮

❼ **estimate**
[ˋɛstəˏmet] 估計

❽ **vote**
[vot] 投票

❾ **reasonable**
[ˋriznəbl̩] 合理的

❿ **logical**
[ˋlɑdʒɪkl̩] 合乎邏輯的

⓫ **rational**
[ˋræʃənl̩] 理性的

⓬ **wise**
[waɪz] 明智的

⓭ **measure**
[ˋmɛʒɚ] 措施

⓮ **add**
[æd] 添加

⓯ **unclear**
[ˏʌnˋklɪr] 不清楚的

專業貼心便條

會議預算包括以下幾方面：

1. 交通費用：出發地至會議地的交通費用；會議期間交通費用；返程交通費用。
2. 會議室費用：會議場地租金；會議設施租賃費用；會場佈置費用；其他支援費用，如廣告、印刷、禮儀等。
3. 住宿費用及相關服務費用。
4. 餐飲費用：早餐；中餐；酒水及服務費；會場茶飲；聯誼酒會。
5. 租賃費用：視聽設備；設備的運輸、安裝調試及技術控制人員支援費用；演員及節目費用。
6. 雜費：會展過程中一些臨時性安排產生的費用，包括列印、臨時運輸及裝卸、紀念品、模特兒與禮儀服務、臨時道具、傳真及其他通訊、快遞服務、臨時保潔、翻譯與嚮導、臨時商務用車、匯兌等等。

SECTION 05

表達贊同或反對
Agreeing and Disagreeing

隨身應急情境句

Track 043

1	What's your attitude towards his suggestion? 您對他的建議是什麼態度？
2	Do you approve of his idea? 你贊同他的觀點嗎？
3	That makes a lot of sense. 非常有道理。
4	I totally agree with her. 我完全認同她。
5	I don't have any objection to it. 我沒有任何異議。
6	I couldn't agree with you more. 我非常贊同你的觀點。
7	I think it's a great idea! 我認為這個想法很棒！
8	I suppose that's true. 我認為那是對的。
9	That's not the way I see it. 我不是那樣看。

10	I rather doubt that. 我非常懷疑。
11	I don't think that's a bad idea at all. 我認為這完全不是個壞主意。
12	It was a sensible idea, I felt. 我覺得這是個明智的想法。
13	How wise of you! 您真明智！
14	I can't favor your plan. 我不能贊成你的計劃。
15	What's the point of making so much trouble? 花那麼多力氣有什麼用？
16	I'm afraid I can't agree with you there. 我恐怕在這個部份上不能同意你的看法。
17	I'm not in favor of it. 我不贊成。
18	I get your point, but there are other things we have to consider. 我明白你的意思，但我們還要考慮其他的事。
19	I agree with much of what you said. 我基本上同意你的意見。
20	What you say is partly right. 你說的有一部分是對的。

萬能好用句型

- Do you approve of ...? 你贊同……？
- I totally agree with .... 我完全認同……。
- I couldn't agree with you more. 我非常贊同。
- I suppose that's true. 我認為那是對的。
- How wise of you! 您真明智！
- I'm not in favor of it. 我不贊成。
- I agree with much of what you said. 我基本上同意你的意見。
- Thanks for your comment. 謝謝你的意見。

職場應答對話

✦ 謝謝你的意見 Thanks for Your Comment ✦

James First of all, the DVD campaign. I just want to remind everyone that we will be launching this campaign at the end of the month.

詹姆斯 首先，是 DVD 活動。我只是想提醒一下各位這個月底我們就要展開這項活動。

Ann Actually, James, can I just ask you—sorry to hold the meeting up—can I ask you about this time frame, because I thought that we were going to launch this campaign the month after next, and I understand that you have your deadlines, but I do feel quite strongly that we're bringing this out too soon.

安 事實上，詹姆斯，我能不能問一下——抱歉耽擱下一會議——我能不能問一下活動時間表，因為我以為我們會下下個月展開活動，我理解你有截止期限的壓力，但我真的覺得我們太早開始了。

James	Thanks for your comment, Ann.
詹姆斯	謝謝妳的意見，安。
Ann	I just believe we should think about this more carefully.
安	我只是認為我們應該考慮得更謹慎一點。
James	You're right. Does anyone else have any thoughts before I comment on that?
詹姆斯	妳說得對。在提出我的意見之前，其他人還有什麼想法嗎？

- launch [lɔntʃ] v 發起，發動
- campaign [kæmˋpen] n 運動，活動
- time frame 時間表

關聯必備單字

❶ **agree**
[əˋgri] 同意

❷ **disagree**
[ˏdɪsəˋgri] 不同意

❸ **approve**
[əˋpruv] 贊成

❹ **disapprove**
[ˏdɪsəˋpruv] 不贊成

❺ **in favor of**
支持

❻ **dislike**
[dɪsˋlaɪk] 不喜歡

❼ **objection**
[əbˋdʒekʃən] 反對

❽ **unacceptable**
[ˏʌnəkˋsɛptəbḷ] 不能接受的

❾ **awful**
[ˋɔfʊl] 糟糕的

❿ **terrible**
[ˋtɛrəbḷ] 糟糕的

⓫ **ideal**
[aɪˋdiəl] 理想的

⓬ **absolutely**
[ˋæbsəˏlutlɪ] 絕對地

⑬ **totally**
[ˋtotl̩ɪ] 完全地

⑭ **unanimously**
[jʊˋnænəməslɪ] 全體一致地

⑮ **excellent**
[ˋɛksələnt] 極好的

⑯ **partly**
[ˋpɑrtlɪ] 部分地

專業貼心便條

都市會議模式可分為下面這三種：

1. 旅遊市場導向型：

依附著名的旅遊目的地或中轉過境地，借助該地的觀光旅遊優勢，依託旅遊市場，開發會議需求，形成觀光旅遊型會議聚集地，包括以會議方式存在的獎勵旅遊和福利旅遊等。

2. 城市商務導向型：

由大都市的商務會議市場需求拉動，產生聚集效應，形成商務接待與商務會議型會都。這些會議區多位於經濟繁華大都市的郊區。

3. 資源支撐型：

由特色、新奇或珍稀的資源所支撐，尤其是與休閒度假緊密相關的資源，如溫泉、滑雪、海濱等，形成休閒度假目的地。

SECTION 06

做好會議總結
Drawing a Conclusion

隨身應急情境句

Track 044

1	Is there anything we might have left out? 我們是不是漏掉了什麼？
2	Have we missed anything? 我們有遺漏什麼嗎？
3	Did we overlook anything on the agenda? 我們有遺漏任何議題嗎？
4	Let's go over the agenda again to see if we've missed anything. 讓我們再跑一遍議程，看有沒有什麼漏掉了。
5	We skipped Item No. 4. 我們漏掉了第四項。
6	Please allow me to give a brief conclusion. 請允許我做一個簡單的總結。
7	I'd like to summarize the main points of today's meeting. 我想要總結一下今天會議的要點。

8	Before we close the meeting, I'd like to run through the main points again. 在會議結束之前，我想要再跑一遍重點。
9	We are all ears. 我們洗耳恭聽。
10	Finally, we do appreciate the contribution that everybody makes for the company. 最後，我們非常感謝大家為公司所作出的貢獻。
11	We would like to thank Mr. Smith for his tremendous contribution. 我們要感謝史密斯先生作出的巨大貢獻。
12	For any further questions, please feel free to contact me. 有任何進一步的問題，請隨時聯繫我。
13	If you have any questions, please do not hesitate to contact us. 如果你有什麼問題，請隨時聯繫我們。
14	I believe we have achieved a lot in this meeting. 我相信這次會議讓我們有很多收獲。
15	I declare the meeting closed. 我宣佈會議結束。
16	You're dismissed! 散會！

17	That concludes today's meeting. 今天的會議到此為止。
18	If nobody wants to add anything, we can draw the meeting to a close. 如果沒有人要補充的話，會議就到此結束。

萬能好用句型

- We skipped....
  我們漏掉了……。
- Before we close the meeting, I'd like to....
  在會議結束之前，我想要……。
- We are all ears.
  我們洗耳恭聽。
- For any further questions, please feel free to contact me.
  有任何進一步的問題，請隨時聯繫我。
- That concludes today's meeting.
  今天的會議到此為止。
- We've worked really hard to reach this point.
  我們為此都付出了很多努力。
- Let's make our plan a perfect reality!
  讓我們將計劃變成美好的現實吧！

職場應答對話

✦ 記住會議內容 Remember the Contents of the Conference ✦

Chairman Well, everybody … we have achieved a lot in today's meeting.

主席 好的，各位……今天的會議讓我們收穫了很多。

John Yes, we have worked really hard to reach this point.

約翰 是的，我們為此都付出了很多努力。

Chairman True. I want to thank everyone for working so hard to get this far.

主席 的確是。我想要感謝每一個人為現在取得的成績所付出的努力。

John Let's remember what we talked about today and put it into practice.

約翰 讓我們記住今天討論的內容，並付諸行動。

Chairman Yes. By following our plan, we are sure to be successful! So everyone please remember your role. When each individual part does its job well, then we will have a smooth-running and efficient machine!

主席 是的。按照我們的計劃行事，我們肯定會成功的！所以請每個人記住自己所扮演的角色。當每一個單獨的零件部位都有效發揮作用時，我們便將擁有一台運轉平穩、效率高的機器。

John Very good analogy!

約翰 很棒的比喻！

Chairman Now, team … let's make our plan a perfect reality!
主席 現在，夥伴們……讓我們將計劃變成美好現實吧！

- achieve [əˋtʃiv] v 達到，完成
- follow [ˋfɑlo] v 跟隨，遵循
- smooth-running [ˏsmuðˋrʌnɪŋ] adj 平穩運行的
- analogy [əˋnælədʒɪ] n 類比

關聯必備單字

1. **decision** [dɪˋsɪʒn] 決定
2. **conclusion** [kənˋkluʒn] 結論
3. **finish** [ˋfɪnɪʃ] 結束
4. **main** [men] 主要的
5. **point** [pɔɪnt] 要點
6. **summary** [ˋsʌmərɪ] 概要
7. **brief** [brif] 簡短的
8. **abstract** [ˋæbstrækt] 摘要
9. **objective** [əbˋdʒɛktɪv] 客觀的
10. **skip** [skɪp] 跳過
11. **sum up** 總結
12. **declare** [dɪˋklɛr] 宣佈
13. **dismiss** [dɪsˋmɪs] 解散
14. **overlook** [ˏovɚˋlʊk] 忽略
15. **motion** [ˋmoʃən] 提議
16. **hesitate** [ˋhɛzəˏtet] 猶豫
17. **vote** [vot] 得票（數）
18. **define** [dɪˋfaɪn] 為……下定義

專業貼心便條

你知道什麼是圓桌會議嗎？圓桌會議，沒有主席位置和隨從位置，是一種平等對話的協商會議形式，圓桌會議有下面這四個規則。

1. 角色對等規則：

角色對等是指與會成員發言權的平等，表決權的平等和決策權的平等。

2. 議事不議人規則：

預先發給大家客觀實際的調查材料，讓大家根據工作需要，提名相對適合的人選，而不是把重點放在議論人上，尤其不能放在議論人的缺點上。

3. 非人數優勢規則：

圓桌會議不能輕易按照少數服從多數的原則裁決。其重點是弄清每個方案的利弊，盡可能的做到以理服人。

4. 非決定規則：

不是每一個圓桌會議都要作出決定，即使是這個圓桌會議開得很成功也可以不作任何結論。圓桌會議產生的激烈爭論，可以在下次會議繼續討論而不必當場作出決定。

CHAPTER 08

談判高手 Becoming a Good Negotiator

SECTION 01

介紹自己及公司
Presenting Yourself and Your Company

隨身應急情境句

Track 045

1	If you don't mind, I'd like to introduce myself. 如果你不介意，我想介紹一下我自己。
2	May I introduce myself first? 我先自我介紹一下好嗎？
3	How are you? I'm John Smith. 你好嗎？我是約翰．史密斯。
4	How are you? Glad to meet you. 你好嗎？很高興見到您。
5	Hi, I am Jim Brown and I work for ABC company. 嗨，我是吉姆．布朗，我在 ABC 公司工作。
6	Hi, my name is Kate Jones and I am with ABC company. 嗨，我叫凱特．瓊斯，我在 ABC 公司工作。
7	I'm Katherine Jones, but please call me Kate. 我叫凱薩琳．瓊斯，但請叫我凱特吧。
8	Just call me John. 就叫我約翰吧。

9	It's an honor to meet you. 很榮幸認識您。
10	It's a pleasure to meet you. 很高興見到您。
11	You're from France, aren't you? 您來自法國，是嗎？
12	I joined the company five years ago. 我是五年前進公司的。
13	I've been with the company for over ten years. 我為這家公司已經工作十多年了。
14	I am responsible for developing business with small and medium-sized enterprises. 我負責與中小企業開展業務工作。
15	I am in charge of marketing. 我主管行銷。
16	I'm in charge of the sales department. 我負責業務部。
17	There are over 7,000 employees in the company, in five different countries. 公司總共有 7000 多名員工，分佈在五個國家。
18	There are six main divisions in the company. 公司設有六個主要部門。

19	Our main business is energy supply and services. 我們的主要業務是能源供應和服務。
20	Our current objective is to work with international partners to jointly explore the international market. 我們當前的目標是與國際夥伴合作，共同開拓國際市場。

萬能好用句型

- How are you? Glad to meet you. 你好嗎？很高興見到你。
- Hi, I am … and I work for …. 嗨，我是……，我在……工作。
- Hi, my name is … and I am with …
  嗨，我叫……，我在……工作。
- It's a pleasure to meet you. 很高興見到你。
- I am responsible for … 我負責……
- I am in charge of … 我負責……
- There are … employees in the company.
  公司總共有……位員工。
- Our main business is … 我們的主要業務是……。
- Our current objective is … 我們當前的目標是……。

職場應答對話

✦ 介紹公司 Present the Company ✦

Client Could you please tell me more about the company?
客戶 能告訴我貴公司的更多資訊嗎？

Jeff Of course. We have been handling the marketing and advertisements of major sports teams and well-known athletes for over twelve years now.

傑夫 當然可以。我們負責一些大型的運動團隊和知名運動員們的行銷和廣告業務已長達 12 年。

Client Who are some of the big clients you've had?

客戶 貴公司的大客戶都有哪些呢？

Jeff We have worked with Kobe Bryant, Michael Phelps, and Hope Solo, to name a few.

傑夫 我們和科比・布萊恩、麥克・菲爾普斯以及霍普・索羅都有合作，就列舉這幾例吧。

Client Wow, I am impressed. But how familiar are your agents with the interests of a real athlete? Not many people can relate to us.

客戶 哇，很棒啊。但你們的代理人員對一名真正運動員的切身利益能瞭解多少呢？沒有多少人能理解我們。

Jeff Many of our agents are former athletes themselves, so we relate more with our customers than other firms.

傑夫 我們的很多代理都是退役的運動員，因此跟其他公司相比，我們更能理解客戶。

Client Really? Your company has a great advantage then.

客戶 真的嗎？那貴公司就擁有了極大的優勢。

Jeff That's our goal.

傑夫 那是我們的目標。

- athlete [ˋæθlit] n 運動員
- agent [ˋedʒənt] n 代理人，代理商

關聯必備單字

❶ **division**
[dɪˋvɪʒn] 部門

❷ **energy**
[ˋɛnɝdʒɪ] 能源

❸ **jointly**
[dʒɔɪntlɪ] 共同地

❹ **current**
[ˋkɝənt] 目前的

❺ **global**
[ˋglobl̩] 全球的

❻ **domestic**
[dəˋmɛstɪk] 國內的

❼ **market**
[ˋmɑrkɪt] 市場

❽ **continent**
[ˋkɑntənənt] 大洲

❾ **middle-sized**
[ˏmɪdl̩ˋsaɪzd] 中型的

❿ **enterprise**
[ˋɛntɚˏpraɪz] 公司，企業

⓫ **marketing**
[ˋmɑrkɪtɪŋ] 市場行銷

⓬ **represent**
[ˏrɛprɪˋzɛnt] 代表

專業貼心便條

初次面對客戶時的話語，被稱為「接近用語」。那麼，你知道接近用語的表達步驟嗎？可分為以下六步進行：

第一步：說出對方的姓名及職位。

第二步：進行自我介紹，要清晰地說出自己的名字和公司名稱。

第三步：感謝對方的接見，態度要誠懇。

第四步：跟客戶寒暄，聊一些對方較感興趣的話題。

第五步：表達自己拜訪的理由。

第六步：表達對客戶的讚美，接著以詢問的方式來瞭解客戶的興趣和需求。

SECTION 02

向對方介紹產品
Introducing Your Products

Chapter 01
Chapter 02
Chapter 03
Chapter 04
Chapter 05
Chapter 06
Chapter 07
Chapter 08
Chapter 09
Chapter 10
Chapter 11

隨身應急情境句

Track 046

1 In the next half an hour or so, I'm going to talk about our new product.
下面我用半小時左右的時間談談我們的新產品。

2 I'd like to talk to you about the new product.
我想要和你談談我們的新產品。

3 When may I introduce our new products to you?
我什麼時候可以向您介紹我們公司的新產品？

4 The company has a number of production lines and a variety of slitting equipment.
公司擁有多條生產線和各種分割設備。

5 We have a number of production lines with advanced production equipment.
我們擁有多條設備先進的生產線。

6 We keep four production lines.
我們擁有四條生產線。

7 What are the characteristics of this product?
這項產品的特點是什麼？

8	This product is characterized by the fine workmanship and durability. 這項產品的特點是工藝精湛，經久耐用。
9	Our items are of high quality and very popular among the young people. 我們的產品品質很好，而且很受年輕人的喜愛。
10	Our products are presented more attractively and also safer. 我們的產品外觀比較有吸引力，也比較安全。
11	Our products are lower priced than the competition. 我們的產品價格比競爭對手的更低廉。
12	This item is superior in quality and reasonable in price. 這個產品物美價廉。
13	Our products had sixty percent of the market in China. 我們的產品在中國佔有百分之六十的市場佔有率。
14	Our latest products sell pretty well on domestic markets. 我們的最新產品在全國各地都十分暢銷。
15	Our products have entered the international market. 我們的產品已經打入了國際市場。

16	Some products have entered the world market. 部分產品已進入國際市場。
17	The products are sold to customers in 57 countries. 這項產品銷往全球 57 個國家。
18	Our products are sold all over the world. 我們的產品銷往世界各地。

萬能好用句型

- Our items are very popular among the youngpeople.
  我們的產品很受年輕人的喜愛。
- This item is superior in quality and reasonable in price.
  這項產品物美價廉。
- Our product had … percent of the market in …
  我們的產品在……佔有百分之……的市場佔有率。
- Our products sell well on domestic markets.
  我們的產品在全國各地都十分暢銷。
- The product has entered the international market.
  這項產品已經打入了國際市場。
- The products are sold to customers in … countries.
  產品銷往全球……個國家。

職場應答對話

✦ 介紹產品及服務 Introduce Products and Services ✦

Annie Tell me more about the services you offer.

安妮 跟我多說一點你們提供的服務吧。

Ryan Our "products" or services encompass a wide range of things. As a comprehensive insurance agency, we offer not only housing and car insurance, but health and life insurance among others.

萊恩 我們的「產品」和服務涵蓋範圍十分廣泛。作為一家綜合性保險代理公司，我們不僅提供住宅和汽車保險，而且提供健康及人壽保險等。

Annie Well, I was only looking to switch my car insurance, but I also recently purchased a small fishing boat. Do you cover that, and have flood insurance?

安妮 好吧，我只是想換一下車險，但最近我也剛買了一艘小漁船。你們能替它保險嗎，有沒有洪水保險？

Ryan Of course. We can always come out and give you a quote.

萊恩 當然。我們隨時都能過去，並提供給您一份報價。

Annie Great. We live right on the beach, and I know each summer is a hurricane season.

安妮 太好了。我們就住在海邊，我知道每年夏天都是颶風季節。

Ryan Yes, it is. You want to be insured in case of a storm.

萊恩 對，是這樣的。您想要投保以預防暴風雨。

Annie Thanks for the information.

安妮 謝謝你給我提供的資訊。

- encompass [ɪnˋkʌmpəs] v 包含，包括
- comprehensive [ˏkɑmprɪˋhɛnsɪv] adj 綜合的，廣泛的
- quote [kwot] n 報價
- hurricane [ˋhɝɪˏken] n 颶風
- storm [stɔrm] n 暴風雨

關聯必備單字

1. **product** [ˋprɑdʌkt] 產品
2. **latest** [ˋletɪst] 最新的
3. **percent** [pɚˋsɛnt] 百分比
4. **competition** [ˏkɑmpəˋtɪʃən] 競爭
5. **competitive** [kəmˋpɛtətɪv] 競爭的
6. **appliance** [əˋplaɪəns] 器具
7. **material** [məˋtɪrɪəl] 材料
8. **durable** [ˋdjʊrəbḷ] 耐用的
9. **economic** [ˏɪkəˋnɑmɪk] 經濟的
10. **type** [taɪp] 類型
11. **encompass** [ɪnˋkʌmpəs] 包含
12. **insurance** [ɪnˋʃʊrəns] 保險
13. **insure** [ɪnˋʃʊr] 投保
14. **switch** [swɪtʃ] 轉換
15. **slit** [slɪt] 切割
16. **workmanship** [ˋwɝkmənˏʃɪp] 工藝
17. **domestic** [dəˋmɛstɪk] 國內的
18. **durability** [ˏdjʊrəˋbɪlətɪ] 耐久性

專業貼心便條

向客戶介紹產品是要講究技巧的，你知道有哪些技巧嗎？

(1) 步驟 1：

要進行提前演練，在每一次產品介紹前要確定介紹內容、介紹順序和介紹方式。產品介紹的內容應熟記在心。

(2) 步驟 2：

介紹時要清楚自己要達到什麼目的，不是每一次產品介紹都有機會成交，但每次介紹都在為最後的成交作鋪墊。

(3) 步驟 3：

要以客戶的興趣為中心。在介紹產品時，應該要因人而異，用客戶喜歡的方式來解說。

(4) 步驟 4：

將產品的優點與客戶的需求連接起來。介紹產品功能和優勢，以及能夠為客戶帶來的利益。

SECTION 03

討論合作的可能性

Discussing Cooperation Opportunities

隨身應急情境句

Track 047

1 We would like to recommend our company as a suitable agent for your products.
我方想自薦成為貴方產品的代理商。

2 We are very interested in acting as your sole agent.
我方很有興趣做貴公司的獨家代理。

3 We want to know if you could appoint us as your agent of your latest product.
我方想知道貴方是否願意任命我方為貴方新產品的代理。

4 We learn that you are anxious to expand your market.
我們得知貴方急於拓展市場。

5 If you make us your agent in China, we will try our best to push and publicize your products.
如果貴方授權我方為中國地區代理，我方將竭盡全力推廣宣傳貴方產品。

6 We have many advantages to act as your sole agent.
我方擁有很多優勢，有能力擔當貴方的獨家代理。

7 We believe that our experience in the field will entitle us to win your trust.
我方相信我方在這個領域的經驗可以讓貴方信任我方。

8 We can be a good agent because we have a group of well-trained salesmen.
我方可以成為很好的代理商，因為我方有一個訓練有素的銷售團隊。

9 We are able to work as your sole agent because we have wide connections.
我方有能力擔任貴方的獨家代理，因為我們有龐大的關係網。

10 If we may have the honor to act as your sole agent in our territory, no doubt such ties will do good to expand our mutual trade.
如果我方有幸成為貴公司在我方地區的獨家代理，毫無疑問，這些關係網可以幫助我們拓展雙方的貿易。

11 We are willing to negotiate with you on your proposal to act as our agent.
我方想就任命貴方擔任我方代理一事進行洽談。

12 We feel inclined to agree to your proposal.
我方擬同意貴方的提議。

13 I hope we can work together in the future.
我希望將來我們可以合作。

14 We look forward to starting business with you.
我方期望能與貴公司建立貿易關係。

15	If you can push the sales successfully for the next six months, we may appoint you as our agent. 如果貴方能夠在接下來的六個月成功推動銷售，我方可能會指定貴方作代理。
16	We hope that you will redouble your efforts in your sales pushing. 我方希望貴方可以加倍努力進行推銷。
17	We have already appointed another company as our agent in your territory. 我方已經在貴方地區任命了另一家公司為代理商。
18	We are not going to take the question of sole agency into consideration for the time being. 我方目前還沒有設立獨家代理的打算。
19	We regret that we are unable to accept your proposal. 我方很遺憾不能接受貴方的提議。

萬能好用句型

- We want to know if you .... 我方想知道貴方是否⋯⋯。
- If you make us your agent in ..., we will ....
  如果貴方授權我方為⋯⋯地區代理，我方將⋯⋯。
- We believe that ... will entitle us to win your trust.
  我方相信⋯⋯可以讓貴方信任我方。
- We are willing to negotiate with you on ....
  我方想就⋯⋯一事與貴方進行洽談。

➲ We feel inclined to .... 我方傾向……。

➲ We look forward to starting business with you.
我方期望能與貴公司建立貿易往來。

職場應答對話

✦ 保險業務合作 Cooperation of Insurance Business ✦

Helen I just started up a boat and jet ski rental company in town, and I was told your insurance agency was the place to come.

海倫 我剛在鎮上成立了一家租賃船和水上摩托車的公司，聽別人說要投保的話應該來你們這家保險代理公司。

Ryan Yes, we have many clients in the area, both individual and commercial. So I assume you want to insure all of your water vehicles.

萊恩 是的，我們在這個領域有很多客戶，有個人，也有公司。我猜您是要為所有的水上交通工具投保。

Helen Yes, but what about the company itself? Being an entrepreneur isn't easy these days.

海倫 是的，不過能為公司本身投保嗎？現在當一位企業家可不簡單。

Ryan I understand. You can purchase liability insurance, or casualty and property insurance.

萊恩 我明白。您可以購買責任保險或者意外事故險及財產保險。

Helen I am interested in several different types, and also I need to take care of my employees.

海倫 我對幾種不同種類的保險非常感興趣，而且我也要照顧好我的員工。

Ryan Why don't we set up a meeting later this week to discuss the possibilities?

萊恩 這個禮拜晚一點我們開個會來討論一下這幾種保險怎麼樣？

Helen Sure, sounds good.

海倫 好的，聽起來不錯。

- jet ski 水上摩托車
- commercial [kəˋmɝʃəl] adj 商業的
- entrepreneur [ˏɑntrəprəˋnɝ] n 企業家
- casualty [ˋkæʒʊəltɪ] n 傷亡人員，意外事故

關聯必備單字

❶ **cooperation**
[koˏɑpəˋreʃən] 合作

❷ **share**
[ʃɛr] 分享

❸ **proposal**
[prəˋpozl̩] 提議

❹ **entitle**
[ɪnˋtaɪtl̩] 授權，使有資格

❺ **territory**
[ˋtɛrəˏtorɪ]（營業）地區

❻ **publicize**
[ˋpʌblɪˏsaɪz] 宣傳

❼ **assume**
[əˋsjum] 假定

❽ **enthusiastic**
[ɪnˏθjuziˋæstɪk] 熱心的

❾ **liability**
[ˏlaɪəˋbɪlətɪ] 責任

❿ **property**
[ˋprɑpətɪ] 財產

⓫ **dominance**
[ˋdɑmənəns] 優勢，控制

⓬ **rental**
[ˋrɛntl̩] 租賃的

⓭ **sole**
[sol] 唯一的

⓮ **publicize**
[ˋpʌblɪˏsaɪz] 宣傳

⓯ **well-trained**
訓練有素的

⓰ **mutual**
[ˋmjutʃʊəl] 共同的

⓱ **incline**
[ɪnˋklaɪn] 傾向，傾斜

⓲ **regret**
[rɪˋgrɛt] 對……感到遺憾

⓳ **globalization**
[ˏglobəlaɪˋzeʃən] 全球化

⓴ **inject**
[ɪnˋdʒɛkt] 投入（資金）

㉑ **projected**
[prəˋdʒɛktɪd] 預計的

㉒ **risk free**
零風險的

專業貼心便條

在正式交談開始之前，應有幾句話的寒暄或問候，它本身並不正面表達特定的意思，但它在溝通中是必要的。寒暄能讓人相互認識和熟悉，還能使沉悶的氣氛變得活躍。尤其是初次見面，幾句得體的寒暄會使氣氛變得融洽。下面是幾點建議，希望會對你有所幫助：

1. 寒暄要流露出真摯的感情，避免讓別人感覺到你是出於應酬才說出關懷的話。
2. 可以用詢問工作進展、身體狀況等方式來展開談話內容；即使是身為公司新人也要敢於同客戶交流，找出合適的話題，避免冷場。
3. 最常用的話題包括對方家鄉的風土人情、旅遊中的見聞、個人愛好等。
4. 寒暄中避免涉及對方的隱私，如收入、家庭等。
5. 細心地判斷對方是否有時間，如果對方很忙，就要言簡意賅。

SECTION 04

進行價格談判
Negotiating the Price

隨身應急情境句

Track 048

1	This is a detailed sheet of our offer. 這是我方的詳細報價單。
2	What's the rate of commission you want to charge? 貴方希望收取多少傭金呢？
3	What commission would you expect? 貴方希望收取多少傭金呢？
4	What about the commission? 傭金是多少？
5	Our price is net without commission. 我方的報價是淨價，不含傭金。
6	Our price is in line with the world market. 我方的報價與世界市場行情一致。
7	Our quotation is subject to a 7% commission. 我方報價包括 7%的傭金在內。
8	The quotation includes a 7% commission. 報價中包含 7%的傭金。
9	If we order 5,000, what would be your offer? 如果我方訂 5000，貴方報價是多少？

10	What's your best price? 貴方的最低報價是多少？
11	Would you tell me your target price, please? 能否告訴我貴方的目標價格嗎？
12	This is the best price we can give you. 這是我方所能提供的最低報價了。
13	The price we offer you is the lowest, and we can't do better. 我方給貴方的報價是最低的，不能再低了。
14	I am sorry to say that your prices are about 8% higher than those offered by other suppliers. 我很遺憾貴方的報價比其他供應商提供的高出 8%。
15	Your competitors are offering considerably lower prices. 貴方的競爭對手的報價要低得多。
16	The offer is made on a moderate level. 這個報價很適中。
17	Our products are modestly priced. 我方的產品報價適中。
18	The commission you give is too little. 貴方給的傭金太少了。
19	We find your prices are too high to be acceptable. 我方認為貴方的價格太高了，難以接受。

萬能好用句型

- What commission would you expect?
  貴方希望收取多少傭金呢？
- Our price is .... 我方的報價是……。
- If we order ..., what would be your offer?
  如果我方訂……，貴方報價是多少？
- What's your best price? 貴方的最低報價是多少？
- The offer is made on a moderate level. 這個報價很適中。
- The commission you give is too little. 貴方給的傭金太少了。

職場應答對話

✦ 保險報價 The Quote of Insurance ✦

Ryan So you want property, casualty, liability and workers' compensation insurance?

萊恩 那麼妳想要財產險、意外事故險、責任險，以及工傷保險？

Helen Yes, what are the price quotes?

海倫 是的，報價是多少？

Ryan We have a package of property and casualty for $25,000 every six months, or $45,000 annually.

萊恩 我們有財產險和意外事故險的整套合約，價格是半年 25,000 美元，或者是一年 45,000 美元。

Helen Okay, that sounds reasonable. What about the other types? Can't you throw in liability with that?

海倫 好的，聽起來很合理。其他險種呢？責任險不能算到裡面嗎？

Ryan	I can give you a 20% discount on the liability.
萊恩	責任險我可以給妳 20%的折扣。
Helen	How about 30%? I'll be purchasing workers' compensation and business interruption as well since this is a risky venture.
海倫	30%怎麼樣？我還會買工傷保險和營業中斷險，因為這是一項很有風險的事業。
Ryan	True. Okay, I can do 25% off the liability, and the same for business interruption since you'll be paying full price for worker's comp.
萊恩	的確是。好吧，責任險我可以給妳 25%的折扣，營業中斷險也是，但工傷保險要付全價。
Helen	Oh, I'll have to think about it.
海倫	哦，我要考慮一下。

- business interruption 營業中斷險
- comp [kɑmp] n 補償，賠償（compensation 的縮寫）

關聯必備單字

1. **commission** [kə`mɪʃən] 傭金
2. **price** [praɪs] 價格，報價
3. **quote** [kwot] 報價， 開價
4. **quotation** [kwo`teʃən] 報價
5. **offer** [`ɑfɚ] 出價
6. **moderate** [`mɑdərɪt] 適度的
7. **profitable** [`prɑfɪtəbl̩] 有利可圖的
8. **compensation** [ˌkɑmpən`seʃən] 賠償金

⑨ **profit**
[ˋprɑfɪt] 利潤

⑩ **net profit**
純利，淨利

⑪ **gross profit**
毛利

⑫ **business profit**
營業利潤

⑬ **commercial profit**
商業利潤

⑭ **detailed**
[ˋditeld] 詳細的

⑮ **net**
[nɛt] 純粹的，淨餘的

⑯ **target**
[tɑrgɪt] 目標

⑰ **discount**
[ˋdɪskaʊnt] 折扣

⑱ **overvalued**
[ˏovɚˋvæljud] 高估的

專業貼心便條

國際貿易所採用的代理方式按委託授權的大小，可分以下幾種：

1. 獨家代理 (Sole Agency)：是指在特定地區內、特定時期內享有代銷指定商品的專營權，委託人在該地區內不得再委派第二個代理人。
2. 一般代理 (Agency)：又稱傭金代理，是指在同一地區、同一時期內，委託人可以選定多個客戶作為代理商，根據推銷商品的實際金額付給傭金，或者根據協定規定的辦法和百分比支付傭金。
3. 總代理 (General Agency)：是在特定地區和一定時間內委託人的全權代表。除有權代表委託人進行簽訂買賣合約、處理貨物等商務活動外，也可以進行一些非商業性的活動，而且還有權指派分代理，並可享有分代理的傭金。
4. 特約代理 (Special Sales Agency)：有些國家的廠商和跨國的托拉斯集團公司，常在國外指派特約代理，為其推銷技術性的工業產品或為其提供技術和維修服務。

SECTION 05

協商合約細節
Negotiating the Contract

隨身應急情境句

Track 049

1	Let's have a word about packing. 我們來談談包裝問題。
2	Buyers always pay great attention to packing. 買主總是很注意包裝。
3	We wish our opinions on packing will be passed on to your manufacturers. 我們希望我們對包裝的意見能傳達到你們廠商那裡。
4	We wish the new packing will give our clients satisfaction. 我們希望新的包裝會使我們的顧客滿意。
5	The next thing I'd like to bring up for discussion is insurance. 下面我想討論一下保險問題。
6	What do you expect for delivery pattern? 貴方希望怎麼樣出貨？
7	We always send goods by train. 我們都是用鐵路出貨。

8	As we are in urgent need of the goods, we would like you to ship them by air freight. 由於我們急需這批貨物，我們希望貴方可以使用空運。
9	How do you like the goods dispatched, by railway or by sea? 貴方希望如何運送貨物，透過鐵路還是海運？
10	What's your requirement of packing? 你們對包裝有什麼要求嗎？
11	What do you expect for the insurance? 你們對保險有什麼要求嗎？
12	Please send us the shipment by sea. 請利用海運出貨給我方。
13	Please ship the goods by the first available steamer early next month. 請於下月初用第一班輪船出貨。
14	We hope that you could pack them in cartons of 8kg each, and please see to it that each carton is sealed. 我方希望貴方能用紙板箱打包，每個箱子裝 8 公斤貨物，並請確保每個紙板箱都是密封的。
15	You'd better pack them in cartons of 15kg each. 貴方最好用紙板箱打包，每個箱子裝 15 公斤貨物。

16	Please mark the packages with the same lot numbers as given on the order sheet in order to avoid being mixed up. 請在包裹上標明和訂單一致的批號以避免混淆。
17	We wish to insure against all risks. 我們要保全險。
18	We shall insure the goods in your behalf. 我們將為貴方的貨物投保。
19	Please insure for us these products for 120% of the invoice value. 請按發票金額的 120% 為我們投保這些產品。
20	We'd like to cover the goods we ordered against WPA for 110% of the invoice value according to our usual practice. 根據我們的慣例，我們要按發票金額的 110% 為我們所訂的貨物投保單獨海損險。

萬能好用句型

- Let's have a word about .... 我們來談談……。
- The next thing I'd like to bring up for discussion is ....
  下面我想討論一下……。
- What do you expect for ...? 貴方希望怎樣……？
- What's your requirement of ...? 你們對……有什麼要求嗎？
- Please send us the shipment by ... 請利用……出貨給我方。

職場應答對話

✦ 23%更合適 23% Is More Realistic ✦

Jeff So you don't think 30% is fair?

傑夫 那麼您認為 30%不合適嗎？

Ella No. You are not representing my client; you are merely helping to promote his image.

艾拉 是的。貴方並不代表我的客戶，只是 明提升他的形象。

Jeff That is true, however the amount of time we put into finding and negotiating commercial and endorsement deals is substantial.

傑夫 確實如此，儘管我們為商業合作及代言協議的尋找和談判投入了大量的時間。

Ella But there will still be additional negotiating by me on behalf of my client. That's my job.

艾拉 但我還是需要代表我的客戶來進行一些附加的談判。這是我的工作。

Jeff I understand, but we still do the majority of the work.

傑夫 我明白，但絕大部分工作仍是由我方來做的。

Ella I think 23% is more realistic. My client also agrees.

艾拉 我認為 23%更為合理一些。我的客戶也同意。

Jeff Your client is not well-known, which puts him in no position to make demands.

傑夫 貴方的客戶並不是很知名，他沒有立場來提出要求。

Ella Then we will have to take our business elsewhere.

艾拉 那我們就要找別家了。

Jeff I'm sorry you feel that way.

傑夫 我對您的想法感到很遺憾。

- endorsement [ɪnˋdɔrsmənt] n 代言
- on behalf of 代表
- realistic [ˏrɪəˋlɪstɪk] adj 現實的

關聯必備單字

❶ **term**
[tɝm] 條款

❷ **contract**
[ˋkɑntrækt] 合約

❸ **transportation**
[ˏtrænspɔrˋteʃən] 運輸

❹ **freight**
[fret] 貨運

❺ **railway**
[ˋrelˏwe] 鐵路

❻ **marine**
[məˋrin] 海運的

❼ **delivery**
[dɪˋlɪvərɪ] 遞送

❽ **manufacturer**
[ˏmænjəˋfæktʃərɚ] 製造商

❾ **case**
[kes] 箱子

❿ **packing**
[ˋpækɪŋ] 包裝（材料）

⓫ **carton**
[ˋkɑrtn] 紙板箱

⓬ **seal**
[sil] 密封

⓭ **invoice**
[ˋɪnvɔɪs] 發票

⓮ **substantial**
[səbˋstænʃəl] 大量的

⓯ **dispatch**
[dɪˋspætʃ] 發送

⓰ **shipment**
[ˋʃɪpmənt] 運送（的貨物）

⓱ **steamer**
[ˋstimɚ] 輪船

⓲ **mark**
[mɑrk] 作記號

專業貼心便條

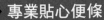

在談判雙方彼此存在長期合作誠意的前提下，成功的商務談判一般會遵循以下三個步驟與原則：

1. 申明價值（Claiming value）：此階段為談判的初級階段。在這個階段，談判雙方應該充分溝通各自的利益需要，申明能夠滿足對方需要的方法與優勢所在。此階段的關鍵步驟是弄清對方的真正需求，也根據情況申明我方的利益所在。
2. 創造價值（Creating value）：此階段為談判的中級階段。在談判雙方申明了各自的實際需要和利益所在之後，這個階段需要雙方盡可能地尋求最佳的方案，以達到雙方利益的最大化，因而這個步驟也就是創造價值。
3. 克服障礙（Overcoming barriers）：此階段往往是談判的攻堅階段。談判的障礙一般來自於兩個方面：一個是談判雙方彼此利益存在衝突；另一個是談判者自身在決策程式上存在障礙。前一種障礙是需要雙方按照公平合理的客觀原則來協調利益；後者就需要談判無障礙的一方主動去幫助另一方順利決策。

SECTION 06

協商付款方式
Negotiating Payment Terms

隨身應急情境句

Track 050

1	What are your payment terms? 貴方有哪些付款方式？
2	Shall we come to the terms of payment? 我們可以談談付款方式了嗎？
3	What's your requirement of payment? 您有什麼付款要求嗎？
4	Which term of payment do you recommend? 貴方推薦哪種支付方式？
5	We propose paying by TT when the shipment is ready. 我方提議裝船後利用電匯付款。
6	We would prefer you to pay in euros. 我方希望貴方用歐元付款。
7	Please conclude the business in terms of US dollars. 請用美元來結算此次交易。

8	As it is the first time for our cooperation, we would like to choose L/C. 因為這是我們第一次合作，所以我方選擇信用證付款。
9	It would be advisable for you to establish an L/C as early as possible so we can effect shipment in due time. 我方建議貴方儘早開具信用證，以便我方可以及時裝船發貨。
10	As usual, we require an L/C issued by a first-rate bank. 和往常一樣，我方要求出具在甲級銀行開立的信用證。
11	As for payment, we require an irrevocable L/C available by draft at sight. 關於付款方式，我方要求不可撤銷的信用證憑即期匯票支付。
12	The payment was made by bank draft. 付款使用的是銀行匯票。
13	We will draw you a documentary draft at sight through our bank. 我方銀行將為貴方開具即期跟單匯票。
14	D/P or D/A is only accepted if the amount involved for each transaction is less than €1,000. 我方只接受每單 1000 歐元以下的付款交單或者承兌交單。

15	As a special case, we may consider accepting your payments by TT. 由於情況特殊，我方可以考慮接受貴方的電匯付款。
16	We can only accept 25% cash payment. 我方只接受 25%的現金付款。
17	TT is only accepted if the amount involved for each transaction is less than $2,000. 我方只接受每單 2000 美元以下的電匯付款。
18	We request a 15% payment at the time of ordering. 我方要求訂貨時交納 15%的預付款。
19	The other 70% by L/C should reach us 15 to 30 days before the delivery. 其餘的以信用證付款的 70%應在發貨前 15 到 30 天郵到。
20	The remaining amount must be paid within 40 days. 尾款須在 40 天內付清。

萬能好用句型

- What are your payment terms?　貴方有哪些付款方式？
- We would prefer you to pay in ….　我方希望貴方用……付款。
- Please conclude the business in terms of ….
  請用……來結算此次交易。
- We would like to choose ….　我方選擇……。

- We can only accept … % cash payment.
  我方只接受百分之……的現金付款。
- We request a … % payment at the time of ordering.
  我方要求訂貨時交納百分之……預付款。
- The remaining amount must be paid within … days.
  尾款須在……天內付清。

職場應答對話

✦ 每半年付一次款 Pay Every Six Months ✦

Emma So how often do I make payments for the insurance policies?

艾瑪 保單要每隔多久付一次錢呢？

Kevin Well, you can choose every month, six-month, or annually.

凱文 妳可以選擇月付、半年付，或者年付。

Emma If I choose to pay annually, then I receive some sort of discount, is that correct?

艾瑪 如果我選擇年付，我就會享受到某種折扣，對嗎？

Kevin Yes, it is. Six-month is a 12% discount each month from the monthly fee, while annually, you would save a total of 18%.

凱文 對，是的。半年付的話，可以享受到每個月的費用為月付費 8.8 折的優惠，而年付則可以節省總額的 18%。

Emma Well, I'm purchasing multiple insurance policies. I want to pay every six months, but is it possible to stagger the payment dates?

艾瑪 好吧，我購買了很多種保險。我想半年付，不過這些保單的支付時間能否錯開呢？

Kevin Sure, that won't be a problem.

凱文 可以，這不是問題。

Emma Great. So if I stagger them, I'll be making a payment every three months and still receive the discount.

艾瑪 太好了。那如果把時間錯開，我每三個月付一次錢，但還是有折扣的。

Kevin Exactly.

凱文 沒錯。

關聯必備單字

❶ **euro**
[ˋjʊro] 歐元

❷ **dollar**
[ˋdɑlɚ] 美元

❸ **pound**
[paʊnd] 英鎊

❹ **yen**
[jɛn] 日元

❺ **cash**
[kæʃ] 現金

❻ **irrevocable**
[ɪˋrɛvəkəbl̩] 不能撤銷的

❼ **modify**
[ˋmɑdɪfaɪ] 修改

❽ **distributor**
[dɪˋstrɪbjətɚ] 經銷商

❾ **commission agent**
傭金代理商

❿ **term**
[tɝm] 條款，條件

⓫ **draft**
[dræft] 匯票

⓬ **TT (telegraphic transfer)**
電匯

⓭ **L/C（Letter of Credit）**
信用證

⓮ **advisable**
[ədˋvaɪzəbl̩]
可取的，明智的

⓯ **effect**
[ɪˋfɛkt] 使發生，引起

⓰ **documentary draft**
跟單匯票

專業貼心便條

國際貿易中主要採用的付款方式有很多種，交易雙方可根據各自的情況商討決定具體採用哪一種方式。

1. 訂貨付現和裝船前付現：前者是指買方須于合約簽訂或訂貨時，或其後指定的時間內，按約定的方式（一般是通過銀行），將全部貨款匯給賣方。後者是指買方應在貨物裝船前若干天，付清全部貨款，作為賣方裝船的條件。
2. 交貨付款：買方只有在賣方按指定地點交貨時，才承擔付款責任。
3. 交單付款：買方在賣方按合約規定交付合格的裝運單據時承擔付款責任。
4. 記帳：又稱專戶記帳。賣方將貨物裝運出口後，即將貨運單據寄給買方，貨款則借記買方帳戶，然後按約定的期限，定期進行結算。
5. 托收：指債權人將金融單據或隨附有關貨運單據委託第三者收取款項或取得債務人對匯票的承兑的行為。在國際貿易上，托收一般是指出口人將金融單據等委託銀行向進口商收取貨款的行為。
6. 信用證：一種由銀行作出的有條件的付款承諾。在國際貨物買賣中大量使用的商業跟單信用證，是銀行應進口人的請求和指示開給受益人，承諾在一定期限內，在受益人遵守信用證所有條件下，憑指定單據，支付一定金額的書面憑證。
7. 分期付款：按工程或交貨進度分期付款。
8. 延期付款：是透過提供中長期信貸以推動出口，尤其是機器設備出口的一種支付方式。

SECTION 07

作出讓步
Making Some Concessions

隨身應急情境句

Track 051

1	Can you consider the order as a special case? 貴方能將此次訂單看作一個特例嗎？
2	Can you cut down the price? 貴方能夠降低價格嗎？
3	Can we meet each other halfway? 我們能不能各讓一步？
4	Can you reconsider your price and give a new bid? Then it's possible for us to meet halfway. 貴方能否再考慮一下貴方的價格然後重新出價？這樣我方才有可能作出讓步。
5	This is our rock-bottom price, and we can't make any concessions. 這是我方的最低價，我方不能再讓步了。
6	We can't make any further discounts. 我方沒法給更低的折扣了。
7	We may consider making some concessions in price. 我方可以考慮在價格上做些讓步。

8	The best we can do is to allow you 3% off our quotation. 我方的最低限度是給貴方提供我方報價的 3% 的折扣。
9	We do not think there is any possibility of business unless you cut down your price. 我方認為除非貴方降價，否則這筆生意不可能談成。
10	We hope you will quote your rock-bottom price, otherwise we have no alternative but to place our orders elsewhere. 我方希望貴方能報出底價，否則我方只好選擇其他公司下單了。
11	We are pleased to give you an 8% discount since you agree to double the order. 由於貴方同意將訂單數量翻倍，我方樂意給貴方 8% 的折扣。
12	If you double the order, we may consider giving you an 8% discount. 如果貴方的訂單數量加倍，我方會考慮給貴方 8% 的折扣。
13	If you increase your initial order to 50,000, then we may consider reducing our price to $50 per unit. 如果貴方的初始訂單增加到 50000 件，我方會考慮每件降價到 50 美元。

14 If you insist on your original offer, it will reduce our profit considerably.
如果貴方還堅持原來的價格，我方的利潤將會減少很多。

15 Sorry, we generally don't quote on a discount basis.
對不起，我方不在打折的基礎上報價。

16 We didn't expect that the discount you offer would be so low.
我方沒有想到貴方提供的折扣這麼低。

17 This is a special offer and we cannot give you any more discount.
這已經是特價了，我方無法再給貴方任何折扣了。

萬能好用句型

- Can you cut down the price?　貴方能夠降低價格嗎？
- Can you reconsider ...?　貴方能否再考慮一下……？
- This is our rock-bottom price.　這是我方的最低價。
- We may consider making some concessions in ....
  我方可以考慮在……上做些讓步。
- We do not think there is any possibility of business unless ....
  我方認為除非……，否則這筆生意不可能談成。
- We are pleased to ... since you agree to ....
  由於貴方同意……，我方樂意……。
- That doesn't make up for my loss.　那也彌補不了我的損失。

職場應答對話

✦ 合約改成 23% Change the Contract to 23% ✦

Client	I still feel that 23% is a fair percentage for your company.
客戶	我還是認為 23%這個比例對貴公司來說很公平。
Jeff	Well, this is the contract we present to all new clients.
傑夫	噢，我們提供給新客戶的都是這份合約。
Client	True, but my client has a lot of options, he wants to see a good deal.
客戶	確實是這樣，但我的客戶有很多選擇，他希望看到一筆很好的交易。
Jeff	If the 30% goes down, more will come out of my paycheck.
傑夫	如果低於 30%，我的薪水會扣更多。
Client	For every million my client makes, we'll give you personally 5%.
客戶	我的客戶所賺得的每 100 萬中，我們將提供給你個人 5%。
Jeff	That doesn't make up for my loss.
傑夫	那也彌補不了我的損失。
Client	But my client is worth more than some of your older clients. He's an Olympic athlete.
客戶	但是我的客戶比你們的一些老客戶更有價值。他是一位奧運選手。
Jeff	Since he has been on a winning streak, I will change the contract to 23%, and you and your client will pay me 5% of each million.
傑夫	由於他連續取得勝利，我會將合約改為 23%，而且你和你的客戶每賺 100 萬都要給我 5%。

- option [ˋɑpʃən] n 選擇
- make up for 彌補
- winning streak 連勝，一連串的勝利

關聯必備單字

❶ **concession**
[kənˋsɛʃən] 讓步

❷ **haggle**
[ˋhægl̩] 討價還價

❸ **agent**
[ˋedʒənt] 代理商

❹ **website**
[ˋwebˏsaɪt] 網站

❺ **risk**
[rɪsk] 風險

❻ **return**
[rɪˋtɝn] 回報

❼ **paycheck**
[ˋpeˏtʃɛk] 工資

❽ **flexible**
[ˋflɛksəbl̩] 可變通的

❾ **ratio**
[ˋreʃo] 比例

❿ **consent**
[kənˋsɛnt] 許可

⓫ **shipping**
[ˋʃɪpɪŋ] 運輸

⓬ **million**
[ˋmɪljən] 百萬

⓭ **alternative**
[ɔlˋtɝnətɪv] 供替代的選擇

⓮ **compromise**
[ˋkɑmprəmaɪz] 妥協，讓步

⓯ **bid**
[bɪd] 出價

⓰ **rock-bottom**
[ˏrɑkˋbɑtəm] 最低的

⓱ **per**
[pɚ] 每，每一

⓲ **waive**
[wev] 放棄，免除

專業貼心便條

企業和公司的類型都有哪些，你知道嗎？

- 國有企業 state-owned enterprise
- 集體企業 collectively-owned enterprise
- 聯營企業 associated enterprise
- 私營企業 private-owned enterprise
- 合作經營企業 cooperative venture
- 合資企業 joint venture
- 內資企業 domestic enterprise
- 外資企業 foreign-invested enterprise
- 獨資企業 exclusive investment enterprise
- 中外合資企業 sino-foreign joint venture
- 外商獨資企業 wholly foreign-owned enterprise
- 港、澳、台商投資企業
  enterprises with Hong Kong/Macau/Taiwan investment
- 股份有限公司 joint stock limited partnership
- 有限責任公司 limited liability company

SECTION

08 雙方簽訂合約

Signing the Contract

隨身應急情境句

Track 052

1	Please go over the contract and see if everything is in order. 請仔細看看這份合約，看看是否都正確。
2	The terms of the contract are acceptable to us. 這個合約的條款我們可以接受。
3	He was empowered by the company to sign the contract. 他被公司授權簽署該項合約。
4	He has been authorized to sign the contract. 他被授權簽署該合約。
5	Now we can sign the contract. 現在我們可以簽合約了。
6	Both parties have signed the contract. 雙方已經在合約上簽了字。
7	Where do you want me to sign? 您要我簽在哪裡？
8	Just sign there on the bottom. 就在下面這裡簽名。

9	Initially the contract will be in effect for four years. 最初，合約的有效期為四年。
10	After negotiation, they tacked three new clauses on to the end of the contract. 透過協商,他們在合約最後附加了三項新條款。
11	An insurance policy was annexed to the contract. 合約上附加了保險條款。
12	The contract is binding for both parties. 這份合約對雙方都有約束力。
13	The agreement will be legally binding. 這項協議將具有法律效力。
14	The contract is binding, so once you sign remember you must fulfill your obligations or else face legal action. 這份合約將具有法律約束力，因此貴方一旦簽訂就別忘了必須要履行，否則將面臨法律制裁。
15	Here's your copy of the contract. 這是您的那一份合約。
16	We will have three hard copies, one for each party, and one on file in the office. 我們會有三份影本，雙方各有一份，剩下一份放辦公室存檔案。
17	Good. I'm glad we're all done. 太好了，我很高興我們都完成了。

萬能好用句型

- … has been authorized to sign the contract.
  ……被授權簽署該合約。
- Now we can sign the contract.　現在我們可以簽合約了。
- Initially the contract will be in effect for … years.
  最初，合約的有效期為……年。
- After negotiation, they ….　透過協商，他們……。
- … was annexed to the contract.　合約上附加了……。
- The agreement will be legally binding.
  這項協議將具有法律效力。
- Great, we are looking forward to finalizing this.
  太好了，我們期望能圓滿成交。

職場應答對話

✦ 今天簽合約 Sign the Contract Today ✦

Jeff　Have you had time to read over the renegotiated terms of the contract?

傑夫　您看過新協定的合約條款了嗎？

Client　Yes, I have. My client and I are satisfied.

客戶　是的，我看過了。我和我的客戶都很滿意。

Jeff　Great, I think the terms we worked out will be mutually beneficial.

傑夫　太好了，我認為我們協定的這些條款是互惠互利的。

Client	So are we going to sign the contract today?
客戶	那我們今天簽合約嗎？
Jeff	Yes, I have had five copies printed. Three for you and your client, two for us.
傑夫	是的，我已經列印了 5 份合約。其中 3 份給您和您的客戶，另外兩份由我們保管。
Client	Great, I'll call my client to come and sign.
客戶	好的，我打電話請我的客戶過來簽合約。
Jeff	Alright, so we can do it over lunch. How does that sound?
傑夫	好的，我們可以在吃午餐時簽合約，您覺得怎麼樣？
Client	Sure.
客戶	當然可以。
Jeff	I called ahead and made a reservation.
傑夫	我提前打過電話，預定了座位。
Client	Great, we are looking forward to finalizing this.
客戶	太好了，我們期望能圓滿成交。
Jeff	And I'm looking forward to doing business with you and your client.
傑夫	我也很期待跟您和您的客戶談成這筆生意。

- renegotiate [͵rinɪˋgoʃiet] v 重新談判，重新協商
- mutual [ˋmjutʃuəl] adj 共同的，相互的

關聯必備單字

❶ **sign**
[saɪn] 簽署

❷ **contractual**
[kən`træktʃuəl] 合約的

❸ **contractor**
[kən`træktɚ] 承包商

❹ **binding**
[`baɪndɪŋ] 有約束力的

❺ **legally**
[`ligḷɪ] 法律上地

❻ **legal**
[`ligḷ] 法律的，合法的

❼ **empower**
[ɪm`paʊɚ] 授權

❽ **authorize**
[`ɔθə͵raɪz] 授權

❾ **finalize**
[`faɪnḷ͵aɪz] 使完成

❿ **tack**
[tæk] 附加

⓫ **clause**
[klɔz] 條款

⓬ **party**
[`pɑrtɪ] （契約的）一方

⓭ **acceptable**
[ək`sɛptəbḷ] 可接受的

⓮ **annex**
[ə`nɛks] 附加

⓯ **fulfill**
[fʊl`fɪl] 履行，完成

⓰ **hard copy**
影本， 列印件

專業貼心便條

當談判成交時，雙方應及時握手以結束談判。在握手時，主談人要對所有達成一致的問題加以核查，以防遺漏，從而為最後的簽約做好準備。這時可以說：「很高興雙方達成協議，艱苦的洽談得以結束。讓我們雙方整理一下已達成的協議，以便形成文字。若有遺漏允許補充。」或者說 「我們很高興能與貴方達成協議，我們將向上級彙報我們的洽談結果。若有什麼問題再商量。」這樣講既能留有餘地，又不失禮節。最後，要將所有談判的結果形成文字，包括技術附件和合約文本。同時，約定好簽約的時間和方式等具體操作性問題。

CHAPTER 09

業務精英 Being the Best Salesman

SECTION 01

進行市場調查
Conducting a Market Survey

隨身應急情境句

Track 053

1	It's very necessary to carry out market research before launching the new product. 在推出新產品前進行市場調查是非常有必要的。
2	We plan to conduct a market survey in November. 我們計劃在 11 月份進行一項市場調查。
3	We just conducted a market survey last month. 我們上個月剛做了一項市場調查。
4	We have done a market survey on this product. 我們已經針對這種產品做了市場調查。
5	A professional marketing survey agency was invited to do it. 我們請的是專業的市場調查公司。
6	Shall we invite a consulting company to do it? 我們要請顧問公司來做嗎？
7	A recent survey showed 70% of those questioned were interested in the new design. 最近的一項調查顯示，接受調查的人群中有 70%的人對新的設計感興趣。

8	The market survey shows that the customers are really interested in our new design. 市場調查表明用戶們對我們的新設計十分感興趣。
9	Most of the people who responded to the questionnaire were interested in our new design. 做了問卷的大多數人表示對我們的新設計很感興趣。
10	She inferred from the market survey that the new product was in great demand. 她從市場調查中推斷出新產品有很大的需求。
11	The sales manager is really disappointed with the result of the market survey. 銷售經理對這次市場調查的結果很失望。
12	The conclusions from the survey of our new product are far from encouraging. 我們新產品的調查結果不容樂觀。
13	Only correct market research enables both production and marketing to thrive. 準確的市場調查才能使產品的出產及銷售皆受惠。
14	I'm not satisfied with the way to conduct the market survey. 我對市場調查的方法不太滿意。
15	After completing the market demand research, the company decided to launch their new product. 這家公司在調查了市場需求後，決定推出新產品。

16	Foreign companies must understand the needs of the local people. 跨國公司必須要瞭解當地人民的需求。
17	Here is our market survey report. 這是我們的市場調查報告。
18	Please allow me to brief the research result. 請允許我簡短地說一下調查結果。

萬能好用句型

- We plan to conduct a market survey in ….
  我們計劃在……進行一項市場調查。
- We have done a market survey on ….
  我們已經針對……做了市場調查。
- A recent survey showed ….
  最近的一項調查顯示……。
- The market survey shows that ….
  市場調查顯示出……。
- Most of the people who responded to the questionnaire were ….
  回答了問卷的大多數人表示……。
- … inferred from the market survey that ….
  ……從市場調查中推斷出……。
- … is disappointed with the result of the market survey.
  ……對這次市場調查的結果很失望。

Chapter 01
Chapter 02
Chapter 03
Chapter 04
Chapter 05
Chapter 06
Chapter 07
Chapter 08
Chapter 09
Chapter 10
Chapter 11

職場應答對話

✦ 幫忙做市場調查 Help with Some Market Research ✦

Annie	Excuse me, sir. Do you have a moment to help with some market research?
安妮	先生，打擾一下。您有時間幫忙做一下市場調查嗎？
Ted	Sure. How can I help?
泰德	當然。我能幫上什麼忙？
Annie	We have two different products here. Can you tell me which product looks better to you?
安妮	我們這裡有兩種不同的產品。您能告訴我您覺得哪種看起來更好嗎？
Ted	Well, I think I like the red one more. It's more visually appealing.
泰德	好吧，我覺得我比較喜歡紅色的這個。它在視覺上比較吸引人。
Annie	Great. How much would you pay for that item?
安妮	好的。您願意出多少錢買這個產品呢？
Ted	It's not something I would really use often. Maybe $15.
泰德	這不是我常常在用的東西。大概 15 美元吧。
Annie	Good to know. How could the product to be changed to something you would use frequently?
安妮	很好。這個產品要如何改變才能成為您會經常使用的物品呢？
Ted	Making it portable would definitely help.
泰德	它如果方便攜帶的話肯定會很不錯。

Annie	Thanks for your time. Have a great day!
安妮	謝謝您抽出時間來。祝您有美好的一天！
Ted	Thanks, you too.
泰德	謝謝，妳也是。

- visually [ˋvɪʒʊəlɪ] adv 視覺上
- appealing [əˋpilɪŋ] adj 吸引人的
- portable [ˋportəbḷ] adj 可攜式的，易攜帶的

關聯必備單字

❶ **market**
[ˋmɑrkɪt] 市場

❷ **survey**
[ˋsɝve] 調查

❸ **investigation**
[ɪnˏvɛstəˋgeʃən] 調查

❹ **salesman**
[ˋselzmən] 銷售人員

❺ **expert**
[ˋɛkspɝt] 專家

❻ **specialist**
[ˋspɛʃəlɪst] 專家

❼ **infer**
[ɪnˋfɝ] 推斷

❽ **demand**
[dɪˋmænd] 需求

❾ **user**
[ˋjuzɚ] 用戶

❿ **encouraging**
[ɪnˋkɝɪdʒɪŋ] 鼓舞人的

⓫ **result**
[rɪˋzʌlt] 結果

⓬ **research**
[rɪˋsɝtʃ] 研究

⓭ **frequently**
[ˋfrikwəntlɪ] 經常地

⓮ **questionnaire**
[ˏkwɛstʃənˋɛr] 調查問卷

專業貼心便條

市場佔有率指一個企業的銷售量在市場同類產品中所占的比重，直接反映消費者對一個企業所提供的商品和服務的滿意程度，表明企業的商品在市場上所處的地位。市場佔有率根據不同市場範圍可分為下面這四種測算方法：

1. 總體市場佔有率：

指一個企業的銷量在整個行業中所占的比重。

2. 目標市場佔有率：

指一個企業的銷量在其目標市場，即它所服務的市場中所占的比重。

3. 相對於 3 個最大競爭者的市場佔有率：

指一個企業的銷量，和市場上最大的 3 個競爭者的銷售總量相比。

4. 相對於最大競爭者的市場佔有率：

指一個企業的銷量與市場上最大競爭者的銷量比。

SECTION 02

展開行銷活動
Starting a Marketing Campaign

隨身應急情境句

Track 054

1	We are about to launch a marketing campaign next month. 我們將在下個月展開一次市場行銷活動。
2	We plan to start a marketing campaign in April. 我們計劃在 4 月份展開一次市場行銷活動。
3	We decided to start a large-scale promotion in winter. 我們決定在冬季發起一次大規模的促銷活動。
4	The marketing plan has to be different this time. We need a strategy. 這次的行銷計劃必須與眾不同。我們需要好好地策劃一下。
5	This marketing campaign needs to be something totally different. 這次的行銷活動需要與以往不同。
6	We need a new concept of marketing. 我們需要一種全新的行銷理念。

7	Our ad campaign is going to focus on the function of the products. 我們的廣告宣傳活動將著重說明產品的功能。
8	Our marketing concept is to make customers know about our products and like them. 我們的行銷理念是讓顧客瞭解我們的產品並喜歡它們。
9	Who's the audience for your ad campaign? 誰是你們廣告宣傳活動的客群？
10	Do you know the budget for the promotion? 你知道促銷活動的預算是多少嗎？
11	What's the budget for the promotion? 促銷活動的預算是多少？
12	We should not cut back the advertising budget. 我們不應該削減廣告預算。
13	We would like to provide promotional leaflets or product samples for distribution. 我們想要提供宣傳單或發放產品試用包。
14	We'll enhance the promotion with catalogs or leaflets. 我們將通過發放產品目錄或傳單來促進促銷活動。
15	I believe we can successfully challenge for market share there. 我相信，我們能夠成功爭取到那裡的市場佔有率。

16	In 2018, we will make up most of the market. 到 2018 年，我們將佔領大部分市場佔有率。
17	Our competitor must not be allowed to get wind of our plan. 千萬別讓競爭對手知道我們的計劃。
18	We need to study and figure out how to beat our competitors. 我們需要研究並找出方法來擊敗我們的競爭對手。

萬能好用句型

- We plan to start a marketing campaign in ….
  我們計劃在……展開一次市場行銷活動。
- We decided to start a large-scale promotion in ….
  我們決定在……發起一次大規模的促銷活動。
- We need a strategy.　我們需要好好策劃一下。
- This marketing campaign needs to ….
  這個次的行銷活動需要……。
- Our ad campaign is going to focus on ….
  我們的廣告宣傳活動將著重……。
- Our marketing concept is ….　我們的行銷理念是……。
- Do you know the budget for the promotion?
  你知道促銷活動的預算是多少嗎？
- In …, we will make up most of the market.
  到……，我們將佔領大部分市場佔有率。

職場應答對話

✦ 尋找目標客群 Look for Target Audience ✦

Adam What are the important things to remember when starting a marketing campaign?

亞當 展開行銷活動時，要記住哪些重要事情？

Jenny First, you have to do your research and find your target audience.

珍妮 首先你必須進行調查，並尋找目標客群。

Mary Once you have your target audience, find out what is already popular with that demographic and try to advertise there.

瑪麗 一旦有了目標客群，找出受這些人歡迎的是什麼，並試著在那方面做廣告。

Adam Both great answers! What else?

亞當 兩個答案都不錯！還有什麼呢？

Jenny Try several different approaches to make sure you are appealing to a wide variety of tastes. For example, make a print ad as well as a commercial or a billboard.

珍妮 要嘗試各種不同的方式，以確保能夠迎合人們不同的品味。例如，製作平面廣告的同時，也要有廣告片和看板。

Mary Be sure you know your budget! It's a bad thing to run out of money without having all the advertising done.

瑪麗 一定要清楚你的預算！如果廣告還沒全做完，就沒有資金了，那可糟糕了。

Adam It definitely is. Good answers.

亞當 沒錯。很棒的答案。

- target [ˋtɑrgɪt] n 目標
- demographic [ˏdɪməˋgræfɪk] n 特定人群

關聯必備單字

❶ **promote**
[prəˋmot] 推銷

❷ **launch**
[lɔntʃ] 發起

❸ **large-scale**
[ˏlɑrdʒˋskel]
大規模的，大範圍的

❹ **concept**
[ˋkɑnsɛpt] 概念，觀念

❺ **leaflet**
[ˋliflɪt] 傳單

❻ **distribution**
[ˏdɪstrəˋbjuʃən] 分發

❼ **campaign**
[kæmˋpen] 活動

❽ **compete**
[kəmˋpit] 競爭

❾ **competitor**
[kəmˋpɛtətɚ] 對手

❿ **rival**
[ˋraɪvl̩] 對手

⓫ **advertise**
[ˋædvɚˏtaɪz] 做廣告

⓬ **spokesperson**
[ˋspoksˏpɝsn] 代言人

⓭ **challenge**
[ˋtʃælɪndʒ] 挑戰

⓮ **budget**
[ˋbʌdʒɪt] 預算

⓯ **vendor**
[ˋvɛndɚ] 供應商

⓰ **supplier**
[səˋplaɪɚ] 供應商

⓱ **billion**
[ˋbɪljən] 十億

⓲ **trillion**
[ˋtrɪljən] 萬億

⓳ **outlet**
[ˋaʊtˏlɛt] 營業據點

⓴ **function**
[ˋfʌŋkʃən] 功能

㉒ **sales volume**
銷售量

㉓ **sales staff**
銷售人員

㉔ **ad campaign**
廣告宣傳活動，廣告攻勢

㉑ **sales figure**
銷售資料

專業貼心便條

在市場行銷組合觀念中, 4P 分別是產品 (Product)，價格 (Price)，管道 (Place)，促銷 (Promotion) 。它們是市場行銷過程中可以控制的因素，也是企業進行市場行銷活動的主要手段，對它們的具體運用，形成了企業的市場行銷戰略。

1. 產品：主要包括產品的實體、服務、品牌、包裝。它是指企業提供給目標市場的貨物、服務的集合, 包括產品的效用、品質、外觀、式樣、品牌、包裝和規格、還包括服務和售後保證等因素。
2. 價格：主要包括基本價格、折扣價格、付款時間、借貸條件等。它是指企業出售產品所追求的經濟回報。
3. 管道：主要包括分銷管道、儲存設施、運輸設施、存貨控制，它代表企業為使其產品進入和達到目標市場所組織、實施的各種活動，包括途徑、環節、場所、倉儲和運輸等。
4. 促銷：指企業利用各種資訊載體與目標市場進行溝通的傳播活動，包括廣告、人員推銷、營業推廣與公共關係等等。

SECTION 03

參加展覽
Attending Trade Shows

隨身應急情境句

Track 055

1	I will be responsible for this year's exhibition. 今年的展覽事宜將由我負責。
2	He has flown to New York to attend a trade show. 他已經飛往紐約參加一個展覽會了。
3	The booth has already been set up. 展位已經準備好了。
4	Welcome to our booth. 歡迎來到我們的展位。
5	Do you have any brochures about your company? 你有公司的宣傳手冊嗎？
6	We do need a few more brochures if you can send some. 如果你們還能送一些宣傳手冊過來的話，我們的確還需要一些。
7	Could you give me a brochure describing your company? 能不能給我一份你們公司的宣傳手冊？

8	Are there any free gift products or samples? 有免費贈品或試用品嗎？
9	Here are some samples of our products. 這裡有一些產品的試用包。
10	Which items are you interested in? 您對哪些產品有興趣？
11	What do you think of our key products? 您認為我們的核心產品怎麼樣？
12	Could you tell me more about the function of this product? 能多介紹一下這個產品的功能嗎？
13	How do I address you? 我該怎麼稱呼您呢？
14	Just call me Tom. 就叫我湯姆吧。
15	I really enjoyed meeting you. Let's keep in touch. 真的很高興認識你。我們保持聯絡。
16	You will meet some interesting people if you attend trade shows. 如果你參加展覽，可能會遇到一些有趣的人。
17	Can I have your business card, please? 能給我一張您的名片嗎？

18	Here's my card. And I'd like to ask a few questions about your new product. 這是我的名片。關於你們的新產品，有幾個問題我想要問一下。
19	We want to be in the American market, how do we get there? 我們想進入美國市場，我們該怎麼做？
20	Are you familiar with the market of our products? 你熟悉我們產品的市場嗎？
21	There is a good market for these articles. 這些商品很暢銷。
22	I am sure your market still has great potential. 我相信你們的市場仍然有很大潛力。

萬能好用句型

- … will be responsible for the exhibition.
  展覽事宜將由……負責。
- He has flown to … to attend a trade show.
  他已經飛往……參加一個展覽會。
- Welcome to our booth.
  歡迎來到我們的展位。
- Could you tell me more about …?
  能多介紹一下……嗎？
- Let's keep in touch.
  我們保持聯絡。

➲ Can I have your business card, please?
能給我一張您的名片嗎？

➲ Are you familiar with the market of our product?
你熟悉我們產品的市場嗎？

職場應答對話

✦ 參加展覽會的意義 The Point of a Trade Show ✦

Rachel I'm taking Friday off to go to the trade show downtown. Please call any clients that have booked and reschedule their appointments.

瑞秋 禮拜五我不在，要到市區參加展覽會。請打電話給已預約的客戶，重新安排會面時間。

Jake Okay, I can do that. What's the point of a trade show?

傑克 好，我會辦好的。參加展覽會有什麼意義呀？

Rachel I'm going to see what other people in the industry are doing and talking about. It's a great way to meet other people in the same profession and network.

瑞秋 我會看到同行們都在做些什麼，談論些什麼。這是認識同行及同一路的人們的一種很棒的方式。

Jake Do you get anything cool when you go?

傑克 離開的時候會拿到什麼好東西嗎？

Rachel A lot of times companies will give away samples of their products. Since this one is all about the beauty industry, I think I'll get to be pampered a little too!

瑞秋 很多時候各公司會發放他們產品的一些樣品。因為這個檔期都是跟美容業有關的，所以我也會狂拿一番！

Jake	Sounds fun.
傑克	聽起來很有趣耶。
Rachel	You should come. You'd learn a thing or two about working in this industry.
瑞秋	你應該要去的。你能學到一些有關從事這個行業的東西。

- beauty industry 美容業
- pamper [ˋpæmpɚ] ⓥ 縱容，使……過量

關聯必備單字

❶ **booth**
[buð] 展位

❷ **trade**
[tred] 貿易

❸ **exhibition**
[ˏɛksəˋbɪʃən] 展覽

❹ **fair**
[fɛr] 展覽會

❺ **organizer**
[ˋɔrgəˏnaɪzɚ] 組織者

❻ **showroom**
[ˋʃoˏrum] 展示廳

❼ **display**
[dɪˋsple] 展出

❽ **heartfelt**
[ˋhɑrtˏfɛlt] 衷心的

❾ **crush**
[krʌʃ] 征服

❿ **terrific**
[təˋrɪfɪk] 極好的

⓫ **breakthrough**
[ˋbrekˏθru] 突破

⓬ **overtake**
[ˏovɚˋtek] 超越

⓭ **hurdle**
[ˋhɝdḷ] 障礙

⓮ **business card**
名片

⓯ **brochure**
[ˋbroʃʊr] 宣傳冊

⓰ **sample**
[ˋsæmpḷ] 樣品

⓱ **function**
[ˋfʌŋkʃən] 功能

⓲ **address**
[əˋdrɛs] 頭銜

專業貼心便條

1890 年，世界上第一個樣品展覽在德國萊比錫舉辦。隨著社會的演變和科技的進步，會展業的各個方面都在不斷調整和變化。從經濟總量和經濟規模的角度來考察，當今世界會展經濟在世界各國的發展很不平衡。

歐洲作為世界會展業的發源地，經過 100 多年的積累和發展，歐洲會展經濟整體實力最強，規模最大。在這個地區中，德國、義大利、法國、英國都是世界級的會展業大國。而亞洲會展經濟的規模和水準應該說比拉丁美洲和非洲要高，尤其展出經濟的規模僅次於歐美。

SECTION 04

爭取客戶訂單
Obtaining Purchase Orders

隨身應急情境句

Track 056

1	We are pleased to give you an order for the items on this sheet. 我們很願意訂購單據上的貨品。
2	We wish to order from you according to this purchase order. 我們想按這張購物單向貴方訂貨。
3	This is our official order for 2,000 printers. 這是我方訂購 2000 台印表機的正式訂單。
4	We can assure you that we shall do our best to execute the order to your satisfaction. 我們可以向您保證，我們會竭盡全力按訂單的要求來做，讓您滿意。
5	How many do you intend to order? 你們想訂多少？
6	I want to order 1,000 dozen. 我們想訂 1000 打。
7	We require a minimum quantity of 1,000 at a time. 我們要求一次至少訂 1000 筆。

8 Since you are so eager to secure an order from us, now we can place an order with you.
鑒於貴方熱切地希望和我方確認訂單，現在我方決定向貴方訂貨。

9 We can now confirm the order for 5,000 computers.
我們現在確認已收到貴方購買 5000 台電腦的訂單。

10 We are glad to receive the order from you.
我們很高興接到您的訂單。

11 We have accepted your order of May 21st for 800 scanners.
我們已經收到了您於 5 月 21 日發出的購買 800 台掃描器的訂單。

12 We thank you for your order of April 25th.
感謝您於 4 月 25 日寄來的訂單。

13 We believe we shall be able to better satisfy our customers quantitatively.
我們相信我們能在數量上使客戶更加滿意。

14 We can supply any reasonable quantity of the merchandise.
我們能提供此類商品任何的合理數量。

15 We regret that owing to the shortage of stocks we are unable to fill your order.
很遺憾，由於庫存不足我們無法滿足您的訂單。

16	We regret that we can't supply the goods you have ordered. 很遺憾，我們無法提供你們所預訂的貨物。
17	It is hard for us to supply the amount you need. 我們很難提供您要求的數量。
18	The most we can offer you at present is 800 dozen. 目前我們最多能提供給你們 800 打。

萬能好用句型

- We are pleased to give you an order for ....
  我們很願意訂購……。
- This is our official order for ....　這是我方訂購……的正式訂單。
- How many do you intend to order?　你們想訂多少？
- We thank you for your order of ....　感謝您於……寄來的訂單。
- We regret that we can't supply the goods you have ordered.
  很遺憾，我們無法提供你們所預訂的貨物。
- The most we can offer you at present is ....
  目前我們最多能提供……。

職場應答對話

✦ 新訂購單和報價 A New Purchase Order and Price ✦

Brian　Hi, is this Helen?
布萊恩　嗨，是海倫嗎？

Helen Yes, this is Helen.
海倫 是的，我是海倫。

Brian Great. I spoke to you yesterday about a large order of plastic tubs. Do you remember?
布萊恩 太好了。昨天我跟妳說了一個關於塑膠桶的大訂單的事，妳還記得嗎？

Helen Yes, I remember. How can I help you?
海倫 是的，我記得。我能為您做些什麼？

Brian The thing is, I never got the purchase order and I'm nervous that the number I told you might not be correct. Can you send me the order so I can double-check?
布萊恩 問題是我沒有收到訂購單，我擔心我告訴妳的數量可能不對。妳能把訂單寄過來方便我再確認一下嗎？

Helen Of course, I'll send it to you right now through email. It says here you requested 20,000 tubs. Is that correct?
海倫 當然，我馬上用電子郵件寄過去給您。訂單上面寫說您要訂購 20,000 個桶子，是這樣嗎？

Brian Oh, no. We only need 15,000. I had the number wrong yesterday.
布萊恩 噢，不是。我們只需要 15,000 個，昨天我把數量搞錯了。

Helen Okay, no problem. I'll fix it and we'll send a new purchase order and price to you later today.
海倫 好的，沒問題。我會處理的。今天晚一點時我們會寄一份新的訂購單和報價給您。

- plastic [ˋplæstɪk] adj 塑膠的
- tub [tʌb] n 浴盆，桶

關聯必備單字

❶ **merchandise**
[ˋmɝtʃəndaɪs] 貨物

❷ **quantity**
[ˋkwɑntətɪ] 數量

❸ **manufacturer**
[ˏmænjəˋfæktʃərɚ] 製造商

❹ **factory**
[ˋfæktrɪ] 工廠

❺ **execute**
[ˋɛksɪˏkjut] 執行，完成

❻ **dozen**
[ˋdʌzn] 一打

❼ **shortage**
[ˋʃɔrtɪdʒ] 短缺

❽ **advance order**
預付款訂單

❾ **additional order**
追加定貨

❿ **back order**
延期交貨

⓫ **delivery order**
交貨單

⓬ **export order**
出口訂單

專業貼心便條

如何更好地完成銷售工作，成為一名銷售精英呢？下面介紹一些銷售技巧：

1. 在無法瞭解客戶的真實意圖時，要儘量試著讓客戶說話，學會傾聽。
2. 理解客戶的感受。當客戶說完後，不要直接回答問題，要感性回避，適當附和，比如「我覺得很有道理」。
3. 要詳細瞭解客戶的需求，讓客戶在關鍵處儘量詳細地說明原因。
4. 確認客戶問題，並且重點回答客戶疑問，用自己產品的益處消除客戶的憂慮。
5. 與客戶真誠溝通，消除彼此之間的隔閡，和客戶建立起相互信任的關係。

SECTION 05

做完美的簡報
Giving a Perfect Presentation

隨身應急情境句

Track 057

1 I'm here today to present the marketing plan of the new product.
今天我在這裡要介紹新產品的行銷計劃。

2 The reason why I'm here today is to present the advertising strategy of the new product.
今天我會在這裡是為了向各位介紹新產品的廣告策略。

3 I'd like to start off by giving a brief review of our research and development work.
首先我想簡單回顧一下我們的研發工作。

4 I'd like to talk briefly about our international market prospects.
我想簡要地談一下我們的國際市場前景。

5 Please turn your attention to the big screen.
請看大螢幕。

6 Now please focus on the screen behind me.
現在請看我身後的大螢幕。

7 Please look at the data of the third chart.
請看第三個圖表中的資料。

8	The slide shows the turnover in the first quarter of this year. 這張幻燈片展示的是今年第一季度的營業額。
9	My point is that we should hold to the local users. 我的觀點是我們要立足於本土用戶。
10	What I'm saying is that we should develop products suitable for the local customers. 我要講的是我們應該開發適合本土顧客的產品。
11	Our goal is to establish a large and stable user group. 我們的目標是建立一個龐大而穩定的用戶群。
12	This presentation focuses on the analysis of our competitors. 這份報告著重對競爭對手的分析。
13	This strategy will allow the company to lap its chief rivals. 該策略讓公司得以領先於主要競爭對手。
14	Our company is well ahead of its rivals. 我們公司遠遠超過了主要的競爭對手。
15	What is the market share of each major product? 各項主打產品的市場佔有率是多少？
16	Is the data reliable? 資料可靠嗎？

萬能好用句型

- I'm here today to present .... 今天在這裡我要向各位介紹……。
- I'd like to start off by giving a brief review of ....
  首先我想簡單回顧一下……。
- I'd like to talk briefly about .... 我想簡要地談一下……。
- Please focus on the screen behind me. 請看我身後的大螢幕。
- The slid shows .... 這張幻燈片展示的是……。
- My point is that .... 我的觀點是……。
- What I'm saying is that .... 我要講的是……。

職場應答對話

✦ 如何做很好的簡報 How to Give a Great Presentation ✦

Ella Can I get some advice? You're really good at presentations and I'm lousy at them. What could I do better?

艾拉 能給我一些建議嗎？你非常擅長做簡報，而我並不在行。我在哪些方面可以改進呢？

Brad First, you need to change your attitude. Giving a great presentation is about seeming confident and like you're having fun.

布萊德 首先，妳需要改變妳的態度。做一次很棒的簡報意味著妳看起來要很有自信，並且樂在其中。

Ella I'll try.

艾拉 我會試試看。

Brad A way to feel more confident is to practice, practice, practice. I start by giving the presentation to myself in the mirror. After that, I ask a friend to watch and give me feedback.

布萊德	讓自己更有自信的一個方法就是練習，練習，再練習。我一開始是對著鏡子裡的自己做簡報。再來，我讓一個朋友來看並給我一些回饋。
Ella	Those are both good ideas, though I think I might feel silly!
艾拉	這兩個想法都很好，雖然說我想我可能會感覺有點傻！
Brad	Trust me, after you do it once it will seem normal. If you are still nervous, you can try to imagine that everyone in the room is a close friend.
布萊德	相信我吧，妳那樣做一次以後，就會感覺正常了。如果妳還是很緊張，妳可以試著想像房間中的每個人都是妳的密友。

- lousy [ˋlaʊzɪ] adj 差勁的，表現不佳的
- feedback [ˋfidˏbæk] n 回饋

關聯必備單字

❶ **demonstration**
[ˏdɛmənˋstreʃən] 演示

❷ **screen**
[skrin] 螢幕

❸ **slide**
[slaɪd] 幻燈片

❹ **local**
[ˋlokḷ] 本地的

❺ **memorize**
[ˋmɛməˏraɪz] 記住

❻ **idiom**
[ˋɪdɪəm] 俚語

❼ **allocate**
[ˋæləket] 分配

❽ **orally**
[ˋɔrəlɪ] 口頭上地

❾ **conversational**
[ˏkɑnvəˋseʃənḷ] 談話的

❿ **jargon**
[ˋdʒɑrgən] 行話，術語

⓫ **data**
[ˋdetə] 數據

⓬ **diagram**
[ˋdaɪə͵græm] 圖表

⓭ **base**
[bes] 基礎

⓮ **chart**
[tʃɑrt] 圖表

⓯ **turnover**
[ˋtɝn͵ovɚ] 營業額

⓰ **stable**
[ˋstebḷ] 穩定的

⓱ **lap**
[læp] 包圍，領先一圈

⓲ **reliable**
[rɪˋlaɪəbḷ] 可依賴的

⓳ **prospect**
[ˋprɑspɛkt] 前景，前程

⓴ **hold to**
信守，堅持

專業貼心便條

如何製作一個高品質的 PPT 呢？創新工廠董事長兼首席執行官李開復提出了下面幾點建議

1. 製作幻燈片首先要遵循 5 秒原則，即打開一頁幻燈片，5 秒後關掉，觀眾還能描述出其中的內容。
2. 標題應該不超過 10 個字，要涵蓋這頁幻燈片的主旨，即做到唯讀每頁的標題，就能夠理解你的演講。
3. 幻燈片中所放的圖要一目了然，自然地支撐這頁的主旨。
4. 每個重點一行講完，不要換行。要記住是用幻燈片點綴你的口才，而非反之。

SECTION 06

需要出差
Being on a Business Trip

隨身應急情境句

Track 058

1	I'm going to Paris for a month on business. 我要到巴黎出差一個月。
2	I'll be away on a business trip. 我要去出差了。
3	Could you tell us how long we're going to be away? 你能告訴我們要去多久嗎？
4	Would you please give me an arrangement for this trip? 請你給我一個行程安排好嗎？
5	It's a tight schedule for the business trip. 出差行程安排得很緊。
6	The accounting department will reimburse you for all your meals and travel expenses. 財務部門會幫你報銷所有的餐費和旅費。
7	Can I have a receipt? I need it for reimbur-sement. 能開收據給我嗎？我需要用它來銷帳。
8	I'll fly business class, because the first class is full. 由於頭等艙已經訂完了，我將會乘坐商務艙。

9	May I check in here for Flight YH329 to New York? 我可以在這裡辦理飛往紐約的 YH329 航班的登機手續嗎？
10	May I check in the direct flight to London now? 現在我可以辦理直飛倫敦的班機的登機手續了嗎？
11	Which counter should we go to have our luggage checked? 我們應該到哪個櫃檯辦理行李托運？
12	Can I have my luggage checked in here? 我可以在這裡辦理行李托運嗎？
13	Can I carry this suitcase with me on board? 我可以帶這個手提箱上飛機嗎？
14	Is this baggage a free carry-on item? 這件行李可以隨身攜帶嗎？
15	May I see your passport? 可以出示一下您的護照嗎？
16	Can I see your boarding pass? 可以出示一下您的登機證嗎？
17	Your passport and entry card, please. 請出示您的護照和入境卡。
18	I'd like to check in. 我要辦理入住。

19 I've already booked a single room in the hotel.
我已經在飯店訂好了一個單人間。

20 I've reserved for you a business suite.
我為您訂好了一套商務套房。

萬能好用句型

- I'm going to … on business.
  我要到……出差。
- I'll be away on a business trip.
  我要去出差了。
- It's a tight schedule for the business trip.
  出差行程安排得很緊湊。
- May I check in here for Flight … to …?
  我可以在這裡辦理飛往……的……航班的登機手續嗎？
- Which counter should I go to have my luggage checked?
  我應該到哪個櫃檯辦理行李托運？
- I'd like to check in.
  我要辦理入住。
- I've already booked … in the hotel.
  我已經在飯店訂好了……。

職場應答對話

✦ 飛往舊金山參加培訓 Fly to San Francisco for Training ✦

Lola This is amazing. I can't believe we just flew to San Francisco for training.

蘿拉 這太棒了。我簡直不敢相信我們飛到舊金山只是為了參加培訓。

Dan I know! The daily budget they gave us for food does seem a little low, though.

丹 我知道！雖然他們給我們每天吃飯的預算確實有點低。

Lola I agree. You have to be on the lookout for cheap restaurants if you want to have all three meals covered.

蘿拉 我同意。如果想要三餐都算進去，就必須找便宜的餐廳。

Dan At least they put us in a really nice hotel. I like that it has a gym and a pool!

丹 至少他們把我們安排到了一家真的很不錯的飯店。裡面有健身房和游泳池，這點我很喜歡！

Lola Let's go use them after we're done for the day.

蘿拉 白天的事情辦完後，我們就到那裡去吧。

Dan Well, I was thinking about meeting some friends from college for a concert and some drinks tonight after work.

丹 嗯，我想的是今晚下班之後跟大學時期的一些朋友去聽音樂會，然後喝點東西。

Lola Sounds fun! Just remember that we have work tomorrow. If you show up too tired, they'll be pretty disappointed.

蘿拉 聽起來很有趣！只是要記得我們明天還要工作。如果你看起來很累，他們會很失望的。

- San Francisco 舊金山
- lookout [ˋlʊk͵aʊt] n 注視
- on the lookout for 尋找
- gym [dʒɪm] n 健身房

關聯必備單字

❶ **reservation**
[͵rɛzɚˋveʃən] 預訂

❷ **reimburse**
[͵riɪmˋbɝs] 報銷，銷帳

❸ **receipt**
[rɪˋsit] 收據

❹ **luggage**
[ˋlʌgɪdʒ] 行李

❺ **flight**
[flaɪt] 班機

❻ **passport**
[ˋpæs͵port] 護照

❼ **counter**
[ˋkaʊntɚ] 櫃檯

❽ **stewardess**
[͵stjuwɚˋdɪs] 女空服員

❾ **boarding card**
登機證

❿ **sleeper**
[ˋslipɚ] 臥鋪

⓫ **train**
[tren] 火車

⓬ **train set**
列車組

⓭ **reimbursement**
[͵riɪmˋbɝsmənt] 報銷

⓮ **browse**
[braʊz] 瀏覽

⓯ **entry card**
入境卡

⓰ **update**
[͵ʌpˋdet] 更新

⓱ **hotel**
[hoˋtɛl] 旅館，飯店

⓲ **accommodate**
[əˋkɑmə͵det] 提供住宿

專業貼心便條

出差之前，首先要回答下面這些問題，做到心理準備，讓商務旅行更加順利。

1. 為什麼要出差？
2. 出差的地點是哪裡？
3. 此次出差都要跟哪些人會面？
4. 此次出差需要多長時間？
5. 此次出差的形式是什麼？
6. 如何安排出差在外的時間？
7. 出差的這段時間是什麼時候？

SECTION 07

升職加薪
Promotion and Getting a Raise

隨身應急情境句

Track 059

1 I'd like to speak to the manager in the matter of my salary.
我要拿我的薪資問題跟經理談談。

2 May I talk to you about my current salary?
我能和您談談我現在的薪資問題嗎？

3 I'd like to have a chance of a pay raise.
我希望能加薪。

4 My salary isn't enough to support the family.
我的薪資不夠我養家。

5 I'm always unable to make ends meet.
我總是入不敷出。

6 My salary has been increased to 6,000 RMB per month.
我的薪水漲到了每月 6000 元。（RMB = 人民幣）

7 I'd like a chance to talk to you about being promoted.
我想找個機會跟您談談關於升遷的事。

8	Could we talk later? You're being considered for a promotion. 我們等一下能聊聊嗎？我們正在考慮幫你升職。
9	He was promoted to sales manager. 他晉升為銷售經理。
10	The new job is a promotion for her. 這個新職務對她來說是升職了。
11	You're up for a promotion! 你要升職了！
12	You've got a promotion. 你升職了。
13	Congratulations on your promotion! 恭喜你升職了！
14	This promotion also comes with a reserved parking space. 升職後還能享有一個專用停車位。
15	This promotion will increase your pay by quite a bit. 這次升職也會讓你的薪水提高很多。
16	Your pay will be raised substantially. 你的薪水也會大幅度地提高。
17	With a pay increase comes more responsibility. 隨著薪資的上漲，工作職責也會更多。

18	Your new responsibilities will mean more pay. 你的新的工作職責將意味著更高的薪水。
19	Does this promotion come with a raise? 這次升職後，薪水會漲嗎？
20	You're a great worker, and we believe you will do well. 你是一名優秀的員工，我們相信你會做得很棒。
21	You're a fantastic worker, and you deserve this. 你是一名優秀的員工，這是你應得的。
22	We think you're the man for the job! 我們認為你是這份工作的合適人選！

萬能好用句型

- May I talk to you about my current salary?
  我能和您談談我現在的薪資問題嗎？
- My salary has been increased to … per month.
  我的薪水漲到了每月……。
- I'd like a chance to talk to you about being promoted.
  我想找個機會跟您談談我升遷的事。
- He was promoted to …. 他晉升為……。
- You're up for a promotion! 你要升職了！
- With a pay increase comes more responsibility.
  隨著薪資的上漲，工作職責也會更多。
- You're a fantastic worker, and you deserve this.
  你是一名優秀的員工，這是你應得的。

職場應答對話

✦ 應該加薪 Deserve a Raise ✦

Michael Thanks for sitting down with me, Kate.

麥可 謝謝妳能跟我坐下來談，凱特。

Kate Sure thing. Tell me, why do you think you deserve a raise?

凱特 好的。請告訴我，為什麼你認為自己應該加薪呢？

Michael Well, first, I've met all of my performance goals for the past two quarters, and even exceeded them last quarter by more than ten percent.

麥可 首先，前兩個季度的績效目標我都達到了，甚至在上一季度超出績效目標的 10% 還要多。

Kate That's pretty good. The company doesn't have a lot of extra money to throw around right now though.

凱特 那確實很棒。可是現在公司沒有太多額外的錢來做這件事。

Michael I understand that, but I was hired with the promise that I would get a significant pay raise after six months. I've been here over a year now and have only gotten a very slight increase.

麥可 我明白，但是公司在雇用我時就曾承諾過 6 個月後我的薪水將會大幅提升。我已經在這裡超過一年了，薪水只是提高了一點。

Kate Alright. You're a good salesman and I want to keep you. You'll get a raise as soon as I talk to accounting.

凱特 好吧。你是一位出色的銷售人員，我希望你能留下。我跟會計談過後，就會替你加薪的。

關聯必備單字

❶ **promotion**
[prə`moʃən] 晉升

❷ **rank**
[ræŋk] 級別

❸ **outstanding**
[aʊt`stændɪŋ] 傑出的

❹ **salary**
[`sælərɪ] 薪水

❺ **contribution**
[ˏkɑntrə`bjuʃən] 貢獻

❻ **increase**
[ɪn`kris] 增加

❼ **raise**
[rez] 加薪

❽ **accounting**
[ə`kaʊntɪŋ] 會計

❾ **confidential**
[ˏkɑnfə`dɛnʃəl] 保密的

❿ **payday**
[`peˏde] 發薪日

⓫ **piecework**
[`pisˏwɝk] 計件工作

⓬ **minimum wage**
最低薪資

⓭ **basic wage**
基本薪資

⓮ **merit pay**
績效薪資

專業貼心便條

如果你認為自己的薪水應該提高了，那麼怎樣跟老闆申請加薪比較好呢？下面這幾點是你要做到的：

1. 瞭解公司的經營狀況與薪酬制度。
2. 確定申請加薪的原因。
3. 收集加薪證據，確認加薪數目。
4. 學習交流技巧，模擬面談過程。
5. 尋找合適的方式及時間與老闆交流。

SECTION 08

迎接年終考核
The Annual Evaluation

隨身應急情境句

Track 060

1	The boss evaluates every employee's performance at the end of each year. 老闆每年年終都會評估每位員工的表現。
2	The company will have a periodic employee appraisal. 公司會定期對員工進行業績評估。
3	How would my performance be evaluated? 怎樣評估我的業績呢？
4	I'm a little nervous about the coming evaluation. 對即將到來的評估，我感到有些緊張。
5	We've been very impressed with your work this year. Please continue! 我們對你今年的工作印象深刻。再接再厲！
6	You've done a great job this year. 你今年的工作表現十分出色。
7	I get great feedback from my boss. 老闆對我的評價非常高。

8	The boss is very pleased with my work. 老闆對我的工作表現很滿意。
9	He passed performance goals every quarter this year. 今年每一季度的績效目標他都達到了。
10	You're the best salesman in the office. 你是辦公室裡最棒的銷售人員。
11	Congratulations on your sales last year. 恭喜你去年取得很好的銷售業績。
12	I will continue the efforts. 我會繼續努力。
13	I will work harder. 我會更加努力工作。
14	Our company is setting up a higher sales target this year. 我們公司今年制定了更高的銷售目標。
15	We ought to set precise sales targets for the coming year. 我們要為明年制定出準確的銷售目標。
16	It's hard to exceed this year's target by a large margin. 大大超過今年的指標是很困難的。
17	The annual conference will be held next week. 年會將在下個禮拜舉行。

18	Our company is having the annual conference next week. 我們公司會在下個禮拜舉行年會。

萬能好用句型

- How would my performance be evaluated?
  怎樣評估我的業績呢？
- We've been very impressed with your work this year.
  我們對你今年的工作印象深刻。
- I get great feedback from my boss.
  老闆對我的評價非常高。
- … passed performance goals every quarter this year.
  今年每一季度的績效目標……都通過了。
- You're the best salesman in the office.
  你是辦公室裡最棒的銷售人員。
- I will continue the efforts.
  我會繼續努力。
- The annual conference will be held …
  年會將在……舉行。

職場應答對話

✦ 年終考核 Annual Review ✦

Janice Alright, Steven, are you ready to start your annual review?
珍妮絲 好吧，史蒂夫，你準備好開始進行年終考核了嗎？

Steven Yes, as ready as I'll ever be.

史蒂夫 是的，我隨時都準備好了。

Janice Great. Well, first, you are a great employee and I'm very pleased with your work.

珍妮絲 很好。首先，你是一位很出色的員工，我對你的工作十分滿意。

Steven That's good to hear.

史蒂夫 很高興聽到您這麼說。

Janice This evaluation is broken up into 4 sections and you got a score for each. The highest score is 5. You got three 4s and one 5.

珍妮絲 這次評估分為四個環節，每個環節都給你打了分數。最高分是 5 分。你得了三個 4 分，一個 5 分。

Steven Wow, 5! What category was that in?

史蒂夫 哇，5 分！哪一項得了這個分數？

Janice That was for sales goals. You passed performance goals every quarter this year.

珍妮絲 是銷售目標這項。今年每一季度的績效目標你都達到了。

Steven Wonderful. What about the other areas?

史蒂夫 太好了。其他部分呢？

Janice Working as part of a team is the area that I think you could improve in the most. You don't ask for help very often.

珍妮絲 我想你最需要改善的是團隊合作這項。你很少尋求別人的幫助。

關聯必備單字

❶ **comb**
[kom] 梳子

❷ **shave**
[ʃev] 刮

❸ **necklace**
[`nɛklɪs] 項鍊

❹ **perfume**
[`pɝ͵fjum] 香水

❺ **mirror**
[`mɪrɚ] 鏡子

❻ **cleanser**
[`klɛnzɚ] 卸妝水

❼ **whiten**
[`hwaɪtn] 美白

❽ **tissue**
[`tɪʃʊ] 手巾紙

❾ **blouse**
[blaʊz] 女襯衫

❿ **bracelet**
[`breslɪt] 手鐲

⓫ **boot**
[but] 靴子

⓬ **gown**
[gaʊn] 禮服

⓭ **miniskirt**
[`mɪnɪskɝt] 超短裙

⓮ **essence**
[`ɛsns] 精華液

⓯ **moisturizer**
[`mɔɪstʃəraɪzɚ] 保濕霜

⓰ **wig**
[wɪg] 假髮

專業貼心便條

年終總結的六個要點：

1. 要充分認識到總結的意義。
2. 回顧一年來的工作，總結一年來各項工作的完成情況，全面總結成績。
3. 分析取得成績的原因。
4. 分析導致工作目標沒有達成的失誤和問題。
5. 展望與分析當前形勢。
6. 計劃與安排下一年度的工作。

SECTION 09

拿年終獎金
Getting an Annual Bonus

隨身應急情境句

Track 061

1 The bonus will give the employees an incentive to work harder.
獎金可以激勵員工更加努力地工作。

2 Generally speaking, all companies have a sales commission or bonus.
一般來説，所有的公司都會有銷售傭金或分紅。

3 I hope we'll get the annual bonus this year.
希望今年我們能拿到年終獎金。

4 It's almost the New Year. Do you think we'll get a bonus this year?
新年快到了。你覺得今年我們能拿到獎金嗎？

5 We'll receive a quarterly bonus if quotas are met.
如果我們達到銷售額，就能拿到季度獎金。

6 A bonus should be a reward for exceptional performance.
獎金應該作為對出色業績的一種獎勵。

7 Various proposals were put forward for increasing sales.
大家為了增加銷售額而提出了各種建議。

8	If you get an annual bonus, what would you like to do with it? 如果你拿到年終獎金，你要拿它做什麼？
9	What are you going to do with your annual bonus? 你的年終獎金打算怎麼花呢？
10	What do you intend to do when you get the bonus? 你拿了獎金之後打算做什麼？
11	Every employee receives an annual bonus. 每位員工都得到了年終獎金。
12	I decide to buy some new clothes with my bonus. 我決定用獎金去買一些新衣服。
13	I'm thinking of going on a vacation. 我在想著去度假。
14	How much year-end bonus did you get this year? 你今年拿到了多少年終獎金？
15	May I ask how much the year-end bonus is? 我可以問一下年終獎金是多少嗎？
16	It's very thrilling to get my first annual bonus. 第一次領年終獎金讓我很興奮。
17	I just got my annual bonus. I want to celebrate now. 我剛拿到了年終獎金。現在我想要去慶祝一下。

萬能好用句型

- I hope we'll get the annual bonus this year.
  希望今年我們能拿到年終獎金。
- Do you think we'll get a bonus this year?
  你覺得今年我們能拿到獎金嗎？
- What are you going to do with your annual bonus?
  你的年終獎金打算怎麼花呢？
- What do you intend to do when you get the bonus?
  你拿了獎金之後打算做什麼？
- I decide to … with my bonus. 我決定用獎金……。
- How much year-end bonus did you get this year?
  你今年拿到了多少年終獎金？

職場應答對話

✦ 拿到年終獎金 Getting an Annual Bonus ✦

Melody What's this in the envelope?
美樂蒂 信封裡裝的是什麼？

Justin Well, Melody, we've been so impressed with your work this year that we decided to give you a thank-you gift in the form of a cash bonus.
賈斯汀 哦，美樂蒂，我們對妳今年的工作印象深刻，所以我們決定給妳一筆現金獎勵。

Melody Wow, really? I didn't know the company even did that.
美樂蒂 哇，真的嗎？我之前都不知道公司會發獎金。

Justin This is definitely an exception. In fact, please don't speak to your co-workers about the amount you received or anything along those lines.

賈斯汀 這絕對是個例外。事實上，請不要告訴妳的同事妳拿到的獎勵金額，以及與之相關的事。

Melody Okay, I can do that. Thanks for this. Extra money is always appreciated!

美樂蒂 好的，我能做到。謝謝。額外的報酬總會令人心生感激！

Justin You earned it. Thank you for working so hard for the company. I hope to see more of the same in the coming year.

賈斯汀 這是妳應得的。感謝妳對公司的辛勤付出。希望在未來的一年裡能看到妳有更多同樣的表現。

Melody You definitely will. I'm even more motivated now that I know my hard work will be recognized.

美樂蒂 你一定會看到的。我現在甚至更加有動力了，因為我知道我的努力將會得到認可。

- envelope [ˋɛnvə͵lop] n 信封
- be impressed with 對……印象深刻
- exception [ɪkˋsɛpʃən] n 例外
- amount [əˋmaʊnt] n 數量，總額

關聯必備單字

❶ **bonus**
[ˋbonəs] 獎金

❷ **motivate**
[ˋmotə͵vet] 激勵

❸ **stimulus**
[ˋstɪmjələs] 激勵

❹ **expansion**
[ɪkˋspænʃən] 擴大

❺ **promising**
[ˋprɑmɪsɪŋ] 有前途的

❻ **intend**
[ɪnˋtɛnd] 打算

❼ **aspire**
[əˋspaɪr] 渴望

❽ **coming**
[ˋkʌmɪŋ] 即將到來的

❾ **incredibly**
[ɪnˋkrɛdəblɪ] 難以置信地

❿ **incentive**
[ɪnˋsɛntɪv] 激勵，動機

⓫ **sales commission**
銷售傭金

⓬ **quota**
[ˋkwotə] 限額，定額

⓭ **thrilling**
[ˋθrɪlɪŋ] 令人興奮的

⓮ **count on**
指望

⓯ **endeavor**
[ɪnˋdɛvɚ] 努力，盡力

⓰ **marvelous**
[ˋmɑrvələs] 非凡的

⓱ **reciprocal**
[rɪˋsɪprəkḷ] 互惠的

⓲ **sheer**
[ʃɪɚ] 徹底的

專業貼心便條

年終獎金通常有三種發放形式：

1. 有保證的獎金：如外資企業普遍採用的 13 個月薪、14 個月薪或更多，只要員工年底仍然在職，無論他個人的表現如何，無論公司的業績如何，全員享受，屬於「普惠」，類似於福利性質，表示公司對員工一年來「苦勞」的感謝。
2. 浮動的獎金：一般指根據個人年度績效評估結果和公司業績結果所發放的績效獎金。
3. 紅包：通常是由老闆決定的，沒有固定的規則，可能取決於員工與老闆的親疏、老闆對員工的印象、資歷或重大貢獻等。

CHAPTER 10

遇到特殊情況 Special Circumstances

SECTION 01

上班遲到了
Arriving Late

隨身應急情境句

Track 062

1	Crap! I'm gonna be late! 糟糕！我要遲到了！
2	We need to hurry up. It's getting late. 我們得快一點。要遲到了。
3	I can't be late for work again or I'll get fired! 我上班不能再遲到了，否則我就會被開除了！
4	I am sorry for being late, but something urgent happened. 對不起我遲到了，有一點急事。
5	Sorry, I am late. My watch is 30 minutes slow. 對不起，我遲到了。我的錶慢了 30 分鐘。
6	Sorry, I'm late. There was a diversion. 對不起，我遲到了，繞路了。
7	I'm sorry for being late. 真抱歉，我遲到了。
8	I apologize for arriving late. 很抱歉，我遲到了。

9 I was late because my car broke down.
我遲到是因為我的車拋錨了。

10 I'm late for work today because there's a traffic jam.
我今天上班遲到了，因為路上塞車。

11 I'm sorry, I got stuck in traffic.
對不起，我塞在車陣裡了。

12 I was five minutes late.
我遲到了 5 分鐘。

13 I was late by ten minutes.
我遲到了 10 分鐘。

14 I'm really sorry. It will not happen again.
我真的很抱歉，不會再有下次了。

15 You must be punctual for work.
你必須準時上班。

16 Don't be late anymore, or else you'll be fired.
別再遲到了，否則你會被解雇的。

17 If you are late, you will be fined.
如果你遲到會被罰款的。

18 No late charges I hope.
希望遲到不會被罰。

19 Fines will be deducted directly from your paycheck.
遲到的罰款會直接從你的薪水裡面扣。

萬能好用句型

- I'm gonna be late!　我要遲到了！
- I can't be late for work again.　我上班不能再遲到了。
- I apologize for arriving late.　很抱歉，我遲到了。
- I was late because ….　我遲到是因為……。
- I was … minutes late.　我遲到了……分鐘。
- It will not happen again.　不會有下次了。

職場應答對話

✦ 睡過頭了 Overslept ✦

Mr. Friesen *Ring Ring* (telephone)

費里森先生 *鈴鈴*（電話響）

Susan *Yawn* Helloooo?

蘇珊 （打哈欠）你好？

Mr. Friesen Susan, do you know what time it is?

費里森先生 蘇珊，妳知道現在幾點了嗎？

Susan …

蘇珊 ……

Mr. Friesen Susan, I thought I made myself clear last time about coming into work late. You were expected to be here half an hour ago and we have not heard from you.

費里森先生 蘇珊，關於上班遲到的事我想上次我已經說得很明白了。半小時前妳就應該出現了，而且我們都沒有妳的消息。

Susan I am terribly sorry, sir. I overslept because my alarm did not turn on. My cat must have unplugged it.

蘇珊 我非常抱歉，先生。我睡過頭了，因為我的鬧鐘沒有開。我的貓一定是把電源插頭弄掉了。

Mr. Friesen Do you even have a cat?

費里森先生 妳到底有沒有養貓？

Susan Of course I do, sir. I will bring in pictures if you insist.

蘇珊 當然有，先生。如果您堅持的話，我會拿一些照片過去。

Mr. Friesen I would appreciate that. I have a few cats myself. Maybe they can have play dates some time.

費里森先生 這很不錯。我也有養幾隻貓。也許改天牠們能一起玩。

Susan That would be great! Okay, I am on my way, see you in ten minutes.

蘇珊 那就太好了！好吧，我在路上了，10 分鐘後見。

➲ unplug [ˏʌnˋplʌg] V 拔去……的插頭

關聯必備單字

❶ **punctual**
[ˋpʌŋktʃʊəl] 準時的

❷ **punctuality**
[ˏpʌŋktʃʊˋæləti] 嚴守時間

❸ **lateness**
[ˋletnəs] 遲到

❹ **apologize**
[əˋpɑlədʒaɪz] 道歉

❺ **excuse**
[ɪkˋskjus] 藉口

❻ **frequent**
[ˋfrikwənt] 頻繁的

❼ **traffic**
[ˋtræfɪk] 交通

❽ **oversleep**
[ˏovɚˋslip] 睡過頭

❾ **yawn**
[jɔn] 打哈欠

❿ **minute**
[ˋmɪnɪt] 分鐘

⓫ **strict**
[strɪkt] 嚴格的

⓬ **shift**
[ʃɪft] 輪班

⓭ **absent**
[ˋæbsənt] 缺席的

⓮ **sick**
[sɪk] 生病的

⓯ **absenteeism**
[ˏæbsənˋtiɪzm] 曠職，曠課

⓰ **diversion**
[daɪˋvɝʒən] 臨時繞行

⓱ **break down**
發生故障

⓲ **traffic jam**
交通阻塞

⓳ **fine**
[faɪn] 罰款

⓴ **deduct**
[dɪˋdʌkt] 扣除

專業貼心便條

職場人士要儘量避免上班遲到，但如何才能避免呢？下面是避免上班遲到的小技巧，希望對你有所幫助。

1. 學會安排時間：要制訂嚴格的時間表，張貼在隨處可見的位置，把工作安排標注清楚，並留出足夠的準備時間。
2. 進行換位思考：將自己放在「犧牲者」的位置上，當你被迫等待時，會有怎樣的感受呢？
3. 多做心理調適：讓任何事情都順其自然吧，比如家裡好像沒收拾乾淨，那就讓它亂吧；頭髮有點髒了，那就再忍一忍。長此以往，克服了焦慮情緒，遲到就會減少了。

SECTION 02

需要加班
Working Overtime

隨身應急情境句

Track 063

1	I have to work late tonight. 我今天晚上得加班。
2	Are you working overtime tonight? 你今晚要加班嗎？
3	I have to work overtime this weekend. 我這個週末得加班。
4	There is an urgent task. So I have to work overtime this Sunday. 有一項很緊急的任務，所以我這個禮拜日要加班。
5	I guess I am going to work through the night. 我想我得熬夜工作了。
6	I'm working late tonight. Such a bummer. 我今晚要工作到很晚。真倒楣。
7	Are you busy? Could you work late tonight? 你很忙嗎？今天晚上能加班嗎？
8	I'm staying late tonight. Do you know how long that will be? 我今天晚上要加班。你知道要加班多久嗎？

9	How long should I stay tonight? 我今晚要待多久？
10	Typically I can work late on Thursdays and Fridays. 通常我禮拜四和禮拜五可以加班。
11	I can't work late on Fridays, but weekends are fine. 我禮拜五不能加班，但是週末可以。
12	Could I pick up some extra hours? 我能加班嗎？
13	I can work some extra hours this weekend. 這個週末我可以加幾個小時的班。
14	Will I be paid extra if I stay late? 我加班有加班費嗎？
15	Will I get paid more than usual for staying later? 我加班的話，薪水會比平時多嗎？
16	How do you feel about overtime work? 你對加班有什麼看法？
17	I have no plans tonight so I don't mind staying later. 我今晚沒有安排，所以我不介意加班。
18	I don't want to work overtime. 我不想加班。

萬能好用句型

- Are you working overtime tonight? 你今晚要加班嗎？
- Typically I can work late on … 通常我……可以加班。
- Could I pick up some extra hours? 我能加班嗎？
- Will I be paid extra if I stay late? 我加班有加班費嗎？
- I have no plans tonight so I don't mind staying later.
  我今晚沒有安排，所以我不介意加班。

職場應答對話

✦ 今天晚上不加班 No Overtime Work Tonight ✦

Annie Hi Dave, will you be working late tonight as well?
安妮 嗨，戴夫，你今天晚上也要加班嗎？

Dave Oh no, I will be going to Cirque du Soleil, and I had my tickets booked for months.
戴夫 噢，不加，我要去看太陽馬戲團，幾個月前我就訂票了。

Annie That sounds fun! Hope you have a great time.
安妮 這聽起來很有趣耶！希望你玩得愉快。

Dave I'm sure I will. I went last year and have been waiting to go again ever since.
戴夫 我相信肯定會的。我去年看了，之後就一直想再去一次。

Annie Okay, see you tomorrow then. I have to get back to work.
安妮 好吧，那明天見。我要去工作了。

Dave Alright, see you then!
戴夫 好的，再見！

...

……

Annie Hello sir, I have been working for the past few hours and have finally finished what you had asked for.

安妮 您好，先生。我剛才幾個小時都在工作，最後有完成您交代的任務。

Tom Thank you very much, Annie. Good work! As a special thank-you for working overtime, I would like to give you a gift card to Starbucks.

湯姆 非常感謝妳，安妮。做得不錯！作為加班的獎勵，我給妳一張星巴克的禮品卡。

Annie Oh wow, thank you so much!

安妮 哇，太感謝了！

➲ gift card 禮品卡

關聯必備單字

❶ **typically** [ˋtɪpɪklɪ] 通常

❷ **overtime** [ˋovɚ͵taɪm] 加班

❸ **Monday** [ˋmʌnde] 星期一

❹ **Tuesday** [ˋtjuzde] 星期二

❺ **Wednesday** [ˋwɛnzde] 星期三

❻ **Thursday** [ˋθɝzde] 星期四

❼ **Friday** [ˋfraɪde] 星期五

❽ **Saturday** [ˋsætɚde] 星期六

❾ **Sunday** [ˋsʌnde] 星期日

❿ **workday** [ˋwɝk͵de] 工作日

⓫ **weekend**
[ˌwikˋɛnd] 週末

⓬ **plan**
[plæn]（具體）安排

⓭ **overtime pay**
加班費

⓮ **bummer**
[ˋbʌmɚ]
令人失望或不愉快的局面

⓯ **routine**
[ruˋtin] 慣例，常規

⓰ **swamped**
[swɑmpt] 忙碌的

專業貼心便條

如雇主有使勞工每日工作時間超過 8 小時者，或兩週工作超過 84 小時者，應依法給付加班費，其標準為：

1. 延長工作時間在 2 小時以內者，按平日每小時工資額加給 3 分之 1 以上。
2. 再延長工作時間在 2 小時以內者，按平日每小時工資額加給 3 分之 2 以上。
3. 雇主如遇紀念日、勞動節及其他由中央主管機關規定應放假之日或特別休假，均應使勞工休假。雇主於休假 日使勞工出勤者，該日應加倍給薪。該日出勤 8 小時內不計入每月加班 46 小時範圍。
4. 非屬國定假日或例假日之一般非出勤日，工時 80 至 84 小時間者，工資雙方議定，超過 84 小時者，加班前 2 小時：1/3×加班時數×時薪，加班後 2 小時：2/3×加班時數×時薪。

SECTION 03

向老闆請假
Asking for Leave

隨身應急情境句

Track 064

1	Could I take one day off tomorrow? 我明天能請一天假嗎？
2	Could I take a leave on the 15th? 我 15 號能請一天假嗎？
3	May I ask for leave next Monday? 我下個禮拜一能請一天假嗎？
4	I'd like to ask for a week's leave. 我想請一個禮拜的假。
5	I'd like to take three days off if it's all right with you. 如果可以的話，我想請三天假。
6	I need to take a leave on the 25th of this month. 這個月 25 號，我要請一天假。
7	Is it alright if I take a leave next Friday? 下週五我可以請一天假嗎？
8	I want to ask for leave to go to Milan with my family. 我想請假和我家人一起去米蘭。

9	I'm sorry that may not be possible. You know we're now short of hands. 對不起，那不太可能，你知道我們現在缺少人手。
10	I'm afraid I have to let you down. We're just assigned to an urgent task. 我恐怕得讓你失望了，我們剛分配到了一個緊急任務。
11	He's not working today. 他今天請假了。
12	I need to ask for sick leave. 我要請病假。
13	I got sick. I have to ask for a day's leave to see the doctor. 我生病了。我要請一天假去看醫生。
14	She's on sick leave today. 她今天請病假了。
15	I'm sorry I can't come to work today. I'm running a temperature. 很抱歉我今天不能來上班，我發燒了。
16	I'm not feeling well. I have to tell you I won't be in today. 我感覺不舒服。我得跟你說我今天不能上班。
17	What happened to you? 你怎麼了？

18	What's up? 發生什麼事了？
19	Fill in an absence form, and I will sign it. 填張假條，我來簽字。
20	Submit the absence request, and I'll approve it. 填一下請假申請，我來批准。

萬能好用句型

- Could I take one day off tomorrow? 明天我能請一天假嗎？
- Could I take a leave on …? 我能在……請一天假嗎？
- I'd like to take … days off if it's all right with you.
  如果可以的話，我想請……天假。
- She's on sick leave. 她請病假了。
- What's up? 發生什麼事了？
- Submit the absence request, and I'll approve it.
  填一下請假申請，我來批准。

職場應答對話

✦ 兩個禮拜喪假 Two-Week Leave for Bereavement ✦

Mary Hi Sam, I have filled out these forms in order to have a leave of absence.

瑪麗 嗨，山姆，請假要填的這些表格我都填好了。

Sam Okay, that is great. Let me take a look.

山姆 好的，不錯。讓我看一下吧。

Mary Here you go.

瑪麗 給你。

Sam I see that you wrote that a family member passed away. I am deeply sorry to hear that. Our company offers two weeks off work for bereavement time.

山姆 我看到妳上面寫到一位親人去世了。真的很遺憾聽到這個消息。我們公司允許兩個禮拜的喪假。

Mary Thank you for your sympathy. My grandma had raised me since I was a child, and was like a mother to me. I think that I will need to use the full two weeks, time to take care of everything for the funeral and to take some time to grieve.

瑪麗 謝謝您的慰問。我的外婆撫養我長大，對我來說，她就像媽媽一樣。我想我要用這兩個禮拜的時間來料理葬禮的事情和哀悼。

Sam Not a problem. Please let me know if there is anything more we can do for you.

山姆 沒問題。如果我們還有什麼能幫到妳的，請告訴我。

- pass away 去世
- bereavement [bəˋrivmənt] n 喪親
- sympathy [ˋsɪmpəθɪ] n 同情，慰問
- raise [rez] v 養育
- grieve [griv] v 哀悼，感到悲痛

關聯必備單字

❶ **absence**
[ˋæbsəns] 缺席

❷ **fever**
[ˋfivɚ] 發燒

❸ **illness**
[ˋɪlnəs] 疾病

❹ **faint**
[fent] 頭暈的

❺ **cold**
[kold] 感冒

❻ **sign**
[saɪn] 簽字

❼ **headache**
[ˋhɛdˏek] 頭痛

❽ **leave**
[liv] 休假

❾ **ease**
[iz] 減輕

❿ **bad**
[bæd] 嚴重的

⓫ **cough**
[kɑf] 咳嗽

⓬ **hurt**
[hɝt] 感到疼痛

專業貼心便條

有事外出或請假不上班，要得到老闆或主管批准，同時最好跟辦公室的同事說一聲。即使是臨時出去半個小時，也要跟同事打個招呼。這樣，如果老闆或客戶找你，也可以讓同事幫忙交待。如果你什麼都沒說，又恰好有緊急的事，同事就無法替你處理了。這種互相告知，是工作上的需要，也可以聯絡彼此的感情，增加同事間的信任感。

SECTION 04

開始休假
Taking a Vacation

隨身應急情境句

Track 065

1	When will you take your annual leave? 你打算什麼時候休年假？
2	When will you take the balance of your annual leave? 你打算什麼時候休剩下的年假？
3	How much annual leave do you get? 你有多少天年假？
4	We are entitled to 7 days paid vacation. 我們每年有七天給薪假期。
5	The job includes two weeks' paid vacation. 這份工作包括兩個禮拜的給薪假期。
6	She's away on maternity leave. 她在休產假。
7	I'd really like to go on a vacation. 我真想去度假。
8	Going on a vacation would be nice. 去度假會很不錯。

9	It's a good time of the year to go on a vacation. 這個時候去度假很不錯。
10	I'm taking my vacation the first two weeks in May. 五月份的前兩個禮拜我要去度假。
11	I wonder what kind of places I could travel to. 我想知道我可以去哪些地方旅遊。
12	You could ask a few travel agencies what's available. 你可以去問旅行社看看有什麼地方可去。
13	I want to arrange a trip to Brazil. 我想安排一次去巴西的旅行。
14	I'm thinking of taking a trip to Europe. 我想去歐洲旅行。
15	To celebrate our wedding anniversary, my wife and I will go on a vacation. 為了慶祝我們的結婚紀念日，我和我老婆將要去度假。
16	For my wife's birthday, I'm taking her to Milan. 為了慶祝我老婆的生日，我要帶她去米蘭。
17	I am planning to go to Italy this winter with my parents. I really need a getaway from my everyday life and just to spend some time with them. 今年冬天我打算跟父母去義大利。我真的得出去散散心，並且多陪陪父母。

18	I have a family vacation to go on later in the year. 今年晚一點的時候我們一家人要去旅遊。
19	My family want to take a vacation later this year. 我家人想在今年晚一點的時候去旅遊。

萬能好用句型

- When will you take your annual leave? 你打算什麼時候休年假？
- How much annual leave do you get? 你有多少天年假？
- I'd like to go on a vacation. 我真想去度假。
- I'm taking … to …. 我要帶……去……。
- I really need a getaway from my everyday life.
  我真的得出去散散心。
- When will you be leaving? 你什麼時候去？

職場應答對話

✦ 批准休假 Approve the Vacation Request ✦

Tim Hi Charlotte, I have booked my tickets to Paris and would like to tell you the dates for my vacation.

提姆 嗨，夏洛特，我已經訂了去巴黎的機票。我要告訴妳我休假的時間。

Charlotte Okay, I am ready. When will you be leaving?

夏洛特 好的，說吧。你什麼時候要去？

Tim My wife and I will leave on December 21st and I will return to work on January 4th.

提姆 我和我太太會在 12 月 21 日啟程， 然後我 1 月 4 日會回來上班。

Charlotte I am very happy for you. I am sure you will have a great time on your vacation. I will ask Sean if he will be interested in full time hours to help cover your shifts while you are away.

夏洛特 我真為你高興。相信你在假期裡會玩得很高興。我會問下蕭恩看他能不能在你離開的這段時間幫忙代你的班。

Tim That sounds like a great idea. I know he is always looking to pick up more hours.

提姆 這是個不錯的主意。我知道他一直都想要加班。

Charlotte Okay, then it is settled. I will approve your vacation request, and let Sean know about his new hours.

夏洛特 好的，就這麼決定了。我會批准你的假期，然後告知蕭恩他的新的工作時間安排。

➲ shift [ʃɪft] n 輪班

關聯必備單字

❶ **annual leave**
年假

❷ **vacation**
[vəˋkeʃən] 休假

❸ **hotel**
[hoˋtɛl] 旅館

❹ **maternity**
[məˋtɝnətɪ] 產婦的

❺ **anniversary**
[ˏænəˋvɝsərɪ] 紀念日

❻ **faraway**
[ˋfærəˏwe] 遙遠的

❼ **book**
[bʊk] 預訂

❽ **ticket**
[ˋtɪkɪt] 票

❾ **suitcase**
[ˋsutˏkes] 手提箱

❿ **briefcase**
[ˋbrifˏkes] 公事包

⓫ **baggage**
[ˋbægɪdʒ] 行李

⓬ **flight**
[flaɪt] 班機

⓭ **ferry**
[ˋfɛrɪ] 渡船

⓮ **picturesque**
[ˏpɪktʃəˋrɛsk] 迷人的

⓯ **balance**
[ˋbæləns] 餘額，剩餘

⓰ **maternity**
[məˋtɝnətɪ] 孕婦的

專業貼心便條

台灣的給薪假期通常指的是：

1. 法定假期—元旦；春節；和平紀念日；清明節；勞動節；端午節；中秋節；國慶日。
2. 年休假：工作滿一年以上的員工，可享受給薪年休假。
3. 婚假：本人結婚，可享受婚假 8 天。結婚雙方不在一地工作的，可根據路程遠近給予路程假。途中交通費由職工自理。
4. 喪假：員工的直系親屬（父母、配偶）死亡，可給予以喪假 8 日；祖父母、子女、配偶之父母喪亡者，可給予喪假 6 日；兄弟姊妹、曾祖父母、配偶之祖父母喪亡者，可給予喪假 3 日。途中交通費由員工自理。
5. 生育假及看護假：女性職員生育，產假 8 個星期；男性職員陪同配偶生育，可請陪產假 5 日。員工若進入公司超過 6 個月以上，可申請育嬰留職停薪。
6. 工傷病假：發生工傷事故後，員工治療和休養所需要的時間，視為工傷假。在這段時間，工資照發。

SECTION 05

進行崗位調動
Transferring Jobs

隨身應急情境句

Track 066

1	I'd like to ask you for a transfer. 我想請求調換崗位。
2	I'd like to put in for a transfer. 我想申請調職。
3	She was transferred from the marketing department to the sales department. 她從行銷部調到了業務部。
4	I was transferred to the sales department and became a regional manager. 我調到了業務部，成為區域經理。
5	She wants to be a good salesperson. 她想成為一名優秀的業務人員。
6	He asks for a transfer to the marketing department. 他要求調到行銷部。
7	He was transferred to another post. 他被調職了。
8	There will be a reorganization in the company. 公司要進行人事變動。

9	When she heard about the change, she resigned. 當聽到人事變動的消息時，她辭職了。
10	Changes in top management of the company had been in the wind for weeks. 公司高層管理人員的人事變動已進行了好幾個星期。
11	I am unwilling to transfer to other departments. 我不想被調到其他部門。
12	I don't want to leave here. 我不想離開這裡。
13	I'm looking forward to transferring to the export department. 我很期待調到出口部。
14	I bet you are looking forward to moving to our branch in Pittsburgh. It's a great place to raise a family. 我想你很期待調到我們在匹茲堡的分公司吧。那裡很適合養家。
15	For the time being Mary is working in the export department. 瑪麗目前在出口部工作。
16	I'll try my best to learn the new job. 我會盡最大努力熟悉新職務。

萬能好用句型

- I'd like to put in for a transfer.　我想申請調職。
- I was transferred from … to ….　我從……調到了……。
- I was transferred to ….　我調到了……。
- I ask for a transfer to ….　我要求調到……。
- I am unwilling to transfer to other departments.
  我不想被調到其他部門。
- I don't want to leave here.　我不想離開這裡。
- I'm looking forward to transferring to …　我很期待調到……。

職場應答對話

✦ 願意調職去北京 Willing to Relocate to Beijing ✦

Jane Hi Kevin, there is something I want to ask you.
珍 嗨，凱文，有件事我要問你一下。

Kevin Okay, sure, what is it?
凱文 好的，什麼事？

Jane As you know, our company has been growing tremendously these past few years, and we are finally able to open up a new branch in Beijing. When you were hired you said that you would be available to move if needed, and now is that time. Are you still willing to relocate?
珍 你知道近幾年來我們公司發展的很迅速，我們終於能在北京成立分公司了。我們聘用你的時候，你說過如果有需要你可以調過去，而現在是時候了。你還願意調職嗎？

Kevin Yes, for sure, that would be great! My wife isn't working, so this would be the perfect time for moving. Will I need to have special training before I go?

凱文 是的，當然了，那樣很好啊！我的太太沒有上班，所以現在正合適調職。我去之前需不需要進行特別的培訓呢？

Jane Yes, you will. We have a computer program that goes through everything you need to know, and once you finish that you will be ready to go.

珍 要，你需要培訓。我們有一個電腦程式，裡面包含了你需要瞭解的所有內容。一旦你看完，你就可以準備出發了。

Kevin That sounds great! I will start my training tomorrow morning.

凱文 這聽起來很棒！明天早上我就開始進行培訓。

➲ tremendously [trəˋmɛndəslɪ] adv 極大地，巨大地

關聯必備單字

❶ **relocate** [ˌrɪloˋket] 重新安置

❷ **transfer** [trænsˋfɝ] 調動

❸ **regional** [ˋridʒənḷ] 地區的

❹ **reorganization** [riˌɔrgənəˋzeʃən] 重組

❺ **suspense** [səˋspɛns] 焦慮

❻ **adjustment** [əˋdʒʌstmənt] 調整

❼ **adapt** [əˋdæpt] 使適應

❽ **branch** [bræntʃ] 分公司

❾ **lateral move** 橫向調動

❿ **staff turnover** 員工流動率

⑪ **switch**
[swɪtʃ] 轉換

⑫ **decision**
[dɪˋsɪʒn] 決定

⑬ **management**
[ˋmænɪdʒmənt] 管理

⑭ **unwilling**
[ʌnˋwɪlɪŋ] 不情願的

⑮ **regional manager**
區域經理

⑯ **for the time being**
目前，暫時

專業貼心便條

讓自己快樂工作的心理小秘訣，你知道嗎？

1. 把手放在你的前額，緩解眼睛疲勞。
2. 雙肩放下，垂直坐下。以這個姿勢坐下的時候，會立即讓你感到精力充沛。
3. 儘量及時處理比較棘手的郵件、任務、電話。解決完這些難題後，精神也會變得非常振奮。
4. 對於那些不必知道的東西保持不聞不問。
5. 每天至少出去一次，可以去散散步，沐浴在陽光下心情會十分舒暢。
6. 最好跟每位同事都說「早安」。同事間相處融洽，也能讓你保持愉悅的心情。

SECTION 06

請辭
Resigning

隨身應急情境句　Track 067

1	I'm quite bored with my job. I want to quit. 我厭倦我的工作了。我想辭職。
2	I don't like the job any more. I'm quitting. 我不再喜歡這份工作了。我要辭職。
3	I'm thinking of resigning. I'm tired of my present job. 我正在考慮辭職。我厭煩了現在的工作。
4	Jane is thinking of quitting her job, for she wishes to seek a more challenging one. 珍正在考慮辭職，因為她想找一份更具有挑戰性的工作。
5	I've been thinking about pulling the pin. 我一直在想辭職的事。
6	I really want to quit my job. 我真的想辭掉工作。
7	How has this idea occurred to you out of the blue? 你怎麼突然有了這個念頭？

8	I'd like to have an opportunity to further develop my abilities. 我想有機會更進一步發揮我的能力。
9	You should at least put in a month's notice. 你至少應該提前一個月提交辭呈。
10	I'm not putting in a notice. I quit today! 我不寫離職申請，我今天就要辭職！
11	This is a letter of my resignation. 這是我的辭職信。
12	He has submitted his resignation. 他已經交了辭呈。
13	Excuse me, I want to resign my position as secretary. 不好意思，我想辭去秘書的職位。
14	I just think it's about time for me to leave. 我只是覺得是我離開的時候了。
15	I quit, so I have to clean out my desk. 我辭職了，所以我得清理下我的辦公桌。
16	He quit his job as a sales assistant. 他辭去了業務助理的工作。
17	Mary's quitting. We need to find a replacement for her. 瑪麗要辭職。我們得找人接替她。

18 To each his own, we'll miss you around here.
人各有志，我們會想念你的。

萬能好用句型

- I want to quit.　我想辭職。
- I don't like the job any more. I'm quitting.
  我不再喜歡這份工作了。我要辭職。
- I'm thinking of resigning.　我正在考慮辭職。
- This is a letter of my resignation.　這是我的辭職信。
- Excuse me, I want to resign my position as …
  不好意思，我想辭去……的職位。
- He quit his job as …　他辭去了……的工作。
- To each his own, we'll miss you around here.
  人各有志，我們會想念你的。

職場應答對話

✦ 為了孩子辭職 Resigning for Kids ✦

Lucy Hi, Kevin, I would like to speak with you privately when you have a chance.
露西 嗨，凱文，有時間的話我想跟您私下談談。

Kevin I have some free time right now. Come in.
凱文 我現在就有空。進來吧。

Lucy Thank you, sir. I need to hand in my resignation today.

露西 謝謝，先生。今天我要遞交辭呈。

Kevin Alright, and will you continue to work for the next few weeks while we search for a replacement for you?

凱文 好的，那接下來幾個禮拜我們會找人接替妳，在此期間妳可以繼續留在這裡工作嗎？

Lucy Yes, that would be fine. My husband and I have decided that I will stay at home full time with our kids instead of hiring a nanny. It is important for me to be there for my kids as they grow up.

露西 好的，這沒有問題。我和我丈夫決定不請保姆，讓我全天待在家裡照顧孩子。孩子成長過程中，我能夠陪在他們的身邊，這對我來說很重要。

Kevin I understand, and I appreciate all the hard work and effort that you have put into our company up to this point. You have really helped to build the integrity of our company.

凱文 我明白，而且我很感激妳到目前為止為公司所付出的辛勞和努力。妳的確幫助公司樹立了誠信。

- nanny [ˋnænɪ] n 保姆
- integrity [ɪnˋtɛgrətɪ] n 完整，正直，誠實

關聯必備單字

❶ **stress**
[strɛs] 壓力

❷ **bore**
[bor] 使……厭煩

❸ **quit**
[kwɪt] 辭職

❹ **resign**
[rɪˋzaɪn] 辭職

❺ **resignation**
[ˌrɛzɪgˋneʃən] 辭呈，辭職

❻ **secretary**
[ˋsɛkrəˌtɛrɪ] 秘書

❼ **persuade**
[pɚˋswed] 說服

❽ **integrity**
[ɪnˋtɛgrətɪ] 誠信

❾ **replace**
[rɪˋples] 代替

❿ **hand in**
遞交

⓫ **privately**
[ˋpraɪvɪtlɪ] 私下地

⓬ **submit**
[səbˋmɪt] 提交

⓭ **replacement**
[rɪˋplesmənt] 代替者

⓮ **out of the blue**
突然，出乎意料

⓯ **expiry**
[ɪkˋspaɪrɪ] 期滿

⓰ **job-hopping**
[ˌdʒɑbˋhɑpɪŋ] 跳槽

專業貼心便條

辭職可以按照下面五個步驟來進行。

1. 撰寫辭職信：辭職信一般包括以下內容——離職原因、離職時間、工作的交接、向公司表示感謝的禮貌用語等。
2. 跟主管詳談：得到主管的批准和支援，這是離職過程中十分關鍵的一步。
3. 交接工作：在公司未找到合適的接替者前，要一如既往地做好本職工作；若已有接替者，則要將手頭工作交接完畢才能離職，盡到自己的最後一份責任。
4. 辦理人事手續。
5. 開離職證明。

SECTION 07

被解雇了
Getting Fired

隨身應急情境句

Track 068

1 You're fired.
你被解雇了。

2 We are going to let you go.
我們打算讓你離職。

3 You blew it. And I have no choice but to fire you.
你搞砸了。我別無選擇，只能解雇你。

4 You're always late for work. I'm sorry to tell you but you're fired.
你上班總是遲到。我很遺憾地告訴你，你被解雇了。

5 We had to fire him for dishonesty.
由於他不誠實，我們必須解雇他。

6 He was sacked for laziness.
他因懶惰而被解雇。

7 Your work is average. And you apparently don't work well with others.
你工作成績平平。而且很明顯你跟其他員工配合得不好。

8	I don't want to lose the job. Can I get a second chance? 我不想失去這份工作。能再給我一次機會嗎？
9	Why do you fire me? 你為什麼要解雇我？
10	You'll get some compensation. 你會得到一些資遣費。
11	I just got fired. I can't believe it. 我剛剛被解雇了。我真不敢相信。
12	I can't lose the job. It's unfair. 我不能失去這個工作。這太不公平了。
13	She's got laid off. 她被解雇了。
14	The company has to break up the partnership with you. 公司要終止和你的合作關係。
15	The company is downsizing the workforce. 公司在精簡人員。

萬能好用句型

- We are going to let you go.
  我們打算讓你離職。

- I'm sorry to tell you but you're fired.
  我很遺憾地告訴你，你被解雇了。
- We had to fire him for ...
  由於……，我們必須解雇他。
- He was sacked for ...
  他因……而被解雇。
- Can I get a second chance?
  能再給我一次機會嗎？
- She's got laid off.　她被解雇了。

職場應答對話

✦ 再遲到就解雇 Would Be Dismissed for Lateness Again ✦

Tom　Hi, Lily, we need to talk. Please follow me.

湯姆　嗨，莉莉，我們需要談一談。請隨我來。

Lily　Yes, of course. What would you like to discuss?

莉莉　嗯，當然可以。您想談什麼呢？

Tom　Today you were late again. We warned you last time that you would be dismissed if it happened again. Other companies would have let you go a long time ago, but I wanted to give you a chance to change your habits because you are a very dedicated worker when you are here.

湯姆　今天妳又遲到了。上次遲到我們警告過妳，如果再有一次妳就會被解雇。換做其他公司，早就讓妳走人了。但因為妳在這裡是一名很努力的員工，所以我想給妳一次機會，來讓妳改變自己的習慣。

Lily I understand. I appreciate you giving me the chances and I apologize for letting you down. I won't make any excuses for my lateness. I know it is something I need to change and I will keep trying to do better in future, wherever I work next.

莉莉 我明白。我很感激您給我的機會，並很抱歉我讓您失望了。我不會為我的遲到找任何的藉口。我知道這是我需要改變的一件事，不管今後我在哪裡工作，我會努力做得更好。

Tom That sounds like a good plan. Sorry this didn't turn out differently.

湯姆 這聽起來是個好主意。很抱歉結果竟然是這樣。

- dedicated [ˋdɛdə͵ketɪd] adj 專注的，敬業的
- let sb. down 讓某人失望
- turn out 結果是

關聯必備單字

1. **violation** [͵vaɪəˋleʃən] 違反
2. **tolerance** [ˋtɑlərəns] 容忍
3. **fire** [ˋfaɪr] 解雇，開除
4. **sack** [sæk] 解雇
5. **downsize** [ˋdaʊn͵saɪz] 裁員
6. **recession** [rɪˋsɛʃən] 衰退
7. **terminate** [ˋtɝmə͵net] 終止
8. **laziness** [ˋlezɪnɪs] 懶惰
9. **dishonest** [dɪsˋɑnɪst] 不誠實的
10. **dishonesty** [dɪsˋɑnɪstɪ] 不誠實

⓫ **misconduct**
[ˏmɪsˋkɑndʌkt] 不端行為

⓬ **be sacked for**
因……被解雇

⓭ **average**
[ˋævərɪdʒ] 普通的，平均的

⓮ **lay off**
解雇

⓯ **partnership**
[ˋpɑrtnɚˏʃɪp] 合作關係

⓰ **workforce**
[ˋwɝkˏfɔrs] 勞動力，全體員工

專業貼心便條

在職場遭到解雇，很多時候是由於其表現出來的不服從的態度，下面這些不服從的表現，在你身上出現過嗎？

1. 直接蔑視上級的權威。
2. 完全不服從或拒絕遵照上級的命令，尤其是當著其他人的面。
3. 故意蔑視明確規定的組織政策、規章和程式。
4. 當眾批評上級。與上級對抗或爭執也是消極和不恰當的。
5. 公開無視上級的正當指令。
6. 通過繞過直屬上司的方式提出申訴、建議或採取政治策略來表示對指揮的蔑視。
7. 領導或參與暗中削弱和取消上級權力的活動。

CHAPTER 11

休閒時光 Leisure Time

❶ 部門有聚會 Going to an Office Party
❷ 相約購物 Going Shopping
❸ 大家一起去 K 歌吧 Going to Karaoke
❹ 歡樂的舞會 Going to a Dance
❺ 外出旅行 Going on a Trip

SECTION 01

部門有聚會
Going to an Office Party

隨身應急情境句

Track 069

1. Are you busy this evening?
你今晚會很忙嗎？

2. Do you have any plans for tonight?
你今晚有什麼安排嗎？

3. We're gonna have a party tonight. Would you like to join us?
今晚我們有一場派對。你願意參加嗎？

4. Where is the party?
派對在哪裡舉行？

5. We're gonna have a costume party this Friday night. And I want to dress up as a witch.
這個禮拜五晚上我們要舉辦化裝舞會。我想扮成女巫。

6. It's time to go to the office Halloween party.
我們該去參加部門的萬聖夜派對了。

7. It's a theme party.
這是一個主題派對。

8. All kinds of masks are there in the masquerade.
在化裝舞會上會有各式各樣的面具。

9	I didn't recognize you with your mask on. 你戴上面具我都認不出來了。
10	That's my dream party. 那是我夢想中的派對。
11	It's time to go to Mary's birthday party. She's turning 30 tomorrow. 該去參加瑪麗的生日派對了。她明天就三十歲了。
12	Is everybody here now? 所有人都在這裡了嗎？
13	You are so elegant in the long dress. 你穿著長禮服時非常優雅。
14	Here's to your success! 為你們的成功乾杯！
15	Here's to our friendship! 為我們的友情乾杯！
16	Let's propose a toast for Halloween. 讓我們為萬聖夜乾杯！
17	Do you want to grab some food to celebrate? 你想拿一點吃的去慶祝一下嗎？
18	Want to go to the bar after? 之後想去酒吧嗎？
19	Did you guys enjoy the party? 派對好玩嗎？

20 That party last night was really awesome!
昨晚的派對真的很棒！

萬能好用句型

- We're gonna have a party tonight. Would you like to join us?
  今晚我們有一場派對。你願意參加嗎？
- Where is the party?
  派對在哪裡舉行？
- Is everybody here now?
  所有人都到齊了嗎？
- Here's to …
  為……乾杯。
- Let's propose a toast for …
  讓我們為……乾杯。
- That party was really awesome!
  那場派對真的很棒！

職場應答對話

✦ 部門聚會 The Office Party ✦

Jenifer So far, thirty people have RSVP to the office party, but I expect that at least twice that many will just show up.

珍妮佛 到目前為止，30 人回復了部門聚會的邀請，但是我認為到時參加的人至少是現在的兩倍。

Charlie I think that's reasonable. Do we have enough food for everyone?

查理 我覺得有道理。我們的食物夠嗎？

Jenifer Yes, the caterer brought food for 100.

珍妮佛 夠，酒宴承辦單位準備的食物可以供 100 人享用。

Charlie Great. I'm glad the logistics are taken care of. I love going to office parties. It's a nice change of pace to just spend time with co-workers without having to worry about meeting goals or talking about clients.

查理 太好了。後勤做得很好，我很高興。我喜歡參加部門聚會。這是一個不錯的節奏轉變，就是跟同事們待在一起，不用擔心要完成任務，也不用談論客戶。

Jenifer I agree! Plus every time I go to one of these I meet someone new.

珍妮佛 我同意！而且每次我參加這種聚會，都會認識新朋友。

Charlie Yes, it's incredible. I think that a group of us will go out for drinks after the party is over. Would you want to join us?

查理 對啊，這很棒。我想聚會結束後找大家去喝點東西。妳想和我們一起去嗎？

- RSVP **abbr.**
  使用於請帖之答覆用語（敬請賜覆）
- caterer [ˋketərɚ] **n** 酒宴承辦者
- logistics [loˋdʒɪstɪks] **n** 後勤

關聯必備單字

❶ **banquet**
[ˋbæŋkwɪt] 宴會

❷ **buffet**
[ˋbʊfe] 自助餐

❸ **toast**
[tost] 祝酒

❹ **bar**
[bɑr] 酒吧

❺ **barroom**
[ˋ bɑr͵rum] 酒吧間

❻ **bartender**
[ˋbɑr͵tɛndɚ] 酒保

❼ **beverage**
[ˋbɛvərɪdʒ] 飲料

❽ **alcohol**
[ˋælkə͵hɔl] 酒

❾ **cocktail**
[ˋkɑk͵tel] 雞尾酒

❿ **whisky**
[ˋwɪskɪ] 威士忌

⓫ **Scotch whisky**
蘇格蘭威士忌

⓬ **champagne**
[ʃæmˋpen] 香檳

⓭ **brandy**
[ˋbrændɪ] 白蘭地

⓮ **rum**
[rʌm] 萊姆酒

⓯ **juice**
[dʒus] 果汁

⓰ **lemonade**
[͵lɛmənˋed] 檸檬水

⓱ **smoke**
[smok] 吸煙

⓲ **cigarette**
[͵sɪgəˋrɛt] 香煙

⓳ **cigar**
[sɪˋgɑr] 雪茄

⓴ **surprise party**
驚喜派對

㉑ **cocktail party**
雞尾酒會

㉒ **farewell party**
歡送會

㉓ **birthday party**
生日派對

㉔ **tails**
[telz] 燕尾服

㉕ **attire**
[əˋtaɪr] 衣服，服裝

㉖ **formal attire**
禮服

㉗ **bow tie**
蝶形領結

㉘ **handbag**
[ˋhænd͵bæg] 手提包

專業貼心便條

籌備部門聚會或慶功會時，以下這幾點是需要注意的：

1. 認真地考慮這些事情：

應該選擇一個什麼樣的地方？什麼活動能讓大多數人滿意？什麼可以讓大家放鬆一下？什麼能讓這次活動顯得與眾不同？

2. 注重每一個團隊成員：

要瞭解團隊成員不同的品味和每個人的喜好。

3. 要盡可能多地發出邀請：

發出 e-mail 或是貼出通知宣佈這次聚會的目的等。

SECTION 02

相約購物
Going Shopping

隨身應急情境句

Track 070

1	Wanna go shopping this Saturday? 這個禮拜六想去逛街嗎？
2	Want to come with me to the mall today? 今天想和我一起去賣場嗎？
3	Do you want to go shopping with me? 你想跟我一起去逛街嗎？
4	I need to get some new clothes. 我需要買新衣服了。
5	I need a new pair of pants. 我要買條新褲子。
6	I'd like to see some dresses. 我想看看連身裙。
7	My shoes are starting to wear out. I need some new ones. 我的鞋子快磨破了，我需要買新鞋了。
8	Is everything in the store on sale? 商店裡的所有東西都打折嗎？

9	Are you having a sale now? 你們現在有打折嗎？
10	It's a good deal. 這很划算。
11	It's a real bargain at such a low price. 這麼便宜，真划算。
12	Do you have anything that will fit me? 你們有什麼適合我的東西嗎？
13	Do you have this jacket in my size? 你們這件夾克有我穿的尺碼嗎？
14	What size do you wear? 你穿多大號的？
15	It's the wrong size. Can I have a size larger? 這個尺寸不對。可以給我大一號的嗎？
16	The green coat fits you like a glove. 你穿這件綠色上衣很合身。
17	You look gorgeous in this dress. 你穿這件裙子很漂亮。
18	Which color do you like better? 你比較喜歡哪種顏色？
19	What color do you prefer? 你比較喜歡哪種顏色？

20	This color isn't for me. I prefer pink or green. 這個顏色不太適合我。我比較喜歡粉色或綠色。
21	The color is too dark for you. 這個顏色太暗了，不適合你。
22	This is the latest style. 這是最新的款式。
23	May I use the dressing room? 我能用一下試衣間嗎？
24	What's the price of this shirt? 這件襯衫多少錢？
25	How much are you selling these for? 這些東西賣多少錢？

萬能好用句型

- Do you want to go shopping with me?　你想跟我一起去逛街嗎？
- It's a good deal.　這很划算。
- What size do you wear?　你穿多大號的？
- Can I have a size larger/smaller?　可以給我大／小一號的嗎？
- You look gorgeous in …　你穿……很漂亮。
- This color isn't for me.　這個顏色不太適合我。
- How much are you selling these for?　你這些賣多少錢？

職場應答對話

✦ 跟麥特去購物 Going Shopping with Matt ✦

Kate	Thanks for inviting me to come shopping with you. I'm having a lot of fun.
凱特	謝謝你邀請我跟你一起逛街。我逛得很開心。
Matt	Sure thing. I'm glad you're here. Tell me, what do you think of this suit?
麥特	那當然。我很高興妳能來。告訴我，妳覺得這套西裝怎麼樣？
Kate	I don't really like it. The color is too bright.
凱特	我不太喜歡。顏色太鮮豔了。
Matt	You're right. Hey, after we're done here, do you want to get some lunch?
麥特	妳說得對。嘿，等我們逛完了，妳想去吃午餐嗎？
Kate	I actually already ate lunch, but I wouldn't say no to some ice cream.
凱特	其實我已經吃過午餐了。但我不會拒絕去吃點冰淇淋。
Matt	Great idea. I know a place on the waterfront where you can get huge scoops for not very much money.
麥特	好主意。我知道在濱水區有一家店，一大勺冰淇淋還不用花很多錢。
Kate	That sounds perfect! Before that I have to go into the electronics store. My iPod broke and I need another one.
凱特	那個聽起來很不錯耶！但在那裡之前，我要去一趟電子產品專賣店。我的 iPod 壞了，我需要一台新的。

Matt Oh, okay. I should go there too to look at iPhones.
麥特 噢，好的。我也該去那裡看看 iPhone。

- waterfront [ˋwɔtɚ͵frʌnt] n 濱水區，（城市的）碼頭區
- scoop [skup] n 勺，一勺的量

關聯必備單字

❶ **mall**
[mɔl] 商場，購物中心

❷ **store**
[stor] 商店

❸ **counter**
[ˋkaʊntɚ] 櫃檯

❹ **fashion**
[ˋfæʃən] 時尚

❺ **stylish**
[ˋstaɪlɪʃ] 時髦的

❻ **popular**
[ˋpɑpjəlɚ] 流行的

❼ **in style**
流行

❽ **expensive**
[ɪkˋspɛnsɪv] 昂貴的

❾ **pricey**
[ˋpraɪsɪ] 過於昂貴的

❿ **cheap**
[tʃip] 便宜的

⓫ **clothes**
[kloz] 衣服

⓬ **coat**
[kot] 上衣

⓭ **jacket**
[ˋdʒækɪt] 夾克

⓮ **uniform**
[ˋjunə͵fɔrm] 制服

⓯ **suit**
[sut] 套裝

⓰ **jeans**
[dʒinz] 牛仔褲

⓱ **shorts**
[ʃɔrts] 短褲

⓲ **shoe**
[ʃu] 鞋

⓳ **lipstick**
[ˋlɪp͵stɪk] 口紅

⓴ **color**
[ˋkʌlɚ] 顏色

專業貼心便條

色彩第一夫人卡洛爾·傑克遜發明「四季色彩理論」，此理論是把生活常用色按照基調的不同，進行冷暖劃分和明度、純度劃分，進而形成四大組和諧關係的色彩群。你屬於哪一種呢？

1. 春季型：膚色——淺象牙色、暖米色，細膩而有透明感；眼睛——像玻璃球一樣熠熠發光，眼珠為亮茶色、黃玉色，眼白感覺像湖藍色；髮色——明亮如絹的茶色，柔和的棕黃色，栗色。春季型人的服飾基調屬於暖色系中的明亮色調，使用範圍最廣的顏色是黃色、橙紅、橘紅。
2. 夏季型：膚色——粉白、乳白色皮膚，帶藍色調的褐色皮膚，小麥色皮膚；眼睛——目光柔和，整體感覺溫柔，眼珠呈焦茶色、深棕色；髮色——輕柔的黑色、灰黑色，柔和的棕色或深棕色。夏季型人適合穿深淺不同的各種粉色、藍色和紫色，以及有朦朧感的色調，適合在同一色相裡進行濃淡搭配。
3. 秋季型：膚色——瓷器般的象牙色皮膚，深桔色、暗駝色或黃橙色；眼睛——深棕色、焦茶色，眼白為象牙色或略帶綠的白色；髮色——褐色、棕色或者銅色、巧克力色。秋季型人的服飾基調是暖色系中的沉穩色調。
4. 冬季型：膚色——略暗的橄欖色，帶青色的黃褐色，冷色調的看不到紅暈的膚色；眼睛——眼睛黑白分明，目光銳利有神，眼珠為深黑色、焦茶色；髮色——烏黑發亮、黑褐色、銀灰、深酒紅。 冬季型人適合穿純色及有光澤感的面料，混合色不適合冬季型人。

SECTION 03

大家一起去 K 歌吧
Going to Karaoke

隨身應急情境句

Track 071

1	Let's go to a karaoke bar later. 我們一會兒去卡拉 OK 唱歌吧。
2	What are you going to sing? 你想唱什麼歌？
3	You sing first. 你先唱。
4	Now it's my turn. 現在該我了。
5	I'd like to request a song. 我想點一首歌。
6	I'm tone-deaf. 我五音不全。
7	I sing out of tone. 我唱歌會走音。
8	I'm a little nervous to sing in front of everyone. 我在大家面前唱歌會有點緊張。
9	Don't be too nervous. 別太緊張了。

10	Shall we sing a duet? 我們來個二重唱怎麼樣？
11	I picked the song for you. 我幫你點的歌。
12	Tonight I'm gonna sing one of my favorite songs. 今天晚上我要唱一首我非常喜歡的歌。
13	Who sings this song? 誰要唱這首歌？
14	This song is for my dearest colleagues. 這首歌獻給我最親愛的同事們。
15	I'd like to dedicate this song to all of you. Thank you for helping me all the time. 我想把這首歌獻給你們所有人。謝謝你們總是幫助我。
16	Could you turn down the background music? 可以把背景音樂調小聲一點嗎？
17	You have a beautiful voice. 你的聲音真好聽。
18	You're a good singer! 你唱得真棒！
19	Your voice is incredible. 你的嗓音真是太棒了。
20	It's such a beautiful song. I enjoy it so much. 這首歌真美啊。我非常喜歡。

萬能好用句型

- What are you going to sing? 你想唱什麼歌？
- I'd like to request a song. 我想點一首歌。
- I'm tone-deaf. 我五音不全。
- This song is for .... 這首歌獻給⋯⋯。
- You're a good singer! 你唱得真棒！
- Your voice is incredible. 你的嗓音真是太棒了。

職場應答對話

✦ 勇敢獻唱 Be Brave to Sing ✦

Nick Allison! You made it!

尼克 愛麗森！妳來了！

Allison Hey! Yes, Jason convinced me to come. Wow, there're a lot of people from work here.

愛麗森 嘿！是啊，傑森說服我來的。哇，這裡有很多我們的同事啊。

Nick Definitely. You should go grab a drink right away. I'm going to go up and sing next and I'd hate for you to miss it.

尼克 當然。妳快去拿一杯喝的。我要上臺了，我唱下一首。我可不想要妳錯過。

Allison You're actually going to sing in front of everyone? I'm way too scared to get up there.

愛麗森 你真的要在大家面前唱歌？我很害怕上去唱歌耶。

Nick You're scared? That means we're definitely going to get you up there tonight. It's so fun!

尼克 妳會害怕？那今晚我們一定會讓妳上去唱。這很有趣的！

Allison We'll see. I'm not a very good singer.

愛麗森 看看吧。我唱得不太好。

Nick That's not the point! The point is to be silly and have fun. Plus, the more you get out of your shell, the more the people around you will do the same.

尼克 這不是重點！重點是不要怕犯傻，要玩得開心。另外，妳越是不再畏縮，妳身邊就會有越多的人跟妳學習。

關聯必備單字

❶ **music**
[ˋmjuzɪk] 音樂

❷ **song**
[sɑŋ] 歌曲

❸ **sing**
[sɪŋ] 唱歌

❹ **microphone**
[ˋmaɪkrə͵fon] 麥克風

❺ **listen**
[ˋlɪsn] 聽

❻ **lyric**
[ˋlɪrɪk] 歌詞

❼ **tone**
[ton] 音調

❽ **solo**
[ˋsolo] 獨唱

❾ **duet**
[duˋɛt] 二重唱

❿ **trio**
[ˋtrio] 三重唱

⓫ **cheer**
[tʃɪr] 歡呼

⓬ **bass**
[bes] 男低音

⓭ **tenor**
[ˋtɛnɚ] 男高音

⓮ **alto**
[ˋælto] 女低音

⑮ **soprano**
[sə`præno] 女高音

⑯ **rock**
[rɑk] 搖滾樂

⑰ **country music**
鄉村音樂

⑱ **hip-hop**
[`hɪp͵hɑp] 嘻哈音樂

⑲ **electrophonic music**
電子音樂

⑳ **band**
[bænd] 樂團

㉑ **concert**
[`kɑnsɚt] 音樂會

㉒ **club**
[klʌb] 俱樂部

專業貼心便條

一些職場員工由於在公司聚會上的出格行為或不當言辭而遭到解雇，因此為了避免此類後果發生在自己身上，以下這些事情在聚會時可別做唷！

1. 不要喝太多。聚會時還是少喝兩杯吧，不要讓酒精影響了你的判斷力。
2. 不要有過多的抱怨。既然事實不能改變，就試圖從中找到樂趣吧，如果實在不喜歡，也可以提前退場。
3. 不要繼續談論工作，或提及晉升或獎金之類的事情。
4. 不要談論某個現在已經成為競爭對手的前同事。
5. 不要太八卦，辦公室戀情還是不要討論了。

SECTION 04

歡樂的舞會
Going to a Dance

隨身應急情境句 Track 072

1	When does the ball begin? 舞會幾點開始？
2	Would you have a dance with me? 你願意和我跳支舞嗎？
3	Let's have a dance. 我們跳支舞吧。
4	Can I have the favor to dance with you? 我可以跟你跳支舞嗎？
5	May I have the first dance? 我可以跟你跳第一支舞嗎？
6	I'm engaged for the social dance. 這支社交舞我已經有約了。
7	I've already promised someone. 我已經答應別人了。
8	I'm Lisa's partner. 我是麗莎的舞伴。

9	I'm sorry to turn you down. 我很抱歉拒絕你。
10	Which dance do you like best? 你最喜歡哪一種舞？
11	I really love cha-cha. 我很喜歡恰恰。
12	You're so graceful. 你的舞姿真優美。
13	I can hardly recognize you. You are so elegant. 我幾乎認不出你了。你太優雅了。
14	I never knew you were such a good dancer. 我從來不知道你舞跳得這麼好。
15	The tuxedo really suits you. 禮服很適合你。
16	I'm not too much of a dancer. 我不太會跳舞。
17	I cannot do the tango. 我不會跳探戈。
18	We had a great time. 我們玩得很開心。
19	It's amazing! We have a lot of fun tonight. 太棒了！今晚我們玩得非常開心。

萬能好用句型

- Would you have a dance with me?
  你願意和我跳支舞嗎？
- May I have the first dance?
  我可以跟你跳第一支舞嗎？
- I've already promised someone.
  我已經答應別人了。
- I'm sorry to turn you down.
  我很抱歉拒絕你。
- Which dance do you like best?
  你最喜歡哪種舞？
- I'm not too much of a dancer.
  我不太會跳舞。

職場應答對話

✦ 很棒的舞會 A Great Dance ✦

Robin Hey, everyone. There is a great dance tonight at a bar near my house. I'm going, and so are Laura and Amber, so it would be great if more people came.

羅賓 嘿，各位，今晚在我家附近的酒吧有一場很棒的舞會。我會去，蘿拉和安布林也會去，要是有更多的人去就更好了。

Katie What kind of music will they play?

凱蒂 他們會放哪種類型的音樂？

Robin Modern stuff. Very upbeat and easy to dance to.

羅賓 現代的。很歡樂又容易跳的。

Katie Okay, that sounds good. If you all are going, I'll come check it out. I'm not a very good dancer, so as long as no one laughs at me I'm there!

凱蒂 好的，那聽起來不錯。如果你們都去，我就去看看。我跳得不太好，只要沒人笑我的話，我就去！

Robin Oh, me either! That's why everyone should come. The more the merrier. Plus, you stand out less in a big crowd.

羅賓 噢，我也是！這也是大家都該參加的原因。人越多，玩得越開心。另外，在一大群人裡妳也不會那麼顯眼。

Katie I agree! Okay, that's it, everyone else should come too. Plus, it will just be fun.

凱蒂 我同意！好吧，就這樣，其他人也都應該去。而且，這會很好玩的。

- upbeat [ˋʌpˏbit] adj 歡快的
- merry [ˋmɛrɪ] adj 愉快的
- stand out 突出，顯眼

關聯必備單字

❶ **rumba**
[ˋrʌmbə] 倫巴舞

❷ **waltz**
[wɔls] 華爾滋舞

❸ **disco**
[ˋdɪsko] 迪斯可

❹ **ballet**
[ˋbæle] 芭蕾舞

❺ **samba**
[ˋsæmbə] 森巴舞

❻ **cha-cha**
[ˋtʃɑˋtʃɑ] 恰恰舞

❼ **foxtrot**
[ˋfɑksˏtrɑt] 狐步舞

❽ **Latin dance**
拉丁舞

❾ **social dance**
社交舞

❿ **tango**
[ˋtæŋgo] 探戈舞

⓫ **jazz**
[dʒæz] 爵士樂

⓬ **orchestra**
[ˋɔrkɪstrə] 管弦樂隊

⓭ **modern**
[ˋmɑdɚn] 現代的

⓮ **classical**
[ˋklæsɪkl̩] 古典的

⓯ **dancer**
[ˋdænsɚ] 舞者

⓰ **step**
[stɛp] 舞步

⓱ **charming**
[ˋtʃɑrmɪŋ] 有魅力的

⓲ **elegance**
[ˋɛləgəns] 優雅

⓳ **partner**
[ˋpɑrtnɚ] 搭檔

⓴ **ball**
[bɔl] 舞會

㉑ **graceful**
[ˋgresfəl] 優美的

專業貼心便條

在舞會上，下面這些事情是需要注意的：

1. 化妝：

與通勤妝相比，舞會妝可以相對濃一些。

2 服裝：

乾淨、整齊、美觀、大方。有條件的話，可以穿格調高雅的禮服、時裝或民族服裝。

3. 邀請：

按照慣例，在舞會上一般應當是由男士邀請女士。當男士邀請女士時，女士可以拒絕。有時候，女士亦可邀請男士，然而男士卻不宜拒絕。

4. 一曲一舞：

在舞會上一對舞伴只宜共舞一支曲子。第一支舞曲，男士要去邀請與自己一同前來的女士共舞，還可以在演奏舞會的結束曲時再同跳一次。

5. 選擇舞伴：

要選擇年齡相仿、身高相當、氣質相同、舞技相近的人。男賓應當邀請的舞伴有舞會的女主人、被介紹相識的女士、自己熟悉的女伴，以及坐在自己身旁的女士。

6. 順序：

自舞會上的第二支舞曲開始，男主人應當前去邀請男主賓的女伴跳舞，而男主賓則應回請女主人共舞。接下來，男主人還需依次邀請在禮賓序列上排位第二、第三位男士的女伴，這些男士則應同時回請女主人共舞。

SECTION 05

外出旅行
Going on a Trip

隨身應急情境句

Track 073

1 Would you like to take a road trip?
你想進行一次公路旅行嗎？

2 Taking a road trip might be cool.
公路旅行應該會很酷。

3 I'm going on a trip to Hong Kong with my co-workers.
我要跟同事們一起去香港旅行。

4 Would you like to go to the beach?
你想去海灘嗎？

5 How long will the trip take?
這次旅行要多久？

6 How long is this tour?
這趟旅行要多久時間？

7 Is this a long or a short tour?
這是長途旅行還是短途旅行呢？

8 We'll have a week to do sightseeing in this beautiful city.
我們會有一個禮拜的時間遊覽這座美麗的城市。

9	I've never dreamed it would be so beautiful. 我從沒想到它會這麼漂亮。
10	Did you pack enough food for the picnic? 你帶夠野餐的食物了嗎？
11	What a spectacular view! 景色太壯觀了！
12	What a beautiful pacific place this is! 多麼美麗寧靜的地方啊！
13	I want to enjoy things that are different from cities. 我想領體會一些與城市不同的東西。
14	I want to enjoy some natural scenery. 我想欣賞一些自然風光。
15	It's so wonderful to take a walk here. 在這裡散步真是好極了。
16	It's great weather for a sea trip. 這天氣真適合搭船旅行。
17	The mountain here is really beautiful. 這裡的山真美。
18	Those mountain views are absolutely breathtaking. 那些山間美景真是讓人歎為觀止。
19	Take a photo of that. 幫那個拍張照吧。

20	Take a snapshot of that. 幫那個拍張快照吧。
21	Would you take a picture of us? 您能替我們照張相嗎？
22	Did you have a good journey? 你旅途開心嗎？
23	Time flies when you're having fun. 玩得開心的時候就感覺時間過得快。
24	This is the coolest trip I've ever had. 這是我度過的最美好的旅行。
25	I've just come back from Macao with my co-workers. It's a very fascinating place. 我和同事剛從澳門旅行回來。那真是個迷人的地方。

萬能好用句型

- I'm going on a trip to … with my co-workers.
  我要跟同事們一起去……旅行。
- Would you like to go to …? 你想去……嗎？
- How long will the trip take? 這次旅行要多久？
- What a spectacular view! 景色太壯觀了！
- It's so wonderful to take a walk here. 在這裡散步真是好極了。
- Did you have a good journey? 你旅途愉快嗎？
- How was the trip? 這次旅行怎麼樣？

職場應答對話

✦ 海濱之旅 A Trip to the Coast ✦

Ben How was the trip?

班 這次旅行怎麼樣？

Kristen It was good. I had a lot of fun but I was pretty tired. I got to know some people I hadn't really talked to before so it will be fun to see them this week at work.

克麗絲塔 還不錯。我玩得很開心，但也很累。我認識了一些之前沒怎麼說過話的同事，所以這個禮拜上班碰見他們會很有趣。

Ben Oh, did you go with co-workers?

班 噢，妳是跟同事去的嗎？

Kristen Yes. It was a work sponsored trip to the coast. We did some team building exercises, but mostly we just got to explore the city and spend time in the water. At night we all got together, made a big bonfire and shared stories about ourselves.

克麗絲塔 對啊。這是公司舉辦的海濱之旅。我們進行了一些團隊建設活動，但大部分時間我們都在探索這座城市和在水裡玩。到了晚上我們都聚在一起，點上篝火，分享彼此的故事。

Ben That sounds really nice. Did you meet any handsome men?

班 這聽起來還真不錯。妳有認識到帥哥嗎？

Kristen Of course, but dating someone from work is not a very good idea.

克麗絲塔 當然，但辦公室戀情可不是個好主意。

- sponsor [ˋspɑnsɚ] v 發起，贊助
- coast [kost] n 海岸，海濱
- explore [ɪkˋsplor] v 探索

關聯必備單字

❶ **trip**
[trɪp] 旅行

❷ **travel**
[ˋtrævḷ] 旅行

❸ **expedition**
[ˏɛkspɪˋdɪʃən] 探險

❹ **route**
[rut] 路線

❺ **travel agent**
旅行社

❻ **resort**
[rɪˋzɔrt] 度假勝地

❼ **view**
[vju] 景色

❽ **scenery**
[ˋsinərɪ] 風光

❾ **heritage**
[ˋhɛrətɪdʒ] 遺產

❿ **natural**
[ˋnætʃərəl] 自然的

⓫ **bonfire**
[ˋbɑnˏfaɪr] 篝火

⓬ **compass**
[ˋkʌmpəs] 指南針

⓭ **sunglasses**
[ˋsʌnˏglæsɪz] 太陽鏡

⓮ **souvenir**
[ˋsuvəˏnɪr] 紀念品

⓯ **waterfall**
[ˋwɔtɚˏfɔl] 瀑布

⓰ **mountain**
[ˋmaʊntn] 山

⓱ **climb**
[klaɪm] 攀登

⓲ **lake**
[lek] 湖

⓳ **fishing**
[ˋfɪʃɪŋ] 釣魚

⓴ **hiking**
[ˋhaɪkɪŋ] 遠足，徒步旅行

㉑ **camp**
[kæmp] 露營

㉒ **sightseeing**
[ˋsaɪtˏsiɪŋ] 觀光，遊覽

㉓ **picnic**
[ˋpɪknɪk] 野餐

㉔ **pacific**
[pəˋsɪfɪk] 平靜的，寧靜的

㉕ **breathtaking**
[ˋbrɛθˏtekɪŋ] 令人讚歎的

㉖ **snapshot**
[ˋsnæpˏʃɑt] 快照

專業貼心便條

自駕旅遊 (Self-driving tour) 也是一種很棒的休閒方式，公司有時會組織大家集體出遊，而自駕旅遊的必備物品都有哪些呢？

1. 車輛備件類：全套隨車工具、備用輪胎、牽引繩、備用油桶、水桶、工兵鏟等。
2. 應急類：多功能手錶、指南針、行動電話、組合刀具、對講機等。
3. 文本類：身份證、駕駛證、保險單、養路費及購置稅／車輛使用稅繳費憑證、公路地圖、信用卡、筆記本、筆等。
4. 藥品類：繃帶、ok 繃、消毒藥水、消炎藥、暈車藥、驅蚊液等。
5. 日用品類：當季衣物、遮陽帽、手套、適宜駕駛的軟底鞋、雨具、電筒、照相器材、洗漱用品等。

Note

語言力 E002

老外都醬說！職場英語

和外國工作夥伴溝通無障礙，工作順暢度立即提昇。

作　　者　【美】梅根・珀維斯／【美】約書亞・H・派克／方振宇
顧　　問　曾文旭
總 編 輯　黃若璇
編輯總監　耿文國、吳國鏞
特約編輯　盧惠珊
校　　對　盧惠珊
內文排版　菩薩蠻數位文化有限公司
封面設計　菩薩蠻數位文化有限公司
法律顧問　北辰著作權事務所　蕭雄淋律師、嚴裕欽律師

印　　製　世和印製企業有限公司
初　　版　2016 年 03 月
出　　版　凱信企業集團 - 開企有限公司
電　　話　（02）6636-8398
傳　　真　（02）6636-8397
地　　址　106 台北市大安區忠孝東路四段 218-7 號 7 樓

定　　價　新台幣 420 元
產品內容　1 書 + 1MP3

總 經 銷　楨彥有限公司
地　　址　231 新北市新店區寶興路 45 巷 6 弄 12 號 1 樓
電　　話　（02）8919-3186
傳　　真　（02）8914-5524

國家圖書館出版品預行編目資料

老外都醬說！職場英語 / 梅根 . 珀維斯 , 約書亞 .H. 派克 , 方振宇作 .-- 初版 . -- 臺北市 : 開企 , 2016.03
面 ;　公分 -- (語言力系列 ; 2)
ISBN 978-986-89597-8-1(平裝附光碟片)

1. 英語 2. 職場 3. 會話

805.188　　105001326